WHEN BEGGARS DYE

Peter Hey

When Beggars dye, there are no Comets ſeen,
The Heav'ns themſelves blaze forth the Death of Princes.

William Shakespeare, Julius Caesar

For Gunner Frank Dye. Sorry, Frank. And sorry, Frances Ellen and both Mabels. I should have tried harder.

I'd also like to mention the boxer George Foreman, if only because he doesn't get hung up on names. Nor should you.

'I named all my sons George Edward Foreman. And I tell people, "If you're going to get hit as many times as I've been hit by Muhammad Ali, Joe Frazier, Ken Norton, Evander Holyfield – you're not going to remember many names."'

I wouldn't stress too much about dates either.

Prologue

It's not the first thing I remember, not quite. But if not my oldest memory, it is my oldest companion. It visits me daily. It whispers without words; it reminds me who I am, why I am. It defines me as it defines him: pirate princess and buccaneering pirate king. His giant frame towers above me on the dockside. He is strong and fearless, my protector. And he climbs aboard his tall, grey ship and he leaves me.

Forever.

Yet as the years have passed, the original colours have been lost to the primary hues of a child's painting. All I see now is the representation of memory: lapping green waves and cloudless blue sky pierced by a flaming yellow sun that silhouettes the black outline of his head, wild haired in the wind. Two simple arcs of white suggest the swooping seagull, screaming in prescience of a lifetime's hurt.

And as I watch, the image melts and moulds, as I change and grow into a gangling teenager, wide eyed amongst the treasures of a Parisian gallery. Infantile shapes become a delicately detailed Orthodox icon: John the Baptist haloed by beaten gold. Am I Salome, my mother's daughter? Do I share the blame?

The lychgate

The two men laid the crudely rolled sheet of lead on the bed of the battered white van. A tatty scrap of carpet helped deaden the sound, but it was largely unnecessary. Those living within earshot knew better than to look out of their windows when their sleep was disturbed by unusual noises in the early hours.

'I'm having that old plaque too,' whispered the man in the darker jacket.

'Can't we leave that, Deano? It don't seem right,' said the other. Despite the quietness of the reply, anxiety was evident in his voice.

'Don't tell me what's right and what's not,' rasped Dean. 'What do you care? Your family's not from round here. My great-uncle's on the thing and you know what? I don't give a damn. Everyone who ever cared is dead. Or so old they're gaga. It's ancient history, and that's a nice lump of bronze that'll melt down easy. No questions asked.'

Dean looked for compliance in his accomplice's face. Seeing only doubt, he gave up on argument. 'Just do as you're told! Pass me that bar.'

Meekly, Steve reached down into the van and slid out the heavy steel crowbar. Dean grabbed it off him and then gestured that he follow. 'I'll need you to hold the bugger when it starts to come loose. If it hits the floor it'll be enough to wake the dead.'

'That's what worries me,' muttered Steve.

'What?'

'Nothing, Deano.'

There had once been the name of a builder across the side of the van, but the lettering had been stripped off years ago and any ghostly trace was indistinguishable in the half-light. The streetlamp directly in front of the church had been out for days and its partner 30 yards away seemed only to deepen the shadows, particularly beneath the pitched roof of the lychgate that led into the churchyard. To aid the darkness, the van was parked so as to mask the two men's movements from the homes on the far side of what some locals insisted on calling the village green. But this was no picture-postcard idyll of rose-clad thatched cottages and duck pond. Dowley's more prosaic history was betrayed by terraces of cheaply built Victorian houses that seemed to have been transported from the backstreets of an industrial northern city. One half of the 'green' had been tarmacked over for a car park; the other was home to a monument to the village's past, a large pit winding wheel sunk vertically up to its axle. The spoked semi-circle of steel was the last trace of a coal industry whose demise had removed any remnants of pride from this small settlement in the Derbyshire countryside. Long before the local pit went the railway, its only memorial a Station Road with no station. Dowley was now an isolated, run-down dormitory, whose few working inhabitants left each morning in their cars and dreamt of moving up the housing ladder and away.

Had someone twitched their bedroom curtains that night and been able to see past the van, they would have witnessed two men of almost identical build and appearance, scurrying around like rodents in the night. Indeed, there was something distinctly rat-like in their thin, pointed faces and closely cropped hair. A student of body language might have sensed a clear hierarchy, one man slightly more stooped and deferential to the other: dark jacket, the alpha male, albeit in a pack of two.

The crowbar made short work of the ancient brass screws as they were wrenched clean out of the wooden frame of the lychgate. Whoever fixed them could never have imagined a time when their security would be challenged.

'It's heavier than I thought,' grinned Dean as the two men carefully lowered it to the ground.

Steve began to gabble. 'It feels like grave robbing. I don't like this, I really don't. My mum says you shouldn't mess with the dead. She says there are things we don't understand. Things that come back and haunt you. We shouldn't—'

'Oh shut up! Your mother's as mental as you are.'

'I'm not mental. I told you, that assessment thing said I had very mild learning difficulties, that's all.'

'Yeah, yeah, yeah, Steve. So you said.' Dean took a breath and switched from derision to reassurance. 'Look, this isn't a grave. No-one named on this thing is buried anywhere near here. Not that I know of. It's just a war memorial. The bodies were all left in France or Germany or God knows where. My gran's brother isn't buried anywhere. He was on a ship that was blown up at sea. He's down at the bottom of the Atlantic and has been for, what, 70-plus years?'

Steve's only reply was a sullen look and Dean continued his justification. 'It's all so long ago no-one cares. A troop of boy scouts marches up here every Remembrance Sunday, but no-one comes now who actually knew any of these blokes. When I was a kid, my gran would drag me up here and go on about her poor brother and how young he was...'

Dean paused and pulled a small penlight from his pocket. He glanced around and then twisted the end to shine a feeble cone of light onto the oxidised green lettering. 'Here he is. Bottom left corner. K R Dye.'

Steve scanned the names. They were laid out in four columns and divided into two main sections. Some 30 men were listed under 1914-1918, but only eight under 1939-1945. Steve tilted his head and looked puzzled. 'So that's World War I and World War II, I guess. I thought from school that World War II was, like, huge. So why are there more names under World War I?'

Dean found himself fumbling in his memory for the answer he'd received when asking the same question as a child. Something came to him, but it was largely derived from different conversations that had moulded his young mind.

'Lots of men were slaughtered in the trenches in the First World War, a whole generation they reckoned. Every family lost someone. By the time of World War II, no-one, I mean no-one, wanted another fight with Germany. The smart ones actually admired Hitler and what he was doing to rebuild his country. It was no skin of our nose if he had a go at them commie-bastard Poles and Russians. That's what strong men do. We had this guy in our country, Oswald Mosley, who thought we should be on the same side as Hitler, but then... It's a long story, but along comes Sir Winston bloody Churchill. He starts a war that bankrupts the country. We only win because we get bailed out by the Yanks. Sixty odd years later, Germany is running Europe and we're the ones swamped with Poles and the Russian mafia.'

Steve wordlessly nodded his head despite struggling to follow. A knowing smile had crept onto Dean's face as he continued the history lecture.

'But here's the thing – a very wise man once said, "It's the victors what write the histories." Churchill and his mates wrote the history of the Second World War. Oswald Mosley was painted as the bad guy and the whole country had hated him and wanted to take on Hitler. But if that's the case, why are they so few names listed under World War II? Answer me that, Steve?'

Dean had no intention of waiting for a response. He was enjoying the way his logic constructed such a compelling argument. His hobbyhorse was breaking into a gallop.

'But you and I know things are changing again, don't we Steve? All over the world, people have had enough. They've lost faith in voting and democracy because we always get the same bastards in charge. What do they call them? The liberal elite. Lording it over us, getting rich while we get poorer. Destroying our industries, our communities. Calling us racists...'

Dean stopped himself as he suddenly remembered where he was. He switched off the torch and adopted a more urgent tone.

'Don't get me going. Look, I told you, this plaque is just ancient history. Dodgy history at that. Now let's get this thing in the back and get our arses out of here.'

Silent now, the two men lugged the bronze sheet into the van. They closed the doors as gently as they could and then climbed in the front. Dean used his sleeve to wipe the condensation from the windscreen and his eyes swept the scene for signs of life. Reassured, he turned the key. Like a heavy smoker responding to an early morning alarm, the worn-out diesel engine reluctantly coughed into life. Releasing the handbrake, Dean shifted into gear and steered the van towards the sanctuary of the unlit country lane that led out into the night.

Dean allowed himself a brief smile of relief and satisfaction. He glanced over at Steve and winked. 'A good night's work, that. And don't lose any sleep about that plaque. It's one of them victimless crimes, mate. Nothing's going to come back to haunt you.'

North Atlantic 1941

The petty officer in the recruiting office had decided the young miner would make an ideal stoker. The Royal Navy had adopted oil power a generation before, but the old sea dog from Tiger Bay had a long memory and had always been a proponent of returning to an abundant, native source of fuel. And, he reasoned, there was still room for a fit and healthy coal shoveller on some of the senior service's lesser or more ancient vessels.

'And it'll be finest Welsh steam coal, laddo. None of that Derbyshire rubbish.'

And even if the laddo found himself on an oil burner, a life below decks in the bowels of the ship would suit someone used to a subterranean world.

Ken wanted to say he'd had his fill of dirt, dust and dark confinement, but was intimidated by the older man, and besides, he was relieved to be accepted into the navy. His father had warned him off a life in khaki, the muddy hell of the trenches having claimed several family members a short two decades earlier.

Ken made the train journey home with a huge grin on his face. As the song said, all the nice girls love a sailor, and wearing a beard and bell-bottom trousers, he was going to see the world. His parents and sisters would be proud. He decided not to relay the petty officer's opinion of the black rock his father had spent a life of toil and sweat bringing to the surface.

12 months later, Stoker 2nd Class Dye had the bell-bottoms but not the beard. The sparse whiskers on his youthful, fresh face had not convinced the chief stoker that they were capable of growing into something that the captain would accept as a 'full set' in line with King's Regulations. Dye had at least two consolations. Despite her age, his ship drew her power from tanks of fuel oil. His job was in one of the four cavernous boiler rooms

deep below decks, directly below her twin funnels. He got his hands dirty, but it was oil and grease that smeared his face, not coal dust. The second consolation, and what a consolation, was the identity of that ship. She was the pride of the Royal Navy, for 20 years the largest and most powerful warship afloat, arguably the most beautiful, with 30 knots of speed and armed with eight formidable 15-inch guns. She was HMS Hood.

A total of 24 boilers generated steam for the four massive turbines that each drove a huge manganese bronze propeller, 15 feet in diameter. In her sea trials, her engines had generated the power equivalent to over 150,000 horses and it took some 300 officers and men just to keep the shafts turning.

Ken was on the mess deck when the captain gave the call to action stations. The young rating took one last look at the photograph fixed to his locker door. Stoker 1st Class Jock Brown leaned over his shoulder as he did so.

'Kenny's blowing kisses at his girlfriends again, lads,' said the Scotsman, with a bravado meant to distract from the anxiety he knew they were all feeling in their stomachs.

'As you well know, Jock, they're my sisters,' replied Ken, instinctively playing the game.

'Well if they're not your girlfriends, maybe you could introduce them to Sid, Taff, Tommo and me.'

'Apart from Mary, they're way too young for you lot. And whilst I might introduce my big sister to Sid or Taff, or maybe even Tommo, there's no way on earth I'd let you go anyway near her, Jock.'

'I think you've got me wrong, Kenny. I'm a—'

'Stop squawking like shitehawks and get to your posts!' bawled an officer. 'The ship's got a job to do. The job she was built for. And she needs every one of you to be where you're bloody well supposed to be!'

It was hot in the boiler room, and not for the first time, Ken was glad he wasn't above decks exposed to the bitter cold of a North Atlantic dawn. But at least he might know what was going on up there. Here, below the waterline, amongst a confusion of pipes, taps and valves in a sealed and windowless steel chamber, you read the state of battle through the sounds echoing around you. For nearly three hours, there'd been a constant background din as the throbbing turbines pushed the ship at full speed and every rivet and bolt seemed to be humming with vibration.

Suddenly, there was a colossal blast from the front of the ship and she shuddered from stem to stern.

'Don't worry, son,' said Chief Petty Officer Knox above the noise. 'Those are our guns. We've fired off a salvo from the forward turrets. I wouldn't want to be on the other end of that lot.'

The guns roared again, and high-explosive shells weighing nearly a ton were sent arcing at over twice the speed of sound towards their target, some 13 miles distant.

'Why aren't they using the aft turrets as well, Chief?' said Ken, trying to hide the quiver in his voice.

'We must be going pretty much straight towards the bastards. Taking the fight to them.'

Within two or three minutes there was a different sounding loud crash that seemed to come from directly above.

'They've hit us,' said Knox, nervously looking up at the ceiling. 'Don't worry, son. The old girl can take it. But there'll be dead sailors up there. It's at times like this I'm glad we're down here.'

'Do you think we'd get out, Chief? You know, if they did get us?' Ken's mind was racing through the labyrinth of bulkhead doors and ladders that stood between them and the possibility of escape.

'We're on the Hood, son. The Invincible Hood. It's them poor sods on the Bismarck and the Prince Eugen that need to be scared.'

They felt the ship begin swinging to port.

'Here we go, son. The captain's bringing her about so we can train everything on the bastards. They're going to be sorry.'

HMS Hood had been designed in World War I. She was fast and had the guns of a battleship, but her armour protection was flawed. She was ageing and had been in near constant service for over 20 years. She retained her beauty but desperately needed the major rebuild that had been postponed because of the start of a second great war. The Admiralty knew she was now outclassed by modern capital ships such as Bismarck, but few available big gun vessels could match her speed, and Hood was despatched to hunt the German down before she could wreak havoc on the Atlantic convoys.

The captain knew Hood's vulnerability, but Chief Petty Officer Knox did not. Stoker 2nd Class Dye certainly didn't. Hood's battle was short, her end dramatic and sudden. The shocked official enquiry concluded one of Bismarck's shells had penetrated Hood's armour plate and reached an aft magazine, igniting tons of cordite. When the catastrophic explosion ripped her apart, the captain stayed at his post on the bridge. Knox and Dye had no choice. The lights went out and they were hit by a wall of water that threw them across the room. Dye remained conscious, though totally disoriented by the rushing, icy, salty blackness that engulfed him and pinned him upside down against the hot steel of a boiler casing. Some instinct told him to breathe, to let a quick death flood into his lungs, but he resisted for as long as he could.

Within three minutes the great vessel had slipped beneath the waves. In the forward part of the ship, furthest from the conflagration, men still fought for their lives in the twisting, tilting, tearing, collapsing darkness. Some escaped the hull only to be dragged back as millions of gallons of seawater were sucked into its voids. The steel mistress they'd served and loved refused to let them go. Out of 1,418 crew, only three survived.

Leicester Square underground

The train pulled into King's Cross station just before noon. Jane Madden hadn't been in London since she'd moved back to Nottingham three months previously. When making the journey in the opposite direction, visiting her childhood home and her grandparents, she'd always driven. Now, a two hour train ride seemed infinitely preferable to battling against the capital's traffic and to the hassle and expense of trying to find somewhere to park.

As she walked through the station concourse, she realised she hadn't been there since its refurbishment. The opening had been extensively covered in local news broadcasts at the time, but she found herself disappointed when she looked up at the curved lattice of white steel that swooped organically up and out from a central trunk to form the semi-circular canopy roof. In photographs it looked breathtaking; in reality it somehow lacked scale and drama. She sensed a wave of disproportionate melancholy rolling towards her but she chastised herself. 'New start', she said out loud and the mantra made her back straighten. Though the area was crowded, no-one seemed to notice the tall woman in the bright-green coat talking to herself.

She'd agreed to meet him in a Leicester Square pizza restaurant. It was part of a large chain and catered primarily for families and tourists, but its expansive premises had personal history. Jane and he had first gone there for what they called their 'homework'.

When she emerged from the underground the sun had come out. The pedestrianised road leading to the square itself was crammed with people who by their dress, language and ethnicity appeared to have come from every country on the planet. Though she was 15 minutes early, Jane made her way through to the restaurant as quickly as she could. As she'd expected, he was standing outside waiting for her. He was looking down at the ground and didn't notice her until she spoke.

'Thompson Ferdinand! You're looking well. It's been so long. I've missed you.'

She put her arms around him and gave him a hug. He reciprocated, though somewhat awkwardly.

'Jane, you look well too. You look... yes, you look well. I mean, I guess the move to Nottingham must be doing you good. And I like your coat too. It's very, erm, green.'

'I'm going through a colourful phase, Tommy. Might dye my hair this colour next.' She knew he didn't always recognise when he was being teased but she couldn't resist. She raised her eyebrows and grinned to give him a hint, but he just looked slightly worried.

Tommy checked his watch. 'We probably ought to go inside and see if we can get a table. I'm concerned it might be full up down there. There seem to be so many people about.' His troubled expression seemed to have deepened.

Jane shrugged her shoulders. 'If it is, we'll just have to find somewhere else. It's not exactly wonderful in there. It was just somewhere we both knew. No biggie, as they say. Or maybe they don't anymore?' She grinned again.

Jane's taking charge seemed to smooth the furrows on Tommy's forehead. They descended the narrow flight of stairs and were soon guided past a short queue of larger groups to be squeezed into a small table for two, next to a column at the far side of the extensive, windowless basement. Though busy with families talking loudly, the Babel-like cacophony was strangely deadened. The decor and fittings conformed to corporate standards, but special attention had been paid to the lighting in an attempt to avoid the fluorescent hardness of a hospital or classroom. The success had been limited.

The restaurant was geared to high throughput and they were served quickly. Neither of them needed to dither over the menu, and when they had placed their order, Jane re-started the conversation.

'Talking of hair – as we were, five minutes ago anyway – I love the Afro. Really suits you.'

Tommy reddened slightly. 'I just haven't had it cut for a while. I've never enjoyed going to the barbers. All that, "Have you been away this year, sir?" small talk stuff. It's a lot easier just letting it grow. I think Afros are back in fashion, but that's not really my thing.'

'Well, it definitely looks cool. And you were okay coming into central London today? It's not a problem anymore?'

Tommy's eye line became fixed on the table. 'I don't get into town much, I must admit. Most of my social interaction is still online, I guess. But I can do it if I need to. It was obviously easier knowing I was going to meet you.'

'To think there was a time when we were both scared to leave our front doors.'

'I think agoraphobia was always a bigger problem for me. You weren't ever really frightened – you just couldn't see the point.' Tommy briefly looked up before dropping his eyes again. 'And I've always suspected you pretended a bit, about that at least, so you could help me out.'

Jane ducked her head towards the table to try to enter his field of vision. 'You helped me too, Tommy. You were a good mate when I needed one. Someone to talk to who understood at least some of what I was going through. Dave tried, bless him, but sensitivity was never his strong suit.' Her expression became wistful. 'God, he'd hate this place.'

The East European family sat to Jane's left got up to leave. She shuffled over on the bench seat to allow the son and daughter to edge out between the two adjacent tables. The children were wordless, but their mother said, 'Thank you' on their behalf.

The interruption gave Tommy time to compose his words. 'I was sorry to hear you and Dave had broken up. You always seemed a strong couple. I mean, there always seemed to be a strong bond between you.'

'Me being ill took its toll. I was a total self-centred bitch sometimes, an absolute nightmare to live with. I don't know if I'd have coped had it been the other way around. I alternate between understanding forgiveness and hateful resentment. I'm scared I'd scratch that woman's eye out if I met her again.' An iciness had entered Jane's face. She seemed to gather her thoughts and it receded. 'Shouldn't have said that – you know I don't mean it. Let's change the subject. How about you? You're a good-looking chap, particularly with the new hairstyle. Anyone in your life?'

'No-one that I've ever met in the flesh. People are always dismissive about online relationships, but there's at least one person I feel I know really well, that I get on with really well.'

'What's she look like?'

'Hard to tell in the gaming world. We all tend to hide behind avatars, and if you do see an actual photograph, you're never quite sure it's really them. For all I know, Gabi1701 could be a hideous monster with green hair.'

Tommy looked up and smiled.

Jane grinned back. 'I'm going to dye it now, just to spite you. But, anyway, why don't you and Gabi1701 meet up?'

'Well one reason is the distance. South America's a long way away. Neither of us earns enough to go jetting around the world.'

Jane nodded. 'So tell me about this new job of yours. It sounds like you're back working in IT?'

'Yes and no. I briefly went back to programming, but it requires an intensity of concentration and effort that wasn't doing me any good. I can't switch off. Some people can stop work at 5pm on the dot and then do other things, relax. I like solving problems but I'm always working on the next one in my mind. I guess I'm scared of losing control.'

He paused meditatively before adopting a more upbeat tone, 'So this new job... I work from home as a "search engine evaluator". I'm a self-employed contractor for a company based in California. They employ people from all around the world on behalf of a mysterious client who is never mentioned by name. But, between you and me, that name probably begins with G. Followed by a couple of Os.'

He looked at Jane. She gestured her understanding and he continued, 'Obviously everyone knows who it is, but contractually we're not supposed to say, even to each other. Anyway, it's continually developing its algorithms. Sample results get generated and they need real human beings to check them.'

'Sounds interesting,' said Jane with a hint of a question mark.

'Sometimes. Sometimes it's tedious and repetitive. Sometimes I haven't a clue what I'm doing. The weirdest things get typed into search engines. You have to get into the head of some very odd people.'

'You can be quite odd, Tommy,' said Jane before guiltily adding, 'Sorry, only teasing. Carry on.'

'The good thing about it is I can work from home, and if I want to take time off, I do. So long as I complete a minimum number of tasks every month, my time's my own.'

'So you work nice regular hours?'

'Sort of. Unfortunately they're Californian hours. Tasks tend to come in overnight. The important thing for me is that if I'm not around, someone else will do them. I don't get a backlog building up, so I'm not tempted to overdo it. I have time for things I enjoy – computer games, chatting on forums, that kind of stuff.'

'Where does sleep fit in?'

'I still have trouble sleeping. I've found a lifestyle that fits in with that. I catch the odd hour here and there. It's enough for me.'

Tommy's complexion was a rich caramel that reflected his mother's Caribbean heritage, but Jane noticed the skin beneath his eyes was lined and appreciably darker, suggesting his assessment of adequate rest was flawed.

She decided not to comment and steered the conversation onto the reason she'd made the trip to London that day. 'I was hoping you might go back to working for that genealogy website. After all, you designed and built most of it.'

Tommy shook his head dismissively and Jane pressed on. "You were such a help when we were at the clinic. Tracing my mother's family back kept my mind off all that negative crap I was thinking. Have you lost interest now?'

'No, I still keep my hand in. I spend a lot of time chatting on genealogy forums and help people out if I can. I get a buzz from it. I get to solve problems without them being my problems. And it is just a hobby, after all. If someone can't find their great-grandmother's date of birth, the world doesn't come to end.'

'Have you ever thought of charging people, Tommy? You know, like a consultancy fee.'

'Of course not. It's something I do for fun. If it became work I wouldn't enjoy it anymore.'

'But you were always amazing! You know so much and you have a real talent for unearthing connections and sources that no-one else would think of. I wasn't exactly a novice when we met, and I'm not stupid, but you ran rings round me.'

'I suppose that's how my brain's wired. Logic, patience, persistence. Lateral thinking. Obsession, maybe.'

Jane had got her opening and started on the speech she had semi-rehearsed on the train journey down.

'I've a confession to make. There was an ulterior motive in suggesting we meet up today. Obviously I wanted to see you again and catch up, but I wanted to run something, a business proposition, past you.'

Tommy looked up. Jane didn't read the disappointment in his face and took the eye contact as a signal to carry on.

'When my grandmother died, you know I inherited her house in Nottingham. That and my half of the London flat mean that I've got a level of financial independence, in the short-term at least. It gives me time to sort myself out, work wise. It goes without saying I can't go back to the police force.' Jane glanced away briefly before turning her focus back towards Tommy. 'I tell people it's because I hated working shifts and the sleazy lowlife you have to deal with. That's true, but it's not the truth. You know the real reason. I'm better now, obviously, but...'

Jane felt her emotions starting to freewheel but managed to apply the brakes. 'Look, here's my idea. You can make a living as a professional genealogist. There are lots of successful, well-off people who want to trace their family trees but don't have the time or expertise to do it themselves. It's easier to pay someone else. I've got a fair amount of experience now, as an amateur, and my USP – sorry, unique selling point – is that I'm a former police detective who knows how to rough people up when I need to get information out of them.' She smiled. 'Sorry, that was a joke. But I'm sure there are transferable skills I can bring to bear.'

Jane paused and gazed at Tommy expectantly. There was a palpable delay before he replied.

'I always thought you had a talent for genealogical research, certainly compared to a lot of the people I meet online. And I'm sure you do have transferable skills, but I would have thought you'd need to be, well, an *expert* to do it professionally.'

Jane shrugged. 'I know it would be taking a bit of a flyer, but lots of people learn on the job – it's often the best way. And I can always offer some kind of no ancestor, no fee guarantee, at least when I'm starting.' She stopped again and a tone of uncertainty entered her voice, 'And I have a secret weapon. I hope.'

She scanned Tommy's face for a sign of understanding. Finding it opaque, she laid out her proposition.

'I really don't know if it will take off, but I thought you could maybe help out on a consultancy basis. If I get stuck. I'd share the fees with you and maybe we'd end up with a nice little business. And then you wouldn't have to try to get inside the head of weirdos and the dodgy things they type into Internet search engines. So, what do think?'

Tommy's expression lightened. 'I think you're my friend, and if I'm honest, one of the few who exists in a non-virtual world. If that's what you want to do, I'll obviously try to help as much as I can. But I don't want to be paid – I don't want it to be work.'

Jane beamed with relief. 'You're a nice man, Tommy. I could kiss you. Look, we'll see. When, and if, I've done a couple of commissions, we'll revisit the whole question of finances and sharing the proceeds.'

The pizzas arrived. Jane watched Tommy pick up his knife and fork, and wondered whether he was one of her few real friends too. And whether she was exploiting him.

Pittsburgh proposal

It had arrived in her inbox in the early hours of the morning. That was when Tommy preferred to communicate, but this was from someone else. The corporate email address suggested a different time zone rather than an insomniac.

Tommy had built the website in an afternoon after Jane had spent a fortnight thinking about layout and composing suitable text. The focus was on a daily or hourly rate for bespoke, tailored services rather than off-the-shelf packages of the 'three generations for £300' variety. Jane stressed her willingness to travel as necessary and suggested her location in the 'centre of England' was ideal for visiting register offices around the country. She also spoke of an 'office' in the west London area close by the National Archives. Tommy seemed happy to be described in such terms and Jane felt occasional trips to the government's riverside building in Kew would get him out of the house and do him good.

Jane emphasised she was an ex-Metropolitan Police detective whose time at Scotland Yard had given her the ability to solve problems in a logical and thorough manner as well as strong interpersonal skills. Strictly speaking, she'd never actually been based in the Yard itself, but thought it might help with international recognition, particularly from potentially well-heeled American clients tracing their British roots. She made it clear that those interpersonal skills meant she was willing to interview potential relatives and other sources on a face-to-face basis. She was not a shy, retiring librarian-type, afraid to come out from behind her computer screen or to venture beyond the safe company of the dead and buried.

On balance, she decided it was important to have her photograph on the website. Initially, she sent Tommy a recent one of her looking serious in glasses but quickly replaced it. She told him that it made her appear too much the bookish researcher. In reality, she'd succumbed to the vanity she knew she'd inherited from her mother. When the website went live, it was adorned with Jane's favourite picture of herself, which was taken a few years previously. It was shot from the waist up and showed a woman of athletic build with mid-brown, shoulder-length hair and wearing a smart summer dress; the only background was a warm blue sky. She had been on holiday with Dave before their relationship had fallen apart, and the happiness showed in her face and smile. The image was still a good likeness and only slightly flattering. As Jane looked at it for the hundredth time, she saw a passably attractive woman but one whose strong features must have come from her father; no matter how hard she tried, she could not find the delicate beauty of her mother. It seemed cruel to have her vanity without her looks.

Tommy had used his expertise in search engine optimisation to ensure Jane's website came high on the list of results when people googled professional family history researchers in the UK. He tried to explain exactly what he'd done, but other than picking a good name for the site, it all went over Jane's head. Whatever he'd done, it worked: it was only a few days before the email arrived.

Jane, am interetsed in potential use of your services. Facetime me at above email address at <u>2pm your time tomorrow, Wednesday</u>.
Julian Stothard (Pittsburgh)

Jane scanned the text two or three times, the detective in her trying to read between the lines. It was certainly brief and to the point, business-like and effective. What was required of her was very clear. The underlined specificity of the time and day avoided any confusion over time zones. But there was an arrogance there too. Interested was misspelt; surely that would have been highlighted by a spell-checker, but perhaps the author didn't care. More significantly, the assumption that Jane was free at 2pm and had access to Apple's FaceTime video-calling application spoke of someone who was used to saying what he wanted and getting it. Jane knew she was only one of many offering similar services on the Web. Mr Julian Stothard could easily go elsewhere if Jane didn't fit in with his, clearly busy, schedule.

Fortunately, Jane was free at 2pm and had an iPad with FaceTime. Also, she reasoned, arrogance suggested success and success suggested money. It looked like she might have struck lucky at the first time of asking. This could be the wealthy American client she'd been hoping for.

With no background information in the message, Jane wasn't able to do any real preparation for the video call. She googled Julian Stothard and the company name revealed by his email address, and established he was managing director of a business manufacturing mining machinery. It was based in Pennsylvania, but sold its products all over the world.

Jane decided to wear something neutral, on the casual side of smart. She wasn't one for wearing much makeup, but she thought a hint of lipstick might make her look less anaemic on a video link. She tied her hair back in a simple ponytail. At precisely 2pm she took a deep breath, tried to look calm and activated the connection. It was answered almost immediately.

'Jane. Thanks for being on time. Give me two seconds. I just need to finish with my secretary.'

It was 8am in Pittsburgh. Jane had assumed the time was chosen so she would be calling Julian Stothard at home before he left for work, but clearly he was already in his office. She was also wrong-footed by his appearance and accent. She'd pictured an overweight, balding plutocrat in his fifties or sixties. The face she'd seen, albeit briefly, was of a handsome man in his early forties with a neat mop of straw-blond hair casually swept back from his face. And, whilst there was a hint of mid-Atlantic twang, the voice was unmistakably that of a well-spoken Englishman.

There was a small window on Jane's iPad screen in which she could see herself in the image being transmitted. Instinctively, she lifted the device to try to achieve a more flattering camera angle. After 30 seconds, Julian Stothard reappeared on the main area of the display.

'Jane. Sorry about that. Let's get down to business. Thanks for the FaceTime. I like to see the people I'm dealing with, don't you?'

'Well, yes, Mr Stothard. It does help.'

'Julian. Just call me Julian. Business is conducted on first name terms over here. It's been a while since I left the UK, but I think it's pretty much the norm there too now. Anyway, let's get on with it. I've got an 8:15, I'm afraid.'

Jane nodded, but Julian had already continued talking. 'I saw your website last night. Said all the right things, except I'm a bit concerned about your lack of experience. You have competitors who seem to have been around much longer.'

There was no rising inflection but there was a pause indicating that a question had been asked. It was one Jane had expected and she responded quickly.

'I accept that my main experience is in the Met, but my associate was a lead developer on one of the main family history websites. His expertise is second-to-none. People consult him from all over the world. He's remarkable, if I say so myself, but perhaps a little on the autism spectrum...' Jane felt a pang of guilt as her assessment of Tommy slipped out. 'What I mean is, I'm the people person. I'm also no novice at family history research myself. Between the two of us we make a formidable team.'

It was Julian's turn to nod. 'I would normally look for more in the way of references, but I'm also someone who trusts his judgement. To be honest, my assessment is that the genealogy element is going to be easy. My mother did her research pre-Internet. It took years, but these days it's probably a five minute job – I'd do it myself if I had the time, but I don't. Your website stood out for three reasons. You're based in the right part of the country; you're a woman and you're ex-police. Call me old-fashioned, but I still trust the British police. You suited the uniform, by the way.'

Jane looked puzzled. She hadn't put any photographs of herself in uniform onto the website.

Julian quickly resolved the confusion. 'I did a bit of digging around online. You can find a lot about someone these days. Your Facebook was a dead end, but fortunately your picture got in the paper when you received that commendation. The article said you were praised for the sensitivity with which you handled the victims of that attack. I guess it told me two things – you are who you say are, and also you're the type of person I'm looking for.'

Julian looked at his watch. 'Okay, in the interests of time, let me lay out the complete story. My mother is still in the UK, half an hour's drive from you. She's registered blind and has a live-in carer. I want you to go over to see her. She worked on our family tree twenty-odd years ago, before the Internet took off and before her eyesight went. She got quite far, but it's all on paper. She's tried various accessibility aids but can't get the hang of a computer. Anyway, here's the thing. When her own mother was still alive, they were going through the tree together and her mother let slip that there was something wrong with it. She wouldn't say what. It was something she clearly considered scandalous and she died with the secret. At the time, my mother was intrigued but had other things to worry about. Now she doesn't. She spends a lot of time in her own thoughts and this has become the big unsolved mystery in her life. She's contacted all her living relatives and they can't help. It will make her very happy if you could just tap a few names into the Internet, check her research and see what she's missed. It's going to be a big disappointment, I'm sure. Great-aunt Ethel probably had a child out of wedlock. No more than that.'

Jane sensed the opportunity to interject. 'What if it's something genuinely unpleasant?'

'I'd be very surprised, but my mother says she's prepared for that. She may be blind but she's emotionally robust. Always has been.'

'Okay, but the other problem I foresee is, well, genealogy isn't an exact science, Mr Stothard... sorry, Julian. There are gaps in the records, not everything's written down. Far from it. It isn't as easy as spending five minutes typing a few names into the Internet. At this stage it's hard to know how long this exercise will take. Do you have a budget in mind?'

'I've seen the rates on your website. Rest assured I'll pay whatever it costs, within reason. What price a mother's happiness, eh? But I'm a businessman. I pay on results, particularly when I'm dealing with an unproven supplier like yourself. If you can't deliver, I won't be paying.'

'Mr Stothard, you're asking me to look for something that effectively may not exist anymore. Once you get past living memory, family history, any history, isn't the study of what happened – it's the study of what was written down. I could potentially spend days, weeks of research. I'm sure I'll be able to expand on what your mother found 25 years ago, but that's not what you're asking me to. You're asking me to look for a needle in a haystack, but we're not sure the needle's there anymore. Perhaps we're not sure the needle was ever there. Sorry, I don't want to sound negative but I just want to set your expectations.'

'Jane, thank you for the lesson on the nature of history, and I assure you I have realistic expectations. What I think we're arguing about is payment of your fees. I don't wish to be rude, but my next call is imminent and I need a yes or no.'

Jane considered briefly and then responded, 'As I am in the process of establishing this business, I am prepared to progress on those terms. I must insist, however, that any expenses I incur – travel, ordering of certificates, etc – are covered by you irrespective.'

'Agreed. My secretary will email a brief terms of reference and all the necessary details. Please handle administrative matters through her and update her in, say, two weeks. We'll knock this on the head if you're getting nowhere. I don't want to waste each other's time. Goodbye and good luck.'

The FaceTime session was ended, but Jane continued to stare at the screen wondering what she had just committed to. She'd told Tommy she might be willing to do her first projects on a 'no ancestor, no fee' basis but felt she'd been bullied into this one. On the positive side, it was a start to her new life as a professional genealogist, though she was fairly sure she was unlikely to make money from the deal. She was normally attracted to strong, forceful men but she was also fairly sure she didn't like Julian Stothard.

Beneath the Heights of Abraham

Julian Stothard's estimate of a 30 minute drive proved optimistic, but the sun was shining and Jane took the more scenic route avoiding the motorway. It was on days like these that she appreciated having a convertible sports car, top down and travelling at speed along the A6 as it twisted and turned with the meanders of the River Derwent. The car, a bright-green Mazda MX-5, had seemed so exciting when she and Dave had first bought it. Dave had decided on the specification but allowed Jane the choice of colour. The car spoke of childhood ambitions achieved and a fun couple enjoying the rewards of successful careers. They'd imagined themselves motoring around Europe with permanent grins and hair blowing in the wind. In reality, it was just a car. They used it for shopping and commuting to work. The boot was limiting and the lack of rear seats a regular irritant. On hot days, Jane would often drive with the hood up to get some shade. Longer motorway journeys would also be exhausting unless the top was raised against the buffeting of the wind. When she and Dave had split up, he hadn't put up much of a fight to keep the little green Mazda.

When Jane arrived at Matlock Bath, though, there was a grin on her face. The weather, the car and the beauty of the steeply wooded limestone gorge all contributed, but her mood was buoyed by the happy memory of her previous visit. Her grandparents had brought her as a child, and they'd ridden the then new cable car that climbed Alpine-like over the river and trees to the so-called Heights of Abraham, looking down on the pretty spa town. Seeing it now, Jane was reminded of a passage from the novel Frankenstein which she'd later read at school. The eponymous doctor visits Matlock Bath en route to Scotland and his description of the local countryside resembling Switzerland, albeit without distant snowy peaks, rang true.

A tourist destination for 300 years, the town was little more than a village. Its mix of largely Georgian and Victorian buildings was hemmed in along one side of the river, expansion prohibited by the site's geography. Parking could be a problem, but Jane had been told that Margaret Stothard's house was set back from the road, with space for a car in front. As instructed, Jane turned by the bridge, forked right up a short hill and directly ahead was her destination, a neat modern bungalow hemmed in by terraces of older, stone-built houses. It was set back into the hillside, sitting on top of its garage, with a flight of steps twisting up through a tiny garden to the front door. Jane pulled into what passed for a driveway and killed the engine. She checked the skies, and reassured, decided to leave the hood down. She spent a few more moments gazing up the tall cliffs behind the bungalow to where she could see one of the cable car pylons rising out of the trees. On cue, a daisy chain of three gondolas climbed into view, along with three others on the downward journey. As they overlapped at the pylon, they stopped like old friends meeting in the street. They swung gently for perhaps a minute and then accelerated sharply away.

Jane looked at her watch and then took the steps two at a time. She rang the bell and almost immediately heard a muffled voice somewhere within. A few seconds later the door was opened by a middle-aged, grey-haired woman. She scanned Jane up and down before speaking.

'Can I help you?'

'Yes, my name's Jane Madden. I'm the genealogist. I don't know if it was you I spoke to on the phone? Are you Mrs Stothard?'

'No, Margaret's inside. We were expecting you. Please come through.' There was little warmth in the reply.

Jane was shown into a comfortable sitting room with a wide picture window. Like mobile phone footage on a TV news bulletin, there was a narrow view of the bridge and the far side of the gorge, cropped between the houses opposite. Margaret Stothard was sat in a large, winged armchair with her back to the window. Appearing to be in her late sixties or early seventies, she looked up when Jane entered the room, but there was blankness in her eyes.

Jane spoke first. 'Mrs Stothard, I'm Jane Madden.'

'Ah yes, dear. Thanks for driving all the way over here. Caroline says it's a lovely day out there. The village is probably heaving with visitors. I hope the traffic wasn't bad?'

'No, I had a very pleasant journey.'

'Good. Now, two things – please call me Margaret, and would you like a cup of tea?'

Caroline was despatched to make the refreshments and Margaret chatted casually about her situation and background. She clearly liked to talk and her life story emerged with remarkable brevity. She and her husband had taken an early family holiday in the Peak District. They fell in love with Matlock Bath and had talked of eventually retiring there. He was older than her and built up a successful small business. He always worked too hard, smoked and suffered a fatal heart attack when he was sixty. Their two children, Julian and Jessica, had left home by then, so Margaret decided to move to Matlock Bath on her own. Her eyesight was already bad and she could no longer drive, so the nearby station and bus routes meant she could still get around. Jessica and her family lived in Derby which was just half an hour away by train. Julian moved to America, but was a 'good boy' who phoned regularly and was a great help financially. It was he who paid for Caroline. Caroline had lived with Margaret for several years and was more of a friend than an employee. She was very protective of Margaret, but any initial off-handedness (Margaret whispered at this stage) wore off when she got to know people. As to her own disability, Margaret explained she was now almost completely blind, being left with a very restricted and blurred field of view, like looking down a straw onto a foggy day.

'But I can tell that you're quite tall,' she said. 'Well, I think I can. Maybe Julian said you were tall. I think he was quite taken with you.'

'Really?' said Jane, openly surprised.

'Well, he said you were very nice and I'm sure he said you were attractive. Or perhaps I just inferred that. Since he split up with that supermodel wife of his, I'm always trying to pair him up with somebody or other. Sorry, dear.'

'His wife was a supermodel?'

'No, that's just me being naughty. She acts like she's a supermodel. I can't see it, of course, but I'm told she's a real beauty... and clever... and successful. Still, I wouldn't describe her as nice and that was Julian's assessment of you.'

'That's kind of him, but we only talked for a few minutes. I could have a really nasty streak for all he knows.'

As soon as the words left her lips, Jane regretted them. She was supposed to be putting this vulnerable client at her ease. Fortunately, Margaret recognised their light-hearted intent.

'You don't though, do you, dear? I can tell you're nice and I'm sure you're attractive too.'

Somewhat pointlessly, Jane shook her head. 'I think my mother was always disappointed I wasn't prettier, I'm afraid. But then she was a bit of a beauty too.'

Caroline belatedly arrived with a tray on which sat two fine china cups, a small jug of milk, a bowl of sugar and a plate of biscuits. Both cups contained tea, but one had milk already added. She placed that directly in front of Margaret, mumbled something about leaving them to it and left the room again.

Jane decided it was time to steer the conversation onto the business at hand. 'Julian said you'd done a lot of work on your family tree, but there's some mystery we need to resolve?'

'Yes, dear. I'm not as clever as you, obviously, but I was a very enthusiastic amateur in my day. My day being in the steam age before computers, of course.'

Margaret carefully reached for her tea cup, her hand seemingly guided by heat. She took a small sip and continued. 'I'd get the train up to London for the day and go to St Catherine's House on the Aldwych. Then everything moved to Islington. Do you remember, dear?'

'Before my time, I'm afraid.'

'Well, they had the birth, marriage and death indexes in these huge books, one for each quarter. You'd heave them off the shelves, plonk them on the long table beneath and search through for the surname you were after. If you were looking for someone married around 1890, say, you might start with the first quarter 1885 and work your way through to the last quarter 1895 until you found them. That's what? 40 books? Or is it 44? Anyway, it took ages, but was great fun. Then there were the census records. They were on microfilm. You had to operate these huge, whirring machines which were like big tape recorders. You'd fast forward, stopping and starting until you'd got to the right place. But the census is organised by address of course, not surname. You'd have to hope your ancestor didn't move around very much to have any chance of finding them.'

'It's much, much easier searching on a computer,' contributed Jane while Margaret took another sip of tea.

'So I understand, dear. I get talking books from the library in Matlock. The librarian, he lives locally. Nice man, awful wife. Well, he was telling me that with the

Internet you just type in someone's name and all their details pop up. Simple as that.'

Jane was tempted to ask what was wrong with the librarian's wife, but resisted the diversion. 'It's not always quite that easy, but the Web has totally transformed family history research. And new information is being put online all the time.'

Jane had earlier noticed a somewhat battered hardback ledger, bulging with papers, on a small side table. 'Does the notebook have all your records and findings in?' she asked.

'Yes, dear. Caroline dug it out for me. There are two pages for each ancestor. I wrote down anything I discovered and stuck any certificates or other documents between the pages. It probably looks scruffy, but it worked well enough. At the front there should be a large sheet of paper, folded up, with the full tree drawn out.'

Jane reached for the book, carefully opened the cover and pulled out the sheet. It unfolded to A1 size. She looked around and then laid it on the carpet next to her chair. She knelt down next to it and smoothed it out. After studying it briefly, she looked up at Margaret. 'You got a long way. Well done.'

'Yes. It took years, off and on. But I was helped by relatively uncommon surnames and families that tended to stay in one place, well apart from one big move. I got further on my mother's side than my father's, but that's where we need to focus.'

'Your mother's family tree?'

'Yes. You see I was talking her through all her ancestors, pleased with myself at how clever I'd been, and she said... Well, I can't remember her exact words. She'd always been a bit funny about the whole thing and she made it clear there was a mistake, an omission. Then she clammed up. She said something like: "I shouldn't have opened my mouth. You're better off not knowing. It brought shame on my family, disgrace." It was definitely "my family", but she wouldn't say any more. Part of me always thought I should respect her wishes, leave it be. But she's been dead a long time now and it's nagging away at me. I really want to know, disgrace or otherwise.'

Jane thought this was an appropriate time to express her concern. 'There's a good chance that whatever it was died with your mother.'

'I recognise that, but I definitely got the impression that it was something tangible that I'd missed, something that was there to be found in the official records, if only I'd looked more carefully.'

Encouraged by this revelation, Jane spent another hour being talked through the tree and getting to understand Margaret's method of filing and recording information. Having spent so long working on it, the older woman's recollection of the ledger's contents was still helpfully clear. As well as her trips to the London Family Records Centre, it transpired she had also visited county record offices and several towns and villages from her ancestral past.

Jane learned that Margaret's mother's family, the Dyes, were originally farm labourers in Norfolk, but had moved to mine coal in Derbyshire in the mid 1800s. There was no suggestion of descent from blue-blooded nobility or landowning gentry. Jane would not be needing Burke's Peerage on this project, unless of course, the hidden secret was one of impregnation by a wayward aristocrat, though that seemed fanciful.

Margaret also brought out the family photograph albums. These were harder for her to navigate, but fortunately the images were annotated and largely self-explanatory. The focus was on the older black-and-white pictures, of course, but Jane was intrigued to see the young Julian Stothard in school uniform. He'd certainly been a good-looking boy.

Margaret allowed Jane to take the ledger with her when she left. It would have been impractical to copy so much information and Margaret shared her son's trust of an ex-police officer, particularly when it was the charming young woman she'd just spent a morning with. She was more reluctant to let Jane take the irreplaceable photo albums, so Jane snapped a few pages with her phone. She thought it might be useful to visualise at least some of the people she was researching.

Jane left the bungalow and began descending its steep steps. The day was still bright and clear, and had she looked behind her she would have seen a trio of cable cars silently climbing the cliffs up to the Heights of Abraham. When they reached the pylon, as on every journey, they stopped and began to rock in the gentle wind.

At the same moment, Jane was also brought to an abrupt, swaying halt.

Her mouth parted and her breathing stopped. Her limbs locked solid as if her brain had lost interest and switched off the power.

Only Jane's eyes continued to move.

On the far side of the road, she could see a tall, powerfully built man with wild black hair falling down to near his shoulders. He was smoking a cigarette and walking slowly away. Despite the distance, Jane felt sure she could smell the tobacco in her nostrils. In her mind it mingled with a long-forgotten but familiar aroma, perhaps cologne or hair oil, sweet, pungent and masculine.

Jane continued to stare, fighting the impulse to call out a name. Her rational self knew it wasn't him, couldn't be him, but her emotions had overridden sense and reason. She was transfixed like a scientist witnessing a demonstration of the paranormal, at once convincing yet utterly preposterous.

Jane's eyes remained set on the broad back and the mane of curls. Suddenly, there was a shout and a little boy rushed up from behind to take the man's hand. A wide, bearded face was briefly turned in Jane's direction.

The spell was broken. She began to breathe again.

After a long pause, her pulse rate settled and she regained her composure. She continued down to her car, unlocked the door and lowered herself in. Twisting the rear-view mirror, she gazed at the letterbox of her reflection.

'Silly, silly girl', she said.

A Derbyshire mining family

Jane drove home using the more direct route via the motorway and eventually managed to put the incident outside Margaret's house to the back of her mind. The nagging voice of self-criticism was drowned out by the rallying call of enthusiasm. Jane's first case was strangely intriguing and she wanted to get started on her research. It was going to be fun, even if it did turn out to be a wild-goose chase that Julian Stothard would refuse to pay for.

She was briefly diverted by Margaret's suggestion that her son had described Jane as 'attractive'. She quickly dismissed the thought. His mother was charming and pleasant; the man himself was not.

15 minutes after walking through her front door, Jane had already rattled off an email to update Tommy. She kept it brief because she intended to get as far as she could without his help. She wanted to test her own skills and save his expertise for when it was really required.

Jane was now kneeling on her own living room carpet. She had a stack of documents to check and the expanse of floor gave her space to spread out. On her left side, she'd unfolded the large sheet showing the summary of the family tree. On her right, she had her laptop and a fresh pad of A4 paper. The bulging ledger was directly in front. Margaret's research had been meticulously recorded and she'd been particularly zealous in ordering birth, marriage and death certificates, which were inserted between the leaves at the appropriate point. Handwritten copies of census returns were also included, but these were less complete because of the difficulty of searching through the old, geographically organised microfilm records.

Each individual ancestor had a pair of facing pages, beginning with Margaret herself and her late husband,

John. The sequence then worked back, the allocated space necessarily doubling with each generation. Jane realised it was a system that worked well for recording direct lineage, but was restrictive if you wanted to expand sideways to include siblings, uncles, aunts and cousins. A limited amount of effort had gone into researching John's family. It looked to Jane that Margaret had simply recorded what he might have known personally: details of his parents and grandparents and two great-grandparents. It was Margaret's project and she'd clearly devoted her time to her own line of descent. Even then, Margaret's father was of Irish extraction and the trail had gone cold when the O'Keefes were back in their home country. The majority of names in the ledger therefore belonged to Margaret's maternal line, the Dyes and the families with whom they intermarried.

Margaret's mother had indicated that the disgrace she sought to hide lay buried somewhere amongst those names. Jane picked up the notepad. Up close, shame could feel overwhelming, but she reasoned, everything shrinks and fades with distance, before eventually disappearing into the haze. Jane wrote down her first heading.

FOCUS AREA – Margaret's maternal line, <u>3 generations</u>

Mother:
    ANNE HANNAH DYE (married William O'Keefe)
    – 1 child (i.e. Margaret herself)
Grandparents:
    REUBEN DYE & MABEL BUTLER
    – 4 children. 1 boy (killed World War II), 3 girls
Great-grandparents:
    THOMAS DYE & HANNAH BOWER
    – 14 children (including 3 from 1st wife, Hannah Fox)
    DAVID BUTLER & MARY PADGETT
    – 3 children

Having identified where she should concentrate, Jane continued reading and scribbling notes to flesh out the people who took Margaret's family back into the 19th century.

Margaret's mother, born Anne Hannah Dye in 1925, had one older brother, Kenneth, who never married and was killed in World War II. Her two sisters were younger but were now also deceased. Margaret had contacted their children, living in Wales and Australia, but any family secrets known to their mothers had died with them.

Margaret's maternal grandparents were Reuben Dye and Mabel Butler. Reuben was a Derbyshire coal miner and Mabel had been a housemaid before their marriage. Reuben was the last of 14 children, 12 of whom survived to adulthood. His father, Thomas Dye, was also a miner in the same Derbyshire pit village of Dowley. He married twice. His wives were confusingly both called Hannah, the first dying after producing Thomas's first three children. The family was raised in a two-up two-down terrace, the overcrowding eased by a 30-year age difference between the oldest child and Reuben. Reuben had, apparently, a rather broken relationship with his eldest siblings, a divide forming partly through age but mainly through maternity. The second Hannah was little more than a child herself when she was married to raise her older husband's motherless children. That she did, but in the harsh poverty of Victorian working-class life, she was unable to love them.

The last observation was clearly conjecture rather than a statement of fact. In the ledger, Margaret had credited it to her own mother based on 'impressions from conversation with her father, the late Reuben Dye'.

Margaret's maternal grandmother, Mabel, came from a smaller family of three children. Their father, David Butler, was described as a farm labourer on his daughter's birth certificate. His wife, Mary, gave birth to

Mabel in a farmhouse on the outskirts of a different Derbyshire village. Calling up an online Ordnance Survey map, Jane could see that Mabel's village was perched on a high hilltop, some three miles from Dowley. The route between the two was by a succession of narrow lanes which snaked down, across and up the far side of a wide valley. For Mabel and Reuben it would have been a peacefully isolated country walk. Today it was interrupted by an eight-lane barrier of tarmac and speeding vehicles, the M1, the main artery linking London to the cities of the North. It was a section Jane recognised, and apart from the motorway, the area was still distinctly rural and untouched. The constant, rumbling traffic ran along the valley floor between a sprawl of irregular fields whose hedgerows were planted at least another century before Reuben courted Mabel around the time of the First World War.

In her early teens, Mabel had gone into service working as a maid for the local doctor who had brought her into the world. Jane wondered exactly how the young serving girl had met the miner from the village a few miles distant. It wasn't recorded in the ledger and reminded Jane of the potential futility of the exercise she was undertaking. It was information that had surely died with the people concerned. Perhaps mother had told daughter of her parents' first encounter, but she had now passed away too. The circumstances of that meeting, of love at first sight or initial indifference, were lost forever.

Jane realised she simply had to trust Margaret's conviction that they were looking for something more concrete, something that would have been recorded. As Jane sat back and scanned the family tree in front of her, her initial suspicions fell on one section in particular: the divided family of Reuben Dye. Was it just a stepmother's coldness or could something more sinister have caused the rift? Jane brought up the mobile phone images she had taken of Margaret's photo albums. There had been a single studio portrait of Reuben's parents, Thomas and the second Hannah. Mounted on thick, somewhat battered card, it showed the couple sitting rigidly upright and surrounded by eight of their children. Margaret had dated it to before Reuben was born, and at least one of the children depicted would not live to adulthood. Unsmiling formality was the norm in photography at the time, but was it Jane's imagination or was there a darker tension in the sepia faces staring back at her?

Jane got to work checking the names, dates and relationships that Margaret had unearthed 20 or more years previously. Whereas Margaret had taken days and months, the Internet allowed Jane to find the same information in minutes and hours. She started at Margaret's mother's generation, searching for births with a family name Dye and a mother's maiden name of Butler. Anne Hannah Dye and her three siblings were immediately revealed, all registered in the Derbyshire district which included the village of Dowley. Helpfully, all four children had been given two first names, so tracking their subsequent lives was made easier. The three sisters had married in this country, but one had subsequently emigrated to Sydney in Australia. As she had died less than 30 years ago, the New South Wales website declined to reveal any record of her death, but Jane knew Margaret was still in touch with that branch of the family so reasoned the date in Margaret's ledger was reliable.

The brother, Margaret's uncle, had been killed in World War II. Margaret had written that he was a stoker on HMS Hood and one of over 1400 men killed when the ship was sunk by the German battleship Bismarck in 1941. Margaret had no official documentation relating to his death, and Jane felt vaguely sceptical that it had occurred in probably the most well-known British naval loss of the war. Any thoughts she may have had about

Kenneth Reuben Dye having survived the conflict and being the source of the family disgrace were soon quelled. She found him on a website devoted to the memory of Hood. It included a photograph of a handsome young man, in truth little more than a boy, wearing a new uniform and the confident smile of one about to embark on the huge battlecruiser, seemingly invincible pride of the Royal Navy. It was the same picture Margaret had in her album. Jane searched further and also found him on a site dedicated to Derbyshire war memorials. It included a picture of a weathered bronze plaque mounted in the lychgate of Dowley parish church. Some of the names were indistinct, but beneath the picture was a list of each serviceman commemorated. When Jane clicked on K R Dye, further details opened up confirming that this was indeed Kenneth Reuben Dye, Stoker 2nd Class, RN, who died on May 24 1941, son of Mr and Mrs Reuben Dye of Dowley.

Jane had one last try with this level of the family tree. She looked for illegitimate children born in Derbyshire with Mabel's maiden name in the years before her marriage. Finding no skeletons there, she decided she could finally move on to the previous generation. It was here her suspicions continued to rest, and she hoped something untoward would reveal itself, despite the passage of a century or more since their births.

Jane spent several hours in the long-dead company of Thomas Dye, the Hannahs and their 14 children. Census data being restricted for 100 years, both the 1901 and 1911 surveys had been released since Margaret did her research. Jane was also aided, of course, by modern search technology and had soon confirmed and expanded on Margaret's work. She filled out the lives of all 12 of the Dye children who survived childhood, following them through their own families to their final ends. The elder boys had moved 40 miles north to the coalfields of South Yorkshire, one of them subsequently dying in the mud of a World War I trench. That conflict cast a wide shadow, and Jane was particularly touched by the fate of the oldest girl. The only daughter of the first Hannah, she had stayed in Dowley, married and had three sons of her own. All three joined the army, and one by one, all three fell, to be buried near different battlefields as the Great War stuttered and flared across northern France and Belgium. Jane looked again at the website showing the lychgate war memorial and there they were: T Oakley, W Oakley and G Oakley, finally reunited.

Jane couldn't find any trace of Margaret's grandfather, Reuben Dye, having joined up. The majority of World War I records were destroyed by a German bomb in the second war, but the medal cards were spared and nothing had been awarded to anyone with his name. Campaign medals were given to all combatants, so this seemed noteworthy as Reuben would have been the right age for service and a single man at the time. But he was also a miner. The government considered the extraction of coal vital war work, and being in a reserved occupation, he would have been exempt from the draft. But many of his contemporaries would have volunteered nonetheless. Jane pondered whether this could have been the reason for the family schism. His brother and his nephews did their duty and paid the ultimate price while Reuben stayed at home. Had he been ostracised? Jane felt it was also significant that Margaret's mother didn't seem to know about her cousins who died in the war. She certainly hadn't told Margaret or surely she would have taken her researches sideways down that branch of the family tree? Or maybe that was the point. Maybe this was the shameful family mystery.

Jane sat back and thought. She had found something, but she had found nothing. It was largely conjecture. She tried to put herself in the mindset of the time. Coal was essential for keeping industry and transport running;

mining was a dirty and dangerous job. There was a strong argument that Reuben was doing his bit. In World War II young men, the so-called Bevin Boys, were actually conscripted to work down the pits. Reuben's sister might be full of bitterness because she'd lost her three sons, but would his daughter really consider it an unspeakable disgrace 80 years later?

Jane knew she had to keep going, dig deeper, further. If the answer was there she was determined to find it.

First encounter

Jane had collated a file holding the results of all her work. She'd expanded the tree significantly but was far from convinced she had achieved her principal objective. As well as Reuben Dye's questionable wartime cowardice, she'd now found at least two illegitimate births amongst remoter cousins. Even at the time, these were not as uncommon as people sometimes thought, so could hardly be classified as scandalous.

She considered asking for Tommy's help, but she knew there were still things she could do on her own. And part of her wanted to impress him with answers rather than questions. As a compromise, she emailed him another brief update and planned her next steps.

There were a few extra certificates she needed. They would contain information not available online, though she expected them merely to confirm what she already knew. The quickest way of getting them was to go to the relevant register office, in this case Chesterfield in Derbyshire, and pay for them to be copied there. It was not the cheapest way, but Julian Stothard had agreed to cover such expenses and Jane felt justified in spending his money. Indeed, it gave her a certain childish pleasure and she knew it wouldn't bankrupt him.

She made an early start and arrived at the register office as it was opening. The staff were friendly and efficient, and just over an hour later Jane was back behind the wheel of the Mazda, its hood up against threatening clouds. Her ultimate destination was Margaret Stothard's bungalow in Matlock Bath. Having made the appointment for early afternoon, Jane had time to take a small detour and visit the village of Dowley. She wasn't looking for anything in particular, but thought it might help to see where so much of the story she was immersed in had taken place. Perhaps the ghosts of the past would whisper their secrets in her ear.

Jane pulled into an empty car park whose tarmac had been rippled and broken by the roots of ill-kempt, bushy trees. The village was not what Jane had expected. If its origins were rural, of farmers and markets, at some stage in the 19th century it had been hijacked by the industrial revolution. That circle had turned and now Dowley appeared to have been cast loose again, unwanted and spent. There was an overall air of gloom that could only partially be blamed on the weather.

The car park was in the centre of the village. To one side was an open grassy area dominated by a pit winding wheel standing half-buried in the ground. Jane assumed, correctly, it had come from the headgear above the now-defunct local mine. Jane had driven past where an old map had told her the mine was located, but the buildings were demolished, the land reclaimed and the site now indistinguishable from the fields that surrounded it. It was the houses that were the main monument to the place's past: Victorian, red-brick, two-up two-down terraces, their uniformity broken only by their varying states of disrepair.

Facing the entrance to the car park was the village church. Of similar vintage to the housing, its Gothic Revival windows were set in buttressed yellow stone, though it eschewed a tower in favour of a simple bell turret crowning the central gable wall. The churchyard was entered by a wooden-framed lychgate with a pitched, slated roof. It was a feature of ecclesiastical architecture originally intended for the shelter of coffins before burial, but by the time this example was built its purpose was more decorative than functional. That said, in the 20th century it had found a role: it housed the memorial to the young men of the village who perished in first one, then another great war.

Jane crossed the road to the gate and was saddened by what she found. The list of names cast in bronze had gone; a replacement had been installed, this time set slightly lower down, cemented into the wall that formed the base of the lychgate. At first sight, Jane was horrified at the thought that the new plaque could be made of cheap glass fibre, but it was cold to the touch and she realised it was polished stone, probably granite, whose purple-grey shine would mellow with time. The story was immediately obvious. She had read of war memorials being vandalised for the sake of a few pounds worth of scrap metal. She wondered what a previous generation would have done to the perpetrators of such crimes and lamented that today's punishment would probably be little more than the ticking-off of community service.

Jane began reading the engraved gold letters. She soon reached the three Oakley brothers and found herself unexpectedly beginning to cry. She imagined their mother standing in this same spot, year after year after year, ageing slowly whilst they could not. Jane pictured a broken woman, head bowed and alone with her thoughts, repeatedly asking why and trying never to think of how.

Jane breathed deeply, and through the tears, continued scanning down looking for another name. There were a trio of Wilsons and Jane wondered if they too were brothers, or perhaps a father and sons. As on every other war memorial she'd seen, the casualties in the first conflict outnumbered the second. Jane knew that whilst the worldwide suffering was worse in World War II, four years of slaughter in the stalemate of the trenches had killed a far greater number of British servicemen in World War I.

The name she was searching for was at the very bottom, but when she first read it, it seemed wrong. She reached into her bag for a tissue to wipe her eyes, and as her vision shifted focus, she was suddenly distracted.

On the far side of the street, climbing into a white van that had been there when she arrived, was a man. Jane had the distinct feeling he'd been watching her and had turned away when she'd noticed him.

She only saw his back, but he was tall and powerfully built with unkempt black hair falling down to near his shoulders.

For the second time in a week, Jane was transfixed as she watched the van drive away. This time her rational mind's plea that it couldn't be him was more muted. Her heart was racing and she began to tremble as her emotional gauges spiked, resentful despair fighting a child-like want.

This man could be the right age.

The hair was streaked with grey and it seemed more lank as if its life had sapped away. The body too, though still huge and intimidating, was heavier round the middle. The man's movement, the effort as he climbed up into the driver's seat, had seemed more deliberate, perhaps more tired. The years were taking their toll.

Those years rolled back as Jane was transported into the memory that haunted her. She was the small girl on a quayside, under the looming bows of a vast grey ship, squinting in the sunshine as she stared up at the tall silhouette bent over her, saying goodbye and not understanding what it meant.

After the van disappeared from view, it took a least a minute for Jane to regain any control. She was still crying, but no longer out of sympathy for a long-dead woman.

She began to curse herself for being so foolish. 'That's twice in the space of a fucking week, you stupid fucking bitch!'

She mouthed the words more than spoke them, and only the harder syllables made any sound. Despite there being no-one within sight or earshot to question the

48

outburst, Jane immediately shrank back into the shadows of the lychgate, as if judgemental eyes were burning into her from all directions.

Silent now, her thoughts sought balance and calm. Of course it wasn't him, she told herself. It was just a larger than average, middle-aged man in need of a haircut. A builder, probably, judging by his size and the white van.

This was a fixation Jane thought she'd left behind. She was beginning to worry that she was getting ill again.

Jane normally had a strict zero-tolerance policy on drinking and driving, but she needed something to steady her nerves. She reasoned she'd be okay with one glass of wine, particularly if she had something to eat. She forgot about the war memorial and searched around for a pub.

She didn't have to look far. There seemed to be two, fifty yards away and facing each other on opposite sides of the road. When Jane got there, she realised that the New Inn must have closed down in the relatively recent past. The door was locked. One of its panels had been roughly repaired using chipboard, which was also fixed into place behind all the ground floor windows. The green paint on the sills was peeling, but the blackboard screwed next to the entrance was still promising 'Every Thursday, Bingo from 8:30 pm'. 'Today's' beer prices had been written on one window pane using a chalk pen. Jane wanted to calculate how long ago 'today' had been, but realised she didn't know how much a pint of John Smith's would cost there and then, never mind six months or a year ago.

The White Hart across the road was still in business, freshly painted and with picnic tables laid out on its tarmac forecourt. There was a banner over the door offering 'Sky Sports'. But If the pub had ever needed to compete with its neighbour and advertise the cheapness of its beer, those days were gone.

Jane walked through the door and looked around. It was just before midday, but there were a few stalwarts already spread around the pastel-walled room. Two elderly gentlemen in flat caps sat at separate tables, each silently cradling a half-pint glass. One had a copy of the Daily Mirror laid out in front of him; the other was just staring into space. The large flat-screen TV on the wall was switched off and the only noise was coming from a pair of younger men in one of the corners. Jane studied them briefly. They were slightly built, wore similar hooded jackets, and had the same closely clipped haircut and thin, pointed, rather weaselly faces. They could have been brothers, but something about their features suggested otherwise. Jane found herself instantly pegging them as petty criminal lowlife and had to stop herself. They could easily be roofers or tilers or binmen taking an early lunch. They were certainly none of her business: her days as a policewoman looking for a potential miscreant or a grass were over.

Jane turned quickly away when one of the men spotted her looking in their direction. He said something to the other which she couldn't hear and then they both laughed salaciously.

The landlord, a tall man with a beard, was standing behind the bar and greeted Jane with a broad smile. He checked his watch and then spoke.

'Good morning, duck. What can I get you?'

'A glass of white wine please. A small one.' She emphasised the word small. 'What do you have in?'

'I think we've got a Sauvignon Blanc in the fridge at the moment. That okay?'

'That's perfect. Thank you. And do you do food?'

'We just do rolls during the week. There's cheese and pickle or ham.'

He pointed to a shelf behind the bar with pre-prepared rolls wrapped in cling film. Jane asked for ham and waited as he got her order. She paid with a £20 note, and when he handed over her change, the landlord continued chatting.

'Not seen you round here before. Just passing through?'

Jane was still feeling agitated and not in the mood for small talk. 'Yes. I'm on my way to Matlock. Look, maybe you can help me. There was a man, a big man, sixtyish maybe, long dark hair, getting in a white van, just up the road in front of the church. Do you know him?'

Jane saw the landlord's expression harden. Perhaps he didn't like the police and her past had betrayed her. Whatever the reason, he clammed up abruptly.

'Lots of blokes with white vans round here, duck. Doesn't ring any bells. Anyway, enjoy your roll.' With that, he turned and walked into the room behind the bar.

Jane sat down in the corner furthest from the two men she'd mentally labelled the weasel brothers. She kept her gaze down but could feel them staring at her. It made her uncomfortable, so she reluctantly decided to finish her lunch as quickly as she could.

She'd taken the second bite from her slightly stale ham roll when there was another snort of ribald laughter. She couldn't quite hear what he was saying, but the louder of the weasel brothers appeared to be getting more animated as if egging himself on to come over to talk to her. In her current state of mind, it was the last thing she needed. She felt an anger begin to ferment and fizz within her.

Fortunately, at that moment, she saw the landlord reappear at the bar. He looked sternly towards the two men and they quietened. Jane smiled at him in gratitude; the response was a simple nod.

There were two weasels in a bar...

When the woman had finished her lunch and left the pub, Dean turned to Steve and smirked.

'Well, she was a pleasant distraction. And I don't mean her orange, glow-in-the-dark jacket. She wasn't exactly pretty, but she was fit. Well fit. I've had better looking, but all her bits were in the right place. If you know what I mean. All she needed was a touch more makeup, some nice high heels, and she could have taken me home for a bit of afternoon rest and recuperation.'

'I think she was a bit out of our league, Deano.'

'Fuck off! Out of your league, maybe. You and your "mild learning difficulties", which we all know is code for "thick as a brick".' Steve shuffled uncomfortably, but Dean carried on obliviously. 'I told you, I've had better than her. I turn on the old Smith charm, give 'em a bit of old chat, wow them with my prestigious intellect and wham, bam, thank you very much, ma'am.'

Dean was on his third pint of lager and it was making him cocky. Even so, he wouldn't be so effusive with anyone but Steve. His friend and sometime accomplice was the one person in Dowley who would be bothered to listen.

Dean took another swig of beer and returned to the subject they'd been discussing before Jane had provided them with a brief interlude. He looked around and lowered his voice.

'I'm skint. I need some money. In the past we could have gone out and found ourselves a bit of lead off a church roof, or we did those war memorials for a while, remember? Trouble is, the low-hanging fruit has gone and the law are clamping down on the scrap business these days.' He took another pull at his pint. 'So, you need to nick some stuff from the site. Power tools would be favourite. Always a market for them. Professional ones cost a bomb, and there's always some chippie or sparky willing to slip you a few quid, no questions asked.'

Steve nervously shook his head. 'I told you. I don't like to, Deano. Michael did me a big favour giving me a job again and he'd kill me if he caught me. He's not a man you want to cross.'

Dean brought his face up close to Steve's. 'I'm not a man you want to cross neither. Maybe I'll give you a kicking too. And don't forget, thicko, you owe me. I did time for you.'

Dean gave Steve a sharp slap on the side of the head to suggest its emptiness. Steve cowered submissively but continued his pleas.

'I told you. I don't like to. And besides, you didn't do time for me. You did it to cover your own arse. If I ever told—'

'Shut the fuck up! You ain't telling no-one or you're dead. I've warned you before. Fucking dead.' Dean was whispering now. 'Don't fuck with me, Steve. No other fucker takes me seriously, but you know what I'm capable of when I get pushed too far.'

The wedding album

Jane parked up in front of the bungalow. Opening the car's small boot, she lifted out a yellow leather tote bag. It felt heavy. Whilst she knew most the weight came from her ageing laptop, the volume of paperwork she'd accumulated added psychosomatically to the strain.

Tommy's response to her email had been a text gently reminding her that: 'With time and distance, shame and disgrace become colour and interest. A nastily violent criminal ancestor transported to Australia becomes Ned Kelly.'

It had been Jane's starting point but she already knew she'd lost sight of it. She'd let herself be drawn into the genealogical process and methodology. It had been interesting and it had been consuming. She'd been successful expanding Margaret's family tree; she'd gone back further and much wider, but it was almost certainly a distraction. It was time to refocus. She needed to talk to Margaret in more detail about her closer family and unearth some better kind of clue, something nearer to home.

As before, the door was answered by Margaret's live-in helper, Caroline, and Jane was shown into the sitting room. Margaret was delighted to see her again and fascinated when the younger woman gave her a brief overview of the scope and number of relatives she'd been able to find.

'My dear, you've done so well and it's been so quick! Isn't the Internet wonderful! Well, I'm sure you're wonderful too. I'm sure Julian will be very pleased that he found you.'

'Unfortunately, my contract with your son was to find some kind of scandalous omission, and I don't think I've been successful, despite all my efforts so far.'

'Are you saying he won't pay you for all this work?'

'In short, yes. But I accepted the contract, so I can't complain.'

Margaret looked sad and concerned. 'So you won't let me keep what you've found? I'd love to go through it all properly.' Realising she was sounding selfish, her tone became apologetic. 'Julian takes after his father, I'm afraid. He was a shrewd businessman too, albeit on a smaller scale. Always drove a hard bargain. Wouldn't give anyone "owt for nowt", as he would say.'

Jane shook her head and smiled. 'No, of course you can keep it. I can honestly say I've enjoyed working on it. And it's of no use to me.'

'That's sweet of you, dear.'

Jane leaned forwards. 'I haven't given up, though. I'd like to chat a little more about your more immediate family – aunts, uncles, grandparents, that kind of thing – just to see if there's anything we're overlooking. Before we do, though, there's one idea I'd like to run past you...'

Jane slowly explained her theory about Reuben Dye, Margaret's maternal grandfather, and his avoidance of military service in World War I.

Margaret looked on the verge of tears. 'So the three boys who died were my grandfather's nephews?'

'Yes, though they were the about the same age as Reuben. Their mother was the eldest in the family, Reuben the youngest,' clarified Jane.

'That poor woman. Losing all three of her sons. It's unimaginable. Can't life be cruel?'

'It can. It certainly can. But why do you think your mother didn't know or tell you about them? They were her first cousins after all.'

'I remember something about brothers dying in the Great War. But I always thought they were much more distant family.' Margaret paused briefly. 'You've got to remember there was a rift between my grandfather's siblings. They had two mothers, the two Hannahs. The children of the first felt unloved by the second. That coupled with the gap in ages meant they had little to do with each other.'

'Do you think your grandfather could have been thought a coward for not fighting in the war? You hear stories of people being given white feathers for not joining up.'

Margaret's sightless eyes turned towards the window and seemed to stare distantly at the narrowed view beyond. 'There was a string of five girls before he was born. Reuben means "behold, a son" in Hebrew, you know.'

'Yes, you put that in your ledger,' said Jane, slightly confused by the tangential aside and failing to disguise it in her voice.

'Sorry, dear, my mind isn't wandering. The point is, he was probably mollycoddled by his mother and sisters as a child. Maybe he wasn't the bravest, but the army wouldn't have had him, so it wouldn't matter.'

'Why wouldn't the army want him?'

'I only vaguely remember my grandfather before he died. But I do know he had a bad limp. He was born with a club foot. A doctor messed around with it when he was a baby, but it just made it worse. He was mobile enough to work down the mine. Just. Of course, coming from where he did, when he did, he had little choice.'

'But he wasn't going to pass an army medical,' said Jane, somewhat defeatedly.

'No, and my mother once told me that's why he didn't move to Yorkshire like his older brothers. Dowley was only a small pit and easier for him to get around.'

'Why didn't you mention his club foot in your ledger?' It was not meant as an accusation. Jane was genuinely intrigued why a seemingly meticulous woman would omit such a defining characteristic.

'He was always very embarrassed by his limp, apparently. Got horribly bullied as a child. My mother was very close to him and I thought it might please her if

I let his disability fade from history. She was never enthusiastic about me doing the family tree, so I felt it was a peace offering.'

'But no-one's going to blame an obviously disabled man if he doesn't enlist,' restated Jane, for her own ears rather than Margaret's.

Margaret shook her head in confirmation. 'It could well have been that his elder half-sister – embittered by the death of her sons – resented the fact that my grandfather stayed at home. But I don't think my mother could have thought of it as shameful. He couldn't help it, poor lad, and as I said, she was devoted to him.'

Jane was only slightly disappointed that her one hypothesis had unravelled. She'd never held out much hope and Margaret's revelation was convincing.

The conversation diverted onto other members of Margaret's closer family, and she tried to flesh out some of the people based on her own recollections or what she'd heard from others. Jane began using the photo albums to see just how fat Auntie Ruthie had become in later life, or how short Auntie Lizzie's husband been, and hoping that some clue would emerge from the entertaining but trivial detail. At the bottom of the pile, Jane saw a cover she didn't recognise and queried it with Margaret.

'There's a dark-red one that I haven't seen before.'

'Oh yes, dear, I meant to mention that. It's kept separately with some of my mother's old things, and Caroline didn't bring it out last time. It's my parent's wedding album.'

Jane's eyebrows lifted.

Despite the gesture being lost on her, Margaret seemed to read Jane's thoughts. 'You'd hope that could tell us a story or two. Trouble is, none of the photographs are labelled. I'm told you can recognise a few of the people – my mum and dad and immediate family – but otherwise it's full of strangers. Long-dead strangers, at that.'

'Didn't your mother ever go through it with you when you were younger?'

'No, I don't really know where she used to keep it. On the mantelpiece there was always a framed photo of her and my dad outside the church. I think I assumed that was all you got in the forties – the war hadn't been over long when they married. After she died, her flat was in such a mess. She was starting to get confused at the end. But we found the album when we were clearing all her things. By then, my eyes were really going downhill and I struggled to make anyone out. My daughter, Jessica, took it home for a while, but she's not that interested and gave it back to me for safekeeping.'

Jane opened the leather-bound book. It had obviously been produced professionally, with pages interleaved by crisp, semi-transparent tissue paper. The condition was immaculate and Jane lifted each sheet carefully and slowly to avoid creasing or tearing something that had survived a biblical lifespan undamaged. The images themselves were in sharp black and white, printed on very glossy paper and carefully mounted, one to a page. Jane stopped at one group photograph. Somehow it stood out as odd. It seemed to be posing a question that she knew she couldn't answer. She picked up a different album and flicked through it until she found what she was looking for.

Placing the two open pages side by side, Jane looked up at Margaret and said, 'Your mother had the two sisters, Elizabeth and Ruth – am I right?'

'That's right, dear.'

'And they attended your own wedding and are standing next to your mother in several of the photographs?'

'Yes. You can't miss the fact they're three sisters. There was a very strong family resemblance.'

'Yes, you can definitely see it. But now I'm looking at your mother's wedding album. I suspect you know, but your aunts were the bridesmaids. They're, what, twenty-five years younger, but it's still unmistakably them. As you'd expect, there's a photo of just the bride and bridesmaids together, but the picture facing it has another woman with them. She's roughly the same age, and well, she's got very similar features. Or maybe it's the way they seem to be so at ease with each other. Now, why would you photograph the four of them together? Just them and no-one else. It's almost as if she were a fourth sister.'

The bell and the biro

Jane was back home in Nottingham and was studying the 70-year-old wedding album more closely. She'd been allowed to take it because it promised to offer potential clues, assuming she could identify more of the guests.

There was one photograph Jane kept returning to. The more she looked at it, not only the physical appearance of the mystery fourth woman, but her body language alongside the bride and bridesmaids, the more she was convinced of the closeness of their bond. There was one other visual clue: the woman was wearing a corsage, a floral adornment she shared with the mothers of the bride and groom.

Obviously, she could be a cousin, but Jane had identified most, if not all, of those and none seemed to fit the bill in terms of age. There was also the question of why the woman hadn't been made a bridesmaid. The answer to that appeared to lie in the final group picture, which depicted all of the wedding guests standing outside the hotel that had hosted the reception. Ms X, as Jane had christened her, was standing next to a rather dashing-looking man with jet-black hair. They were each holding a young child and leaning into each other. Ms X appeared to be Mrs X, mother of two. On that basis, she would presumably be ineligible for a bridesmaid's dress at a 1940s wedding.

There was no labelling or annotation in the album, not even a frontispiece to identify the bride and groom. There was, however, a small cardboard pocket inside the rear cover. This held maybe a dozen pieces of confetti, still bright after 70 years, and a delicate little notepad, around two inches tall, with a shiny silver cover and shaped like a bell. When opened, it had only a few leaves of plain white paper onto which people had signed their names. These, then, were the attendees at the wedding, and it was on this document that Jane knew she had to focus her attention.

The names were in columns and written as small as the person could manage in a mixture of blue and black ink. Some were clearly scribed in fountain pen and a few had smudged. The ink hadn't transferred to the facing page and Jane reasoned that the smudges had occurred because drops of liquid had found their way onto the thin paper. She visualised the silver bell being passed around the guests at the reception and sniffed it for traces of champagne. All she found was the musty smell of old books. The last three pages of signatures appeared to have been written with the same blue pen. Under a magnifying glass, the flow of ink seemed to resemble that of a modern ballpoint. Jane thought the wedding was too early for such a pen, but a quick check on the Internet established that they'd been made for RAF crews in World War II, and after the war, a factory in Reading was producing Biros for sale to the general public.

Having discounted anachronistic forgery, Jane concentrated on the names again. Apart from a single unintelligible scrawl, all the signatures were in the legible copperplate demanded in the classrooms of the late 19th and early 20th centuries. Some of the married women signed themselves with their husband's first name or initial, but most used their own forename in full. The few young children at the wedding were recorded in a parent's hand. About a third of the signatures meant nothing to Jane. She presumed these were friends of the bride and groom or their parents. The other two thirds, however, matched the people Jane had found while researching the family tree. In many cases, she could identify the specific person. In others, she at least recognised the surname as being one which had intermarried with the Dyes.

Eventually, Jane felt confident that she'd eliminated the other possibilities and pinned down the identity of the mystery woman, Mrs X, along with Mr X and their two children. Jane was almost certain they were Mary Smith, James Smith, Lois and Ernie Smith. Jane's feeling of success was only slightly tempered by the potential challenge of tracing individuals with England's most common family name.

Having named them, Jane turned her attention and her magnifying glass to their faces. The Dye sisters, the bride and two bridesmaids, took after their father and were not the prettiest of young women. When pictured alongside them, Mary Smith shared the same features, but hers were probably the most attractive. Even so, she was still far from beautiful. Her husband, James Smith, on the other hand, had the looks of a film star. His jet-black hair was Brylcreemed back and a Clark Gable moustache sat over a full mouth and lantern jaw. There were sharp shadows under high cheekbones. Jane was initially drawn to him, but the attraction lessened the more she looked. There was also an arrogance about the man; something in his smile spoke of guile or perhaps shiftiness. It was not a face that inspired trust.

The two young children, one little more than a toddler, had very contrasting appearances. The older, Lois, looked just like her father: jet black hair and, assuming it did not fade with age, a beauty that would break many a young man's heart in years to come. The boy, Ernie, was plainer to the point of ugliness and had very straight, white-blond hair that stood out as unique amongst the guests at the wedding. Jane knew that children's hair often darkens as they grow older, but he was a striking incongruity nonetheless.

Jane now had names and faces. She even had a perception of James Smith's personality, though that it was based on nothing more than intuition, an intuition that had let her down before. The next step was to establish the relationship between Mary Smith and the three sisters she resembled so much. Jane remained convinced they shared some form of close familial bond.

Jane returned to her computer screen. James, Mary and Ernest Smith were very common names, Lois's less so. The key seemed to be finding links between them and back into Margaret Stothard's family tree.

Jane's first step was to look for marriage records uniting Smith with Dye, or Butler, or any of the other surnames she'd found in her previous research. Unfortunately, nothing seemed to fit. There were no James Smiths marrying a potentially suitable Mary.

Jane then turned to the children. She held out great hope with little Lois. It was a name she could only associate with Superman's girlfriend, Lois Lane, and was surprised to find it going back to at least 1837 in towns as un-American as Swaffham and Dewsbury. That said, there were only a handful of Lois Smiths born in England and Wales in the war years, but none had a mother's maiden name that Jane recognised. And there were no illegitimate Lois Dyes, Butlers, Bowers, Padgetts or Oakleys.

Disappointed, Jane moved on to Lois's brother, Ernest. This time there were significantly more matches, but again, nothing that stood out as a possible connection. In particular, there were no Ernest Smiths who might share a mother with a sister called Lois. Jane tried searching for the name Ernie, but that level of official informality appeared unfashionable in the 1940s and led nowhere.

Having drawn a blank with England and Wales, Jane wondered whether the family could have been living in Scotland. It was possible that a pregnant mother might be evacuated north of the border to avoid the bombing in one of England's industrial cities. The Scottish government kept its records separate and maintained its own family history website. Jane switched her attentions there, but ultimately it, too, proved a dead end. After

Scotland, Jane moved to Northern Ireland and then down to the Republic. Again, she drew a blank.

Jane had been searching for hours and her frustration was escalating into dejection. The Smith family seemed to have left no trace of their existence. She started questioning her basic assumptions. Obviously the parents might never have married, but could the surname Smith be a complete invention? Mr and Mrs Smith might be a masquerade adopted when checking into a hotel for an illicit affair, but surely not when you're at a wedding with people you seem to know well? The apparent ages of the children suggested they were born during or shortly after the war. Foreign travel would be difficult if not impossible at that time, certainly for the social class that attended the nuptials of a Derbyshire coalminer's daughter. So why couldn't Jane find a record of Lois's or Ernie's birth, legitimate or otherwise, anywhere in the whole of the British Isles? Was adoption proving the barrier? Was Mary not the natural mother to one or both of the children? Would that explain their differing looks?

Jane's ideas widened to European refugees or to a Private Smith returning to England with the woman and children he'd met on active service abroad, things which Jane knew might be impossible to research.

Ultimately though, her instincts still told her that the mystery woman in the photograph was a local girl and closely related to the bride and her bridesmaids. Jane felt sure there was a link hiding somewhere.

She was tired. It had been a long day and it seemed like she'd made no real progress. She finally conceded that she needed help. Perhaps in anticipation, she'd been working methodically throughout the project and had been typing notes as she went along. She scanned in some extra images and attached the files to a rather rambling email summarising her current thoughts and questions. Feeling guilty, she pressed send and went to bed.

Forensic genealogy

Jane was woken by a bright, warm glow seeping round the curtains of her bedroom window. She had slept in and slept well. She quickly rediscovered the positivity she'd felt when she first saw the mystery woman in the wedding photograph. It was still something tangible, something to work on. Maybe with a new day and a fresh mind, the answers would start to reveal themselves, like daisies opening their petals to the morning sun.

It was then that Jane remembered there was another fresh mind potentially being brought to bear. When she'd sent the email late the previous evening, she'd hoped its recipient would look at it immediately, even work on it overnight, but that had seemed rather unreasonable at the time. Now it seemed totally callous and unfair. Nonetheless, she checked her inbox before she even washed or dressed. There were two unopened items of mail. One was clearly phishing spam asking her to 'Update your Informations!' at an online bank where she'd never had an account. The other was the reply from Thompson Ferdinand.

Hi Jane

Work was slow last night, so I was able to look through everything you sent me and, wow! I'm impressed. Analysing photographs and sources other than the normal records is called 'forensic' genealogy. It makes it sound rather exciting, a bit like CSI on the TV, don't you think? But I guess that's the kind of thing you detectives did all day at Scotland Yard when you were solving murders and stuff.

I was also impressed by how far you extended the Stothard family tree. I only found the one (small) mistake and I don't think that was really your fault. I also don't blame you for not finding any trace of the Smith family. It had me foxed for a while, but I guess I'd seen something similar before so it was easier for me.

I've updated your file with the details, but here's a brief summary in chronological order:

1. Mary Smith was born Mary D Butler in 1922. Obviously, I haven't got my hands on a birth certificate overnight but I wouldn't be surprised if the D stood for Dye. She was born illegitimately to Mabel Butler before she married Reuben Dye. Given the family resemblance, I think we can assume Reuben was the father. So, Margaret Stothard's mother was one of four sisters, as you suspected. (I think you missed Mary's birth because at that time you were concentrating on Derbyshire. The registration district was centred over the border in Nottinghamshire. Searches don't always pick that up.)

2. When her parents married, Mary became Mary Dye. Her birth surname simply got dropped.

3. The next bit is the key to solving the rest of the puzzle: the reason you couldn't find her wedding to James Smith was that she had an altogether different surname by the time they married. She was a young war widow named Mary Jensen.

4. Mary Dye married Woodrow Jensen in Norfolk in the 2nd quarter of 1943. They probably didn't make their first anniversary as he died in March 1944. I found his grave on the American Battle Monuments Commission website. He's buried in the US military cemetery in Cambridge.

5. Mary and Woodrow had a daughter, Lois E(lizabeth) Jensen, in December 1943, i.e. six to nine months after they married. Not long after, Mary found herself a widow.

6. I guess society's conventions go out the window in wartime and it didn't take Mary long to find another husband. Mary Jensen married James Smith only a few months after Woodrow's death.

7. She'd got pregnant again because Ernald J(ames) Smith was born in January 1945. (And you didn't find that because you naturally assumed Ernie was short for Ernest. Ernald's a new one on me too.)

8. The trail goes cold for James and Mary Smith, mainly because their names are so common. I haven't been able to pin down either of their deaths. Who knows, Mary could have married a third time and died with yet another surname.

9. After her mother's remarriage, Lois became a Smith and then changed her name again when she married Robert G(eorge) Aimson in 1963. They died in 2004 and 2005 respectively, but they had one son, Christopher Robert Aimson, in 1973. I can't find any record of him marrying.

10. Ernald is also no longer with us, dying in 1994. He married an Ava Mulligan in 1972 and had one son, Dean Ernald J Smith the same year. Again, there are no further records for Dean.

That's as far as I've got at the moment. I'll let you order the birth, marriage and death certificates. They'll give you exact dates to work from and hopefully confirm any assumptions I've made.

Keep your chin up (I hate that expression, but keep it up anyway ;-),

Tommy x

Hi Tommy

Thank you so much. As I guess you could tell, this thing was starting to get me down but it looks like you've solved everything! I'll get the certificates ordered ASAP.

Now make sure you get some sleep. I feel really guilty that you worked on this all night. I don't know what else to say other than you're wonderful and I love you to little bits!!

Jane xxx

PS 'Forensic' genealogy?! Hmm. And I didn't solve any murders when I was at the Met. I was more the go-to woman for break-ins at newsagents or teenagers smashing up bus shelters!

Jane had rattled off a quick reply in the hope of catching Tommy before he went to bed, assuming he ever did go to bed. She now sat back and re-read his email and the attached file, digesting the implications of the names and dates they contained.

Margaret Stothard had an aunt whose existence had been kept from her all her life. Mary Smith, the mystery woman in the wedding photograph, was raised as Mary Dye, the illegitimate eldest sister of Margaret's mother and her siblings. Mary married twice during the war, her first husband, Woodrow Jensen, being killed on active service in the American air force. It was likely she was pregnant when they married. Tragically, their daughter, Lois, lost her father when she was just a few months old. Mary, grieving and with a young baby, found herself seeking solace with another man, a very handsome man called James Smith. Unfortunately, she got pregnant again and James Smith did the decent thing, like Woodrow Jensen had done before him. By the end of the war, James had a wife and two children, one of them, Ernald, his own. Now they were all dead, but there was another generation, Christopher Aimson and Dean Smith. Jane wondered how much they knew of their parents' and grandparents' story.

When Jane had first read Tommy's email she thought it contained all the answers, but she soon realised there was one huge question glaring like a previously unnoticed scratch on a new car. Certainly, the major error in Margaret Stothard's family tree had been identified. But it was painfully close, high in emotional cost. All families have rows, but why had Margaret's mother been so ashamed of her own sister that she'd been airbrushed out of her life with near-Stalinesque resolution? At first, Jane conjectured it was because Mary had taken up with another man so soon after her first husband's heroic death fighting the Nazis. The trouble with this theory was that Mary was at Margaret's mother's wedding a few years later. The warmth and affection between them came across in the photographs. And would a woman really ostracise her widowed and lonely sister for falling for another man, simply because a respectable period of mourning had not elapsed? It was a time, after all, when no-one knew where the next bomb or rocket might fall: people had to live for the moment.

Finding no immediate explanation, Jane decided she needed more data and her time was best spent getting the documents that Tommy suggested. At present, they were mostly working from the online indexes, which omitted key information and were only accurate to a three-month quarter in each year. There was room for error. As the certificates were issued at various locations around the country, she ordered copies to be sent by post from the central register office in Southport and paid for priority delivery. She was still happy spending Julian Stothard's money. She also knew he could no longer refuse to pay her fees. He'd demanded something concrete, and she and Tommy had found it, the omission that Margaret's mother had alluded to all those years before and had intended to take to her grave. The question of why was still unanswered, but Jane's curiosity was fired. She had no intention of giving up without exposing whatever crime or sin Mary had committed, or perhaps, had been committed against her.

Old memories

It would take a couple of days for the certificates to arrive. Jane knew it was sensible to wait until they could be checked before proceeding with any further line of enquiry. Unfortunately, patience was not her thing. She needed a distraction. She also suspected a day off might do her good.

Jane had always been a gifted sportswoman, excelling at swimming and tennis whilst at school and college. These days she found pounding backwards and forwards in a pool rather tedious, so tennis was her recreation of choice. She and Dave had played regularly when they were together. He was fiercely competitive, though not really in her league in terms of style and finesse. She could also bludgeon him with power if she needed to. But since the breakup of their marriage and her recent move back to Nottingham, she'd not picked up a racquet. She was keen to play again and decided to call in an open invitation from a childhood friend.

It was the most exclusive club in the city and the first-team players could hold their own against any in the county. It also had a number of recreational and social players who were more often seen sinking doubles in the bar rather than playing doubles on the court. Jane had been a member in her teenage years and that was where she'd met Sarah.

Sarah was the poshest person Jane knew and the only one she'd kept in touch with after moving away to London. Sarah's father, known to all as 'Papa', had made his money in the rag trade but was an absolute gentleman of the old school and Jane had always loved him. Sarah had been sent to the finest educational establishments but had never been inclined to work hard. Papa seemed unperturbed. The only thing she ever tried at was tennis, and even then, the strength of her game was based more on innate talent than effort. In their youth, Jane and Sarah had been the backbone of the ladies' doubles team, though Jane did more than her fair share of dashing about the court trying to cover the lines.

'Jane, darling, you look gorgeous! Don't you ever put on weight?'

Sarah was sitting in a wicker chair on an immaculate lawn sipping an orange juice. A peaked visor protected her face from the midday sun, but her immaculate hair caught the light and reflected back a rich red-brown glow. Sarah had a classic beauty and had always oozed class. She still did.

'I'd still give my right eye to look like you,' said Jane, as she took an adjacent seat and kissed her old friend on the cheek. Jane had dug out her tennis whites; she'd correctly assumed they would still be required dress at such a high-class club. They'd seemed in reasonable condition when she found them at the bottom of a drawer, but next to Sarah's pristine outfit they looked decidedly grey. It was the sort of thing Sarah would undoubtedly notice but never comment on.

Instead, Sarah began looking around for her husband. 'Where is the old duffer? He needs to get you a drink.'

'I'm fine,' insisted Jane. 'I've got a bottle of water with me. I'll be okay with that. How is Duff by the way?'

Sarah had been calling her husband 'the old duffer', or 'Duff' for short, for so long that the name had stuck. All their mutual friends referred to him as Duff. Some assumed that was his real name and were confused when anyone called him Gordon, which was what was written on his driving licence. He was ten years older than his wife; they'd met when he was in his early thirties and she'd decided on the sobriquet on almost their first date.

'Oh, the old fool's still breathing, still running his little company – you know, I still really don't understand what it does – still keeping me in the style to which I've become accustomed. So long as we keep out of each other's way, we're happy enough.'

Jane grinned. 'I'm not fooled. I know you too are devoted to each other. You'd be lost without him. And you know very well what his company does.'

'Well perhaps, but it's very dull. Almost as dull as he is. Talking of whom…'

A distinguished looking man with thick head of grey hair and an intransigently black moustache walked over wearing a huge smile and a white tracksuit over a rather ample frame.

'Jane, you're even more fragrant and irresistible than ever. Look, I can't stand another day with Ginge here. Let's run off together, go somewhere romantic. I've heard Skegness described as the Venice of the east coast. It's got a canal anyway.' He tweaked his moustache like a silent movie villain.

Sarah gave him her standard black look. 'Jane has more sense and you are far, far too old for her you silly, silly man. Oh, and I may have mentioned this before: I am a rich, dark auburn. I am not ginger, nor have I ever been. It's getting rather tiring.'

'You're a very tiring woman, my love. It's just that, well, maybe it's just the Sunday sunshine, but you've got a definite gingerish hue today.'

Jane knew this was their standard repartee, being given full rein because they hadn't seen her together for some time. She tried her best to join in.

'I'd normally play hard to get, but Skegness is pretty tempting, Duff. Though maybe we should finish our tennis match before we set off."

'Good plan,' interjected Sarah, 'then you're welcome to him. Now, Duff, get Jane a freshly squeezed orange juice and leave us alone to catch up.'

'At once, my ginger sausage roll.'

Duff beamed amiably at the two women and set off for the bar in the saunter that was his default form of locomotion.

Sarah signed as if exasperated and then turned her attention to Jane. 'You're going to be partnering Adam. He's much better than Duff – who isn't – so the two of you will smash us all over the court. I asked Adam because, well, he's gorgeous and I thought you too might hit it off. Unfortunately, Duff told me on the way over that Adam is irretrievably gay, so I really should have chosen someone nearer Duff's standard of tennis, i.e. rubbish.'

'I seem to recall Duff wasn't that bad and I haven't played for ages. I'm going to be very rusty.'

'Talking of being rusty, is there anyone new in your life yet?'

Jane shook her head. 'I've got other things to think about. I've set up a new business and my partner and I are working on our first contract. We've just made a major breakthrough. It's getting quite exciting.'

Sarah looked interested. 'Partner?'

'Sorry, I shouldn't call him that. He's not a partner in either sense of the word. He's someone who's providing expert assistance on a voluntary basis at the moment. But I hope he will become my partner, business partner that is. Researching people's family history, genealogy, that's what we're doing. We've got a fancy website and everything.'

Sarah wasn't going to be sidetracked and persisted with her primary line of questioning. 'This "he", is he married? Or is he in some other kind of relationship, and I don't mean a business relationship?'

Jane felt slightly embarrassed. 'There's someone he knows on the Internet.'

'On the Internet? That's not a real relationship. I bet he fancies you. What's he look like? Is he the Duff type, by which I mean old and past it, or the Adam type, young and virile, but ideally not quite so gay?'

Jane's face reddened even more. 'Well he's not gay, as far as I know anyway. He's about my age and not bad looking, now you mention it, but he's not my type. And I'm certain I'm not his. He's ever so, ever so clever, but also a bit geeky. I've always been drawn to the stronger, more physical type. Like Dave.'

'Unfortunately, so was the slapper he's now shacked up with.'

'She's not a slapper. She's a nice girl – I used to rather like her. These things happen. I've got to move on, forgive them both and move on. Bitterness just eats away at you if you let it. I don't want to make myself ill again.'

The conversation went quiet before Sarah responded. 'But you're okay at the moment. How's your...' She paused while she searched for the right word, 'How's your temper, darling?'

'I'm in a good place. On an even keel. I'm fine. Thanks.' Jane's gratitude was genuine. She knew her oldest friend was asking out of concern not fishing for gossip.

'I saw Christine Jackson in town the other day,' said Sarah, cautiously.

Jane shuffled in her seat. 'Did you say hello?'

'I don't talk to chavs like her! Sorry, my snobbish side is showing. But, common or otherwise, she was always a nasty piece of work, a bitch and a bully. I don't think anyone ever blamed you for lashing out at her. It was just the scale of it that was a bit over the top.'

'How does she look these days?'

'Monstrously obese. And still ugly. What you did to her face may actually have improved it. No, that's not fair. There are no visible scars.'

'It was only a black eye,' retorted Jane, albeit timidly.

'If you remember, I saw her a few days after the incident, when she was still off school. They lived in those grotty flats near our house, dragging down a very nice neighbourhood. She was getting in her mother's car and her face looked terrible. The whole right side was bruised and swollen. You were really fortunate you didn't do her permanent damage.'

'I know. It was a good job I was only hitting her with my fist. I had my tennis racquet with me – if I'd hit her with that I'd have killed her...' Jane's voice had begun to crack and finally tailed off as she struggled with a memory she normally smothered whenever it threatened to surface.

'Oh, I'm sorry, darling,' winced Sarah. 'I shouldn't have brought her up. I don't know what I was thinking of.'

'It's okay. Christine, at least, was a long time ago now. But, God, if a 15-year-old did something like that these days, they'd end up in court charged with assault. I was so lucky just to be expelled.'

'I think the school knew she'd been picking on you for a long time. Their anti-bullying policy was non-existent. I suspect they were worried about being accused of negligence and happy to cover it up.'

Jane didn't comment, so Sarah continued her analysis. 'And Christine's mother never cared enough about anything to make a fuss. I'm sure she was well aware what her daughter was like and probably thought she had it coming. Anyway, violence is part of a chav's world. Isn't that what it stands for? Council House And Violence? Or is that just an urban myth?'

Duff returning with Jane's drink interrupted the conversation. The past was sidelined and the mood quickly became more light hearted. When Adam joined them, they moved onto the court and began their match. It was less one-sided than Sarah had predicted and Duff's game of nasty slice and spin meant they held their own until he began to tire and slow down. Eventually they lost two sets to one. Sarah was enough of a sportswoman to take the defeat graciously. She was somewhat more miffed that Adam kept shouting, 'Good shot, Ginge!', whenever she played a winner. Duff had obviously convinced him that was the pet name used by all her friends, and Sarah was too much of a lady to complain. Jane tried her best to correct her partner by following up with, 'Yes, well played, Sarah', but Adam didn't seem to notice. Despite blowing hard and dripping with sweat, Duff appeared to enjoy the match enormously.

Norfolk 1943

The farmer's land had been requisitioned by the Air Ministry in 1941 under the Emergency Powers Act. The ramshackle Jacobean farmhouse was deemed unsuitable for military use and its centuries-old brickwork succumbed to the bulldozers in an afternoon. One of the barns survived and was initially pressed into service housing jeeps and ancillary equipment. Eventually, its high, beamed roof and half-timbered walls were repaired and a decent floor laid. The colonel recognised that holding regular dances was vital for maintaining morale and the barn offered a far more suitable space than the corrugated-iron tunnels of the Nissen huts that provided most of the camp accommodation.

Invitations were sent out and girls were brought in by army truck from East Dereham and its surrounding villages. The events were weekly, but alternated between the officers and the enlisted men, their social lives being strictly segregated on the base. Mary, as a land girl, was only invited to dance with the lower ranks. The daughter of a miner, she'd been raised to know her place in society and never felt the snub. She was somewhat more self-conscious about what she was obliged to wear. Her crops officer insisted that, as proud members of the Women's Land Army, the girls should always be in uniform when attending a military site.

And so it was that Mary found herself sitting on a wooden bench that ran the length of one side of an ancient barn, whose roughly hewn timbers curved and bent in organic sympathy with the trees that donated them centuries before. The room was brightly lit, and a parachute had been hung from the rafters like a canopy. Further decoration was provided by United States flags adorning all four walls. One end of the building was given over to a low stage, on which a small band of five musicians did their best to recreate the hits of Glenn Miller and his contemporaries. The American airmen were dancing in their dress uniforms, which apart from the insignia on their sleeves, made them all look like officers, certainly in comparison to anything their British counterparts might be issued. The town girls were wearing their finest frocks and spinning and giggling as their partners tried to outdo each other with ever more elaborate steps.

In her baggy brown corduroy breeches, knee socks and green sweater, Mary felt like an ugly sister but still held her head high. She was doing her bit. She was serving king and country and not just a silly shop assistant or cinema usherette. She also knew she was pretty. She had to be or she wouldn't have caught James' eye.

She was staring up at the parachute when she became aware of a man standing in front of her. Looking down, her eyes quickly flicked away again as she tried to ignore his gaze. He wore a sergeant's stripes but Yanks were supposed to be tall and this one was a head shorter that most of the men in the room. He had thinning blond hair and a narrow, pinched face with a sallow complexion. If anything, he looked malnourished, though everyone knew the Yanks ate like lords, whilst the native population suffered the rigours of shortages and rationing.

Through a toothy smile, he finally found the confidence to speak, raising his voice over the trumpet and clarinet. 'Ma'am, I'd be mighty grateful if you'd do me the honour.'

The voice too was a disappointment, pitched somewhere nearer Ginger Rogers than Fred Astaire. Mary wanted to say no, but couldn't think of an excuse. She opted for damage limitation.

'Of course, but just the one. I'm really not much of dancer.'

It was a realistic assessment of her abilities if not her intentions, but the diminutive sergeant made up for her shortcomings and was soon leading her through a complicated and energetic jitterbug. The boy sure could dance and despite her plan to remain coolly detached, Mary was soon beaming with delight as she lost herself in the music and the whirling happiness of being young and alive. The American introduced himself as Woody, and when the number ended, thanked Mary and offered to show her back to her seat.

'I'm happy to stay on the floor,' she said. 'Unless there's someone else you want to dance with?'

Woody shook his head. 'No, ma'am. I'm already dancing with the finest girl in the room.'

They stayed together all evening, taking occasional breaks from the floor to drink at the makeshift bar. Woody stuck to beer, properly chilled, and Mary sipped Coca Cola whilst tucking into the plentiful supply of cakes and what Woody insisted on calling cookies. They were a treat she'd rarely enjoyed since sugar had become so hard to get hold of.

He told her he was from the cornfields of the Midwest and had never seen the sea until Uncle Sam shipped him over 3000 heaving miles of it. He was a gunner in one of the giant four-engined B-24 bombers, and his small stature meant he could squeeze into one of the key positions defending the plane against fighters coming up from below. Mary asked him what it was like and whether he was ever scared. She expected a bravado answer, but Woody told her it was cold and it was very frightening when the air was filled with exploding flak or a Messerschmitt was blasting its cannons straight at you. He acknowledged the view could be great and then changed the subject. His watery-blue eyes had seemed to age, and it was clear he would rather not talk about the dirty business of war nor reflect on the danger facing those who hit back at occupied Europe from daylight skies.

Mary found herself unexpectedly attracted to him. Like the millions of cinema-going women who had fallen for weedy, odd-looking Fred Astaire, she was partly won over by his dancing but more by his sense of humour and his charm. James was funny and charming too, when he wanted to be, but the American seemed a nice, decent man. Even through the blinkers of her infatuation, she'd never fooled herself that James was either of those things.

Towards the end of the evening, the band struck up a slow waltz. Woody held Mary tight as they shuffled round the dance floor one last time. It was what she expected, but somehow it was sexless, as if he were a little boy clinging to his mother, never wanting to let go because of the terrifying world that lay outside the embrace.

The music stopped and Mary asked Woody if he wanted to go outside for some air. The look in her eyes suggested she was offering something else, and he briefly wondered what his staunchly religious parents back home would think. And then he remembered the Plexiglas gun turret that awaited him, so tight that his parachute had to be left outside and cut by an icy slipstream that threatened frostbite to nose, ears and fingers. He saw planes falling from formation, with broken wings and shattered tails. He saw burning figures throwing themselves to oblivion. Woody knew some of the enlisted men would not make the next dance. He might well be one of them.

Documentation and confirmation

The certificates confirmed all of Tommy's assumptions, even his guess that Mary's birth name had been Mary Dye Butler. Reuben Dye was registered as her father, so he had clearly taken responsibility for his new daughter from the outset. Mary was, indeed, the fourth sister and shared her full parentage with Margaret Stothard's mother.

The paternity of Mary's own children was also clearly documented. Woodrow Jensen, sergeant US Army Air Force, was registered as the father of Lois Elizabeth Jensen. James Smith, small trader, was shown as the father of Ernald James Smith. Having the exact dates also verified that Mary was pregnant on both her wedding days.

Lois died of cancer in her early sixties. Her husband, Robert Aimson, a retired newsagent, was 13 years older and predeceased her by a year. The couple stayed in the same house until the end of their lives and there they raised their only son, Christopher Robert.

Lois's half-brother, Ernald, also had the one child, Dean Ernald James Smith. On Dean's birth certificate, Ernald's occupation was given as 'labourer'. Manual work appeared to have taken its toll: Ernald only made it to 49, dying of heart failure. At that stage he was unemployed.

In terms of locations, Jane knew from her previous research that the Derbyshire village of Dowley appeared to have little attraction for the younger generations of Dyes. Nearly all of them, including three of the four sisters, moved away. The youngest sister emigrated all the way to Australia. Mary had Lois in Norfolk, but then she bucked the trend and moved back to Dowley with her second husband for the birth of Ernald. In time, the pattern repeated and Lois married, had her son and ultimately died some 70 miles away on the outskirts of Birmingham. Ernald travelled less far to the nearby town of Chesterfield, taking his last breaths in its main hospital.

Jane sat back and considered the evidence in front of her. All these people summarised by the registrar's trinity of birth, marriage and death: snapshots of data – occupations, addresses, relationships – standing in for lives, personalities and motivations. She could see nothing to even hint at why Mary became such a pariah that her own sister denied her very existence. The family history databases were offering no more clues. There were no wills to document disputed inheritances, no overlapping family trees linking to distant relatives with a story to tell.

Jane could see only one way forward. She needed to track down Mary's surviving descendants, her grandsons, Christopher Aimson and Dean Smith. Assuming Mary was less secretive than her sisters, the two men might hold the key to solving the mystery.

But first, Jane had some news to break.

Revelation and reconsideration

There was already a car in Jane's usual parking space in front of Margaret Stothard's bungalow. It was a rather grand white Mercedes which, fortunately, had been parked tight against the garage door, allowing Jane to fit the Mazda alongside. She checked the other car over as she walked past it; the number plates were this year's and a rental agreement had been tossed onto the passenger seat. She could just make out Heathrow scrawled in one of the boxes on the form.

Jane had thought it best to update Margaret in person. Whilst she'd said she was prepared for the worst, it was a big secret for her mother to have kept from her.

Jane climbed the steps and rang the bell. This time it was not the live-in helper, Caroline, who appeared at the door, but a handsome man in his early forties with a neat mop of straw-blond hair casually swept back from his face. Jane was only partly surprised to see Julian Stothard standing in front of her. She'd already decided he was a likely candidate for the sort of person who would arrive at an airport and rent a Mercedes rather than a Volkswagen or Ford. She was a little more surprised that he was only of average height: she had always pictured someone bigger.

Julian smiled warmly. 'Jane. Lovely to meet you at last.'

'Julian. Your mother said you were in Europe, but I understood you weren't due to visit her until next week?'

'Last minute change of plan. A business meeting got moved, so I hopped on a plane and came straight over.'

Jane waited to be invited in, but after a slightly awkward pause it became obvious there was something Julian wanted to say out of earshot of his mother.

'Look, I feel I owe you an apology. Mum thinks you're wonderful and I suspect I was a little hard on you when we spoke over the Internet.'

Jane replied with a noncommittal smile and Julian continued. 'I'd got my work head on and I was gearing up for some serious negotiations later that day. Mining's a tough business, getting tougher, and you can't pussy-foot around. I sometimes forget that in the outside world a bit of tact and diplomacy can go a long way. Anyway, will you accept my apology?'

'Of course. It wasn't a problem. I'm not a sensitive flower.' Jane wanted to believe she was being honest.

'Good. Thank you. And, about your fees, I'll happily pay for all your time. That results-only condition was unreasonably stringent.'

Jane nodded, more in acknowledgement than agreement. 'I accepted the terms, but as I told your mother on the phone, we've now found something very significant. I'm confident it's what we've been looking for. It's the what, even though we don't understand the why just yet.'

Julian raised his eyebrows and Jane hoped that indicated he was impressed as well as intrigued.

He gestured towards the first door down the hallway. 'Well, please go through and you can reveal all.' As Jane passed, he added, 'You are tall, aren't you?' and then followed her into the sitting room.

Margaret Stothard was waiting for them. She looked up unseeingly when they walked in.

Julian confirmed what his mother already knew. 'It's Jane, Mum. Prompt and on time as you said she'd be.'

Margaret held out her hand for Jane to take. 'It's lovely to see you again, Jane dear. It sounded very exciting on the phone. You've identified the unknown woman in the wedding photographs. Was she a close cousin as we suspected?'

Jane looked at Julian before replying. She felt like a doctor breaking bad news. 'She was closer than that. If you remember, my initial reaction was that she looked like a fourth sister. I'm afraid that's who she was – your grandparents' first child and your mother's oldest sister.'

Margaret looked shocked. 'But why, dear? Why would my mother keep something like that from me? Are you sure?'

Jane laid out her evidence. The Stothards agreed it was compelling: the names, the dates, the places fitted together faultlessly. Jane gently quizzed Margaret to try to unearth some hidden memory, something her mother or father might once have said, that would explain why the deception had been maintained. The older woman could do little more than shake her head.

Eventually, Julian tried to lighten the mood. 'Well, on that bombshell, to quote Jeremy Clarkson, I need to eat. The sun's shining; it's a glorious day; I'll buy us all lunch in the pub by the bridge.'

Margaret declined. 'No thank you, darling. Caroline has already made something and I'm not in the mood. I'd rather just have a bit of a think. Maybe there is something I'm forgetting.' Sensing an air of concern, she added, 'Don't worry. It was a bit of a shock at first, but I'm actually quite excited now. It's a real life mystery, isn't it? You young people go out and enjoy the sunshine.'

Julian and Jane walked the short distance down the hill and over the main road to the Midland, named after the railway company whose locomotives had once steamed down the far side of the gorge. The pub was on the corner of the bridge and the busy A6, but its rear backed onto the River Derwent, where it had a large number of tables laid out on terraces cut into the riverbank. They ordered at the bar and then Julian led the way down to the lower terrace, a few feet above the gently flowing water. It was a lovely spot and it was easy to ignore the constant background rumble of traffic. Their conversation quickly returned to the reason they found themselves in each other's company.

'So, Jane. What next?'

'I need to track down Christopher Aimson and Dean Smith, your cousins, or rather your second cousins.'

'Do you think that'll be straightforward?'

'Aimson is a very uncommon surname. It might not sound like it, but it is. Are you still registered to vote in this country?'

Julian looked puzzled at the apparent change of subject, prompting Jane to quickly explain. 'Okay, these days you have the choice of whether your name and address should go on the public or private copy of the electoral roll. The public, or open, register is sold to anyone who wants to buy it, including online websites, so people are increasingly opting out.'

'I would for one,' interjected Julian.

'Same here. So does Christopher Aimson, now. But, I've found him living at his parent's old house as recently as 2009. Since then someone else appears to have moved in, but I've written to them asking if they've got a forwarding address. There's also a Chris Aimson on Facebook. The account's locked down quite tightly so you can't see any personal details. The profile picture is of a young child, so this Chris is obviously a parent. Trouble is, I'm not 100% sure if it's Christopher or Christine. They don't accept friend requests, but I've sent them a message. There's been no response yet, but I'll try again and hopefully they'll get back to me.'

Jane took a sip from her coke before continuing. 'If Aimson's uncommon, Smith, of course, is as far in the opposite direction as it's possible to go. Dean's got two middle names, so that ought to help, but he's proving elusive. I can't see any evidence he's ever registered to vote. There are lots of Dean Smiths on Facebook. Too many. I've contacted a couple who look like they might be possibles, but I'm not optimistic they're our man. If not, I've got a few other strings to my bow. Maybe I'll need to call in a favour from my previous life in the police to find Mr Dean Ernald James Smith.'

Julian looked satisfied. 'Sounds like you're the right woman for the job.' His expression suddenly changed. 'You know, that's a weird name, isn't it? Ernald, I mean. But I've got a nagging feeling I've heard it somewhere before.'

Julian took out his iPhone and began tapping on the screen. After 30 seconds, he looked up. 'Yes. That's why it's familiar. My degree was from the old Royal School of Mines at Imperial College in London. But I did an optional module on 20th-century history and one essay I wrote was about the rise and fall of British fascism between the wars. The leader of the British Union of Fascists in the 1930s was Oswald Mosley. I'm sure you know that, but you've probably never heard his middle name. Sir Oswald Mosley, baronet, was Christened Oswald Ernald Mosley in 1896.'

Limehouse 1936

They were standing on a wide cobbled street overlooked by tall, soot-stained dockland warehouses. Behind them was a high brick wall, with spirals of viciously barbed wire fixed on its crest to deter access to the imported riches beyond. The people of Limehouse were poor; many were desperate. The Depression had bitten deep and nowhere were its teeth sharper than on the dark streets and alleys of London's East End.

It was a cold October morning, but none of the assembly wore coats. All the men were puffing on cigarettes, as were several of the boys but fewer of the women. Icy breath mingled with tobacco smoke as if a thin London fog had settled on this one backstreet.

The voices were loud and confident. The mood was expectant and arrogant. They were wearing their uniforms with pride and stood in sufficient numbers to deter any gang of left-wing dockers or their Jewish friends. But if they chose to turn up looking for trouble, the men in black would readily oblige. They would argue, with limited conviction, that they would never start fights, but would always finish them.

A military voice barked out a command. 'He's coming. Form ranks!'

Cigarettes were thrown to the ground and stamped on. Those who remembered wartime parade grounds lined up quickly, and the younger men and women copied as best they could. The Blackshirts stood together, then the cadets and finally the women in their berets and flared skirts. Behind the cadets were the standard bearers holding the Union Flag and the Flash and Circle high above their heads.

The boy next to Jimmy was anxiously fidgeting. He knew he should be standing to attention, eyes fixed dead ahead, but he couldn't resist leaning forward and looking down the line.

'I can see him. The Leader's coming!' he whispered.

Jimmy pulled his shoulders back and stretched his neck. He was taller than the other boys, though not yet as tall as the Leader himself. Few were. The youngster had his jet-black hair slicked back like the Leader's, and his uniform of grey shirt and grey trousers had been freshly pressed by his mother. Jimmy himself had spent hours polishing his black boots and belt. He knew he looked the part and hoped to catch the Leader's eye as he passed. Jimmy fantasised that the great man would stop, perhaps not to speak to the lowly cadet, but simply nod his head in approval at this model of fascist youth and England's future.

There had been a violent row with his father when Jimmy had left that morning. The older man had raised his hand, but then dropped it. Those days were gone. His lungs, scarred by poison gas in the trenches, increasingly sapped his strength and he saw a contempt in his son's eyes that suggested he would now hit back. For his part, Jimmy couldn't understand his father's antipathy towards the fascist movement. It was for old soldiers like him, betrayed by successive governments of weak fools, that the Leader was striving to build a new order. The war had reduced Jimmy's father to a pathetic apology of a man, and the reward for his sacrifice was the poverty of the 1930s and a country increasingly being run by Jewish money and corruption. The Leader made everything clear and he was the one man with an answer. England had to change and the alternative to fascism was the unbearable totalitarianism of the filthy communists and their Russian Bolshevik masters.

The press had been forewarned of the parade and told that thousands of ordinary East Enders would gather to hear the Leader's famed oratory as he laid out his vision for the country and its empire. Since

Rothermere's Daily Mail had baulked at the violence of the fascist rallies and abandoned its support, the Leader knew the papers could be expected to be unanimously hostile. The Battle of Cable Street had happened earlier that month. The fascist propaganda machine, run by a scar-faced man named William Joyce, was telling anyone who'd listen not to believe the lie that the East End had risen up to give the fascists a bloody nose. The fighting had been between the police and a largely imported mob of anarchists, communists, trade unionists, Irishmen and Jews. The Leader, Joyce said, had kept his own men under control for the sake of law and order.

But now the Leader knew he had to demonstrate that he still had support in his heartland and its streets were not forbidden him. Even if Fleet Street's editorials were derisory, he would show he was not afraid to march, though he was careful to avoid Cable Street itself.

The military voice barked out the order and a forest of right arms shot out in the salute that Mussolini's followers believed they were copying from ancient Romans and had been adopted with even greater fervour by the Nazis.

Jimmy's own arm was quivering with intensity, yet his focus almost slipped when the Leader drew level. At close quarters he was even more striking than his photographs suggested. He was wearing the new 'Action Press' uniform: black knee-length jackboots, polished like a mirror, breeches, a tight black tunic with shining buttons grouped in threes, black shirt and tie, and a soldier's black peaked cap. Black on black on black, sharply accentuated by a blood-red armband carrying the party emblem of a lightning bolt cleaving a circle. He looked like a Hollywood vision of a futuristic military commander: noble, lean, strong. Irresistible. He marched quickly, his confident strides largely disguising his limp, a legacy of his own wartime heroism. In that instant, Jimmy's mind flashed forward to a time when he too would be old enough to abandon the grey of a cadet. He saw himself standing at the Leader's side, wearing that tunic and with a similar debonair moustache on his upper lip. Jimmy knew he was one of the few who could properly carry it off. A different image of himself with the tall, aristocratic man interrupted but Jimmy immediately suppressed it. It was an impulse he could not yet accept.

Perhaps it was Jimmy's handsome young face or the backdrop of billowing flags, but a flash gun went off as the Leader passed by. When developed, the picture was so powerful that the editor considered suppressing it. Instead he buried it on the centre pages, heading a suitably dismissive article. Nonetheless it caught the eyes of those in office. In later life, Mosley would accept that Action Press had been a mistake: compared to the simple black fencing shirt that preceded it, it was far too militaristic in appearance. Others noted the similarity to the uniform of the Nazi SS, men who had been responsible for the mass killings during the Night of the Long Knives two years before. The government's response was to rush in the Public Order Act that banned the wearing of all political uniforms from the start of 1937.

By then, Jimmy was lying in a hospital bed anxiously awaiting the removal of bandages that swathed his head. Marching around, preening like a chocolate soldier now seemed a foolish and empty ambition.

American presidents

Jane got back to Nottingham in the late afternoon. On the journey she realised she'd completely reappraised her opinion of Julian Stothard. Contrary to her initial impression, he possessed considerable charm and a good sense of humour. They'd spent over an hour together at the pub and the sunny weather, pretty setting and lively conversation had made it a very pleasant experience. They each shared stories of their marital difficulties and separations, though neither resorted to vindictiveness or bitterness when describing their ex-partners. Julian talked of missing his two young sons but said his wife was a good mother and conceded that the amount of time he spent travelling on business meant it was better they were with her and her family. He was flying back to the States the following day, but suggested he and Jane meet up next time he was in the UK. The excuse was to discuss developments on the family tree, but dinner was mentioned and she allowed herself to infer that her burgeoning attraction to him was not one-sided.

Jane parked outside her house and switched off the ignition. Sitting in the car with the fan still whirring air over the otherwise silent engine, she put Julian to the back of her mind and checked her phone. On Facebook, there was nothing from Chris Aimson; however, one of the Dean Smiths had replied. He said he wasn't and had never heard of anyone called Dean Ernald James Smith, but he thought Jane's profile picture looked hot and wondered if she fancied meeting up. Jane sent him a brief thanks but no thanks. Switching to her email account, she found a new message from Tommy.

Hi Jane

I've been doing some more digging around on the Interwebs. I've found some stuff that I think you'll find really, really interesting. In no particular order (well, building up to a crescendo, actually :-)

1. Ernald, as in (Dean) Ernald James Smith, was Oswald Mosley's middle name. But then it was also the name of a Scottish bishop who died in 1163.

2. I found a old newspaper report (see attached file) from April 1944. It concerns the death of Woodrow 'Woody' Jensen, the first husband of Mary Butler/Dye/Jensen/Smith, our mysterious fourth sister. I'd assumed he'd been killed in action, or at least in some kind of flying accident. He wasn't. Read the article for yourself. It's written under the constraints of wartime censorship and the moral sensitivities of the time, but the message seems clear. Sergeant Woody Jensen was killed by a fellow member of the US Army Air Force, a clerk named Corporal Henry Abrams, who subsequently shot himself. It's heavily implied that it was a row between lovers. They were in a Norfolk cottage rented by Abrams and their 'state of undress called into question the relationship between the two men'. The matter had been handed over from the local constabulary to the US military police, who were understood 'not to be looking for any other suspects in this unfortunate matter'. It goes on to describe Jensen as a veteran of numerous raids over occupied Europe and suggests battle fatigue could explain 'any weakness of character displayed in this sorry incident'. Abrams, on the other hand, 'had a certain reputation amongst locals'. The article ends with the reporter praising

'our American allies who take the war to the Nazi homeland on an almost daily basis' and saying that the 'occasional bad apple will not rot this heroic barrel'.

3. I came across a post on one of the forums I subscribe to. It was from someone looking for Lois Elizabeth Jensen, Woody and Mary's daughter. I made initial contact (see attached transcript) and it turns out it's Woody's younger brother, Herbert Jensen, trying to find his long-lost niece. He lives in Minneapolis and wants to talk on the phone; I'm not great with phone calls and it's best you talk to him anyway. I haven't told him yet that Lois is dead.

The plot thickens! That's about it for now. Let me know how you get on with Herbert Jensen.

All the best,

Tommy x

Jane sat back and digested the revelations in Tommy's email. Woody Jensen was homosexual, or at least bisexual, and was having a relationship with another man, presumably behind his new wife's back. Homosexuality was, of course, illegal at the time and considered shameful in many, if not most, quarters. The circumstances of his death were somewhat sordid. Could this be the reason the Dye family eventually disowned his widow, Mary? Perhaps she hid the story from her sisters and parents and it only came to light much later. But would you really pretend your sister had never been born because of something like this, something unpalatable, but something her deceased husband did, not Mary herself? You might consider it embarrassing and suppress the incident itself. Surely you wouldn't block your own flesh and blood out of your life?

Jane checked the time in Minnesota. It was late morning. Herbert Jensen might hold a few more clues. Even if he didn't, he deserved to know what little information Jane could give him about his niece's life. Jane picked up her phone and dialled.

'Herb Jensen speaking. Good morning and how may I help you?'

'Mr Jensen, my name's Jane Madden. I'm phoning from England. You exchanged some messages with my colleague about Lois Elizabeth Jensen. I understand she was your brother's daughter and you want to find out what happened to her.'

'My dear, thank you so much for calling me. I've been trying to track down little Lois for some time. I'm pretty good on the Internet, well, for an old-timer in his eighties. Yet no matter where I looked, the trail ran cold.'

'We struggled to pin her down too. Her mother remarried and she became Lois Smith.'

'So you can put me in touch with her? I don't know how much time I have left, only the good Lord knows that. I don't want to go to my grave without asking her forgiveness for not seeking her out years ago. Whatever sins my brother may have committed, they were not hers.'

Jane registered the word sins and then spoke in what she hoped was a caring tone. 'Mr Jensen, I'm afraid I have some bad news. You might want to sit down.' She paused long enough for Herb Jensen to guess what was coming. 'Your niece is no longer with us. She was lost to cancer when she was just 61. I'm so sorry.'

The line went quiet and then there was an audible sigh followed by a slightly faltering voice. 'I always knew there'd be a good chance she'd have passed. It's been so long. Thank you for telling me. Did she have any family of her own?'

'Her husband is also dead, but they had one son, whom I'm currently trying to contact. His name is Christopher Aimson. He'd be in his forties now.'

'Your colleague pointed me at your website. I understand you are a professional genealogist. May I ask your interest in my niece's family?'

'I don't think it's betraying commercial confidentiality to say I'm working on behalf of her English relatives. Tell me, Mr Jensen, would you be prepared to talk to me about your brother and what you know of his marriage? It could be very helpful and may help me find his grandson.'

'We were named after the presidents who were in office when we were born, you know. Woodrow Wilson and Herbert Hoover. Our parents set their sights so high. Woody was...'

The voice tailed off. Jane responded to the silence with a gentle prompt. 'He was stationed in England in the war. He married an English girl.'

There was another delay before Herb Jensen replied. 'It was a lifetime ago, but it's still rather difficult for me, I'm afraid.'

Jane tried to address the old man's reluctance. 'Mr Jensen. My colleague is a very experienced and talented researcher. He found a newspaper article from the time of your brother's death. It describes the incident pretty clearly. As I understand it, he was murdered by another man. He himself was guilty of no crime, certainly not in the eyes of the law today.'

'Thank you for your tact, my dear. I know that people are more, well, understanding these days. But we're a Christian family. I forgive my brother but it's still hard. It's still a sin in the eyes of the Lord. It brought great pain to my mother and father. I was only a young boy. Woody was much older than me and he was always my hero when I was growing up. He wasn't the most physically imposing of men, but he seemed to have such moral strength and courage. My parents told everyone, told me, that he'd died when his bomber was shot out of the sky. He was a ball turret gunner in the belly of the plane, crammed in a little glass bubble with two heavy machine guns on either side of him. It was so dangerous, and if the plane was going down it wasn't easy to get out. I used to have nightmares about him being trapped with flames all round him as he crashed to earth. I only found out the truth of how he really died much later, and it hurt me – it hurt me considerably. I'm ashamed to say that, even now, I sometimes wish he'd have burnt to death in that damn turret than…'

The floodgates had opened and Jane had let Herb Jensen disgorge 70 years of remorse and resentment without interruption. Now she could hear him gulping air in an attempt to stop himself breaking down. Despite struggling with some of his sentiments, she began to regret asking such an old man to revisit a painful past.

'I'm sorry, Mr Jensen. I didn't mean to upset you like this. If you'd rather not talk about Woody anymore, then please say.'

'No dear. It's good to talk. That's what they say isn't it? And I've been hiding from this for too long. My parents didn't make any attempt to stay in touch with his widow after he died. And her with a young baby too. I think they assumed she was caught up with it somehow. You see, Woody had sent us a photograph of Lois.'

'She was a beautiful little girl.'

'She was. My brother absolutely adored her. But even at a few weeks old she looked nothing like him. Even my mother wouldn't describe Woody as a good-looking boy. And Lois's colouring was so dark. We're a Nordic American family – we're all very fair.'

Jane's reflex was to defend Lois's parentage. 'Her looks must have come from her mother's side. It's not exactly unusual.'

'Yes, but given how he died, I think my parents decided Lois couldn't be his. He only married to disguise his true inclinations.'

'I've got a copy of Lois's birth certificate. Your brother is clearly registered as her father.'

'I know that's the case. Legally. It's what I've been telling myself – Woody said "she is my daughter" and he loved her as such. That's why I wanted to find her and try to make amends for the way we treated her. Her mother may or may not have been innocent, but the girl certainly was.'

'So please, tell me what you can about her mother. She'd have been called Mary Dye when she met your brother.'

'I only know what Woody wrote in his letters. They're gone – I'm pretty certain my parents destroyed them after he died – but I read them so many times as a kid I could almost recite them out loud, even though it's been 70 years. That's how it feels, anyway.'

'So what did the letters say?'

'Mary was working on a farm near to the airbase. The local girls would come to dances and that's how Woody met her. She wasn't the prettiest, nor perhaps the brightest, but Woody told us he fell for her the first time he met her. She was pregnant on their wedding day. It shocked my parents at the time, but it was wartime and they understood that these things happen. And at least Woody was making sure his child wasn't born out of wedlock. My parents and I never met her, of course. We saw her photograph, but we never knew her. I really can't tell you much more. Oh, there was one thing. She wasn't actually a local girl; she came from another part of England. After all these years, I couldn't tell you where.'

Jane answered the question. 'She was from a small coal mining village called Dowley in the county of Derbyshire, about 150 miles away. She had a brother and three sisters. Her brother was in the Royal Navy and died when his ship, HMS Hood, was sunk in 1941.'

'Yes. I remember now. That's coming back to me. She was very proud of her brother, though very, very sad at his death. He was only a boy too. They were all just boys.'

'Is there anything else you remember? Anything that might cause her to become estranged from her own family, if not then, later in life? Sorry, I know that's probably a stupid thing to ask. You weren't in contact after Woody's death.'

'I don't know if it's stupid, but I can't think of anything. From what Woody wrote, she was a nice, ordinary girl. Maybe a bit flighty sometimes.'

'Flighty?'

'Oh, you know, head in the clouds, rather than feet on the ground. It was just an impression, nothing tangible.'

After a few more questions, Jane began to realise she was unlikely to glean any more from the call. 'Mr Jensen, thank you for your time. As I said, I'm trying to track down your brother's grandson, Christopher Aimson. When and if I do, I'll tell him of your interest and give him your contact details. Obviously, it will be up to him if he gets in touch, but I assume that's what you'd like me to do?'

'Please, my dear, I'd be very grateful. Look, I never married. I took over the family business. Rightfully at least a share of it should have been Woody's. The business prospered. I wouldn't say I was rich, Miss Madden, but I have no children, nor do I have other nieces or nephews. Assuming this Christopher is, well, a decent, normal young man, then what money I've got should probably go to him.'

Jane thanked Herb for his time and promised to update him on any progress she made finding his great-nephew. In return, she asked that he let her know if anything should come to mind that might shed light on Mary's relationship with her family.

When Jane put down the phone she had a slightly uneasy feeling. There was a newly added financial carrot that might make her job easier, but she wasn't sure what Herb Jensen had meant by 'a decent, normal young man'. Either way, everything still hung on her tracing Mary's surviving descendants.

A favour

Jane had made progress in her search for Mary's grandchildren. She'd sent another message to Chris Aimson's Facebook profile, this time stating that there was an elderly and childless American gentleman searching for his brother's lost grandson. She didn't explicitly mention any form of inheritance, but knew it was an obvious inference. The next morning there was a reply. Chris Aimson's full name was indeed Christopher Robert Aimson. After a brief exchange, she established that he was single parent living in a flat in north London, and he agreed to her calling on him in two days' time.

Locating Dean Smith, however, was proving a more intractable problem. Jane realised the time had come to make the phone call she'd been dreading. She didn't like asking for favours, particularly from someone she sometimes wished she would never see or talk to again.

'Dave speaking'

'Dave, it's Jane. You got a minute or two?'

A slight pause. 'Yeah, yeah. What can I do for you, sweetheart?'

Another pause whilst the historic endearment sank in at both ends of the line. 'I need to ask you a favour. Sorry, how are you first? And how's Bridget?' Jane tried hard to pronounce the name of her replacement evenly and without bitterness.

'We're well, thanks. And you? You're keeping on the straight and narrow?'

'Yes, don't worry, I'm good. Look Dave, I've set up this business. You know I got into family history? Well, I'm doing it professionally now and my current case involves tracking down someone who's still alive. Normally I'll be looking for relatives who are long dead, but this is very much the exception. And I need some help.'

'You're not asking me to break the law, are you, Janey?'

'Since when did you become a stickler for the rules? I'm just asking you to tap a name into a computer. No-one is ever going to find out and you know I'm an ex-policewoman who understands the rules of the game. I'm not some madwoman who's going to leave you in the shit.'

'Are you sure you're not a madwoman, Janey? No-one knows better than me that you've had your moments.'

'So we'll have something on each other and, besides, you owe me for… for Bridget.' The bitterness was no longer suppressed.

'We already have something on each other, my love. And I thought I gave you the car because I owed you.'

'Dean Ernald James Smith.' Jane spelt out Ernald. 'Despite being a Smith, Ernald is pretty unique. There's only going to be one. Have you written it down yet?'

'Oh, bloody hell. Where's my pen? Okay, Dean Ernald James Smith. I'm not at work right now. I'll see what I can find and call you back. When I get a chance. Could be tomorrow, I'll see. Oh, and Jane? This is a one-off. For Bridget you get one car and one phone call. Kapeesh?'

The following morning, Jane was gazing at clouds through the window of the small bedroom she considered her office, when her thoughts were interrupted by the ringing of her mobile phone. Dave's face came up on her screen. He looked handsome, reliable and strong. It was her favourite photo of him. She made a mental note to delete it.

'Dave, thanks for calling back.'

'The things I do for you, Janey.'

'So what have you got? Hang on, I'll just switch on my tape recorder so I can blackmail you at some future date.'

'Ha ha. Very funny. Do you want the lowdown on Dean Ernald James Smith or not?'

'I would like the lowdown on Mister Smith, Dave. Thank you very much.'

'Well, it was an easy one. Turns out Dean is well known to our colleagues in the Derbyshire Constabulary. He's no stranger to their chums in Nottinghamshire either. I went through training with a DI who's based in Chesterfield. I stuck my neck way out for you, gave him a call and pulled the old pals act. He knows Dean all right. Proper little tealeaf. Convictions for shoplifting, handling stolen goods, burglary, fiddling his electricity meter, drunk and disorderly, you name it. All pretty minor-league stuff.'

Jane found herself slipping back into the mindset of a policewoman. 'Still, he must have been sent down at least once with that sheet.'

'He did a stint for doing over a car accessory shop just outside Derby. Listen to this – as well as a deficiency in honesty, he's not the brightest of God's creatures either. He was wandering around in full view of the CCTV. He had his hood up, but you see him looking straight at the camera in one shot apparently. Our Mastermind candidate then pulls a tin of spray paint off a nearby shelf and squirts the camera. What did he think that was going to do once he's looked into the thing? Burk. Not only is he stupid, but he's not popular either. Someone grassed him up almost immediately. The local uniform raided his council flat and all the stuff from the car shop was piled up inside the hallway. The hoodie he was wearing in the video was in a pile of dirty washing in the kitchen. I don't think he bothered entering a not guilty plea. He may be an idiot, but he's not totally brain-dead.'

'So you've taken a liking to the guy, Dave?'

'Yeah, right. My type of fellah. The sort of bloke that makes a policeman's world go round. Scumbag.'

'So, how can I get in touch with him? Do you have the address of that council flat?'

'Jane, hold your horses. Two things – a) he got kicked out of the flat for, well, being a scumbag. And b) he can turn nasty. If you were still in the force, I wouldn't let you go near him without backup. A bit of muscle to give him a slap if he got lively. He's a bit of a runt, apparently, but a runt with a temper. The sort who knocks his girlfriends around. One used to call 999 on him, but always got cold feet when it came to pressing charges.'

'I'll go and see him with Tommy. He's my partner in this family history business.'

'Tommy? You mean that streak of piss who lives on the Internet and is frightened to leave his own front door? What fucking good would he be?'

'He looks the part. Sort of. I'll do the talking. Look, we'll be fine. I'll be careful. I'm not exactly a novice when it comes to handling lowlife. And top of the class in self-defence at police college, don't forget.'

'Amongst the women.'

'Don't be sexist, Dave. So, where do I find Dean Smith?'

Dave answered with obvious reluctance in his voice. 'No fixed abode. Living in or around a place called Dowley in Derbyshire. Sleeping on other people's sofas, you know the drill. That's all I've got.'

Jane's ears had pricked up at the name of the village. 'Hopefully it's enough. I've been to Dowley and it's pretty small. I can ask around locally. Should be able to find someone who knows him.'

'Jane love, be careful. Watch yourself. If you do find him and he does turn nasty, just tell him your husband's a six-foot-four copper who'll rip his arms out of their sockets if he dares lay a finger on you.' Mid-sentence, Dave's tone had flipped from pleading to menacing.

'You're not my husband anymore, but thanks, Dave. Thanks for caring.'

'I always cared, Jane. I know I let you down. I know I hurt you, but it wasn't because I didn't care. It was just because…' Dave struggled for a cogent explanation. 'Because these things happen. I'm sorry, sweetheart.'

The line went quiet as dormant feelings broke the surface, like desert flowers in the rain. They wilted back almost immediately. Both Jane and Dave knew their relationship was too far gone to ever blossom again.

Jane decided it was time to end the call. 'Dave, you're a star. I probably owe you now. And don't worry, I'm a big girl. And not a stupid one either. See you around.'

'Not if I see you first,' replied Dave. There was intended humour in the words, but no levity in his voice.

Jane hung up. Another trip to Dowley beckoned. She had lied about taking Tommy. It would be unfair to ask him and Dave's assessment of his utility was accurate. This was something she would handle on her own. She was, after all, a big girl.

Chris Aimson

Chris Aimson lived in a modest apartment in an unfashionable part of north west London. The three-storey 1980s block was a 15-minute walk from the nearest tube station, on one of the outer branches of the network. Driving had seemed a much easier option, and Jane had no difficulty parking in the street outside. She climbed the open stairs to the first floor and rang the bell of flat number six. She heard noises within but it was a good two minutes before the door cracked open on its chain. A good looking though pale man in his forties, jet-black hair peppered with grey, peered through the gap. He scanned Jane briefly before releasing the chain and opening the door properly.

Jane spoke first. 'Chris? I'm Jane Madden. Thanks for agreeing to see me.'

'Jane. Lovely to meet you. Thanks for coming all this way. Nottingham, you said. I haven't been there for years. Nice city.'

'Yes, it's my home town, but I lived in London for a while. I'm not sure I miss the hustle and bustle of the Big Smoke, as my grandad used to call it.'

Chris nodded slowly as if his capacity for small talk was becoming exhausted. 'Please come on through,' he said eventually. 'I'm sorry we're in a bit of a mess. I meant to tidy up but I'm having one of my days, I'm afraid.'

He turned and started down the short hallway. He was leaning on a stick, and his movements were slow and deliberate like those of a much older man. He led the way into a bright sitting room and gestured that Jane sit opposite him on a trendy-looking sofa. He himself took a more upright wooden chair next to the window. It seemed to be an effort lowering himself down, but he immediately began to rise again.

'Oh, I'm sorry. I should have offered you a drink. What would you like?'

Jane gestured him to stay seated. 'I'm absolutely fine, thank you. I drink far too much coffee anyway. Makes me jumpy if I'm not careful. Please don't worry.'

Chris smiled in gratitude and then answered Jane's unspoken question. 'Multiple sclerosis. It was undiagnosed for years then it really kicked in. I go up and down. Today I'm a bit down. Jean Paul was being a bit of a bugger earlier. Wore me out. Fortunately, I got him off to sleep. He's in the next room.'

'Jean Paul is your son?'

'That's right. Happiest day of my life when the adoption came through. It's been rather downhill since then. First the MS diagnosis and then Henri had his stupid motorbike accident.'

'Henri?'

'My partner. He had one those enormous Harley Davidsons and a bright chrome helmet. I told him bikes were death traps, but he thought he looked so cool. And then one day he was hit by a truck and it was goodbye and adieu, Henri.'

'I'm sorry. That must have been awful.'

'Jean Paul kept me going. Apart from the odd tantrum, he's an adorable little boy. I worry what this damned illness is going to mean for us. I know they're going to take him away from me at some stage.' Chris hesitated and tried to sound more business-like. 'Anyway, you didn't come to listen to me moan. You wanted to ask me about my ancestry?'

Chris stopped talking but quickly interrupted his own silence. 'Oh look, I'm sorry I ignored your messages at first. It's just that when I'm not feeling great, I don't want to talk to anyone. And then you mentioned an elderly American relative. I'm really not a grasping gold-digger in search of an inheritance.'

'Of course,' said Jane.

'It's just that…' Chris's face suggested a man more tired than guilty. 'I don't have anyone, no family of my own, and Henri's parents totally disowned him when he came out. I had this sudden fantasy that Jean Paul and I could be rescued by an unknown benefactor on the other side of the Atlantic. I'm sure that's not how life works, but you grasp at straws sometimes.'

Something told Jane that she should be wary of raising Chris's hopes. 'I don't know my American contact's full intentions, I'm afraid. But if we double-check that you and he are related, then who knows? He's certainly said he wants to get in touch with you, assuming you're happy with that.'

Chris confirmed his full name and birthdate and those of both his parents. All the details checked out. Jane explained she was working on behalf of a different branch of his family which, like his American great-uncle, was estranged from Chris's mother and grandmother. Jane didn't elaborate on the reasons but asked Chris what he knew of his maternal line.

'Mum was from Derbyshire. She left home when she was no more than 16, I think. Got a job at a factory in Birmingham. She didn't like talking about her childhood, but I know she hated her father.'

Jane's eyes widened. 'Was he her father or stepfather?'

'Her father, I'm sure. She never said anything about a stepfather.'

Jane briefly pondered whether the truth about her parentage could have been kept from Lois herself. 'Sorry for interrupting, Chris. Please tell me anything you remember.'

'Mum's dad was a drunken bully with really extreme right-wing views. She once told me he lost the sight in his right eye during a fracas with anti-fascists before the war. It wasn't the Battle of Cable Street, but something like that.'

Jane nodded her understanding and Chris carried on. 'Needless to say, the bastard was on the wrong side, marching with Mosley's Blackshirts. Mum said the injury didn't spoil my grandfather's pretty face and he could be a real charmer when he wanted. Led my grandmother a right dance. Knocked her around more than once as well. My mum inherited his looks – she was a stunner when she was young – but fortunately not his personality or his politics.'

Chris's expression glazed as his mind reached back to a beautiful and caring young woman, the only one he might ever love. He breathed deeply and then pressed on with her story.

'When she left home, she swore never to have anything to do with him ever again. She still saw her mum occasionally. I vaguely recall meeting an old lady when I was very small, but my grandfather found out and that was that. It's easy to say my grandmother should have left him, but I guess it's not always that easy. She'd always idolised him, apparently. There was definitely some kind of hold.'

Chris shrugged his shoulders to indicate he had no more to tell, so Jane probed further. 'Did your mother ever speak about your grandmother's family?'

'Yes and no. She never mentioned any names, but she did tell me that my grandfather had started some kind of fight and it led to a permanent falling-out.'

'You don't know what the fight was about?'

'Sorry, no. As I said, my mum really didn't like talking about it. It brought back the ghosts of an unhappy past. And I think she felt guilty about losing touch with my grandmother.'

'Did your mum ever talk about having a brother?'

'Oh sorry, yes. I forgot about him. Nasty piece of work, she said. Took after his father, without the looks and charm. She was happy to cut him out of her life, too.'

'Did she ever mention a US airman who was killed during the war?'

Chris shook his head and looked blank. Jane asked a few more questions but it became clear he'd divulged all he knew. It was her turn to slot pieces into the mosaic of his family background.

He sat and listened quietly as she drew out his genealogy, restricting herself to the last two or three generations. The fact that his grandmother had been disowned by her family fitted with his recollection of the quarrel caused by his grandfather. On the other hand, Chris struggled to believe that his mother had been fathered by another man. In response, Jane produced the paper trail that showed Woodrow Jensen was Chris's real grandfather, not James Smith, the drunken fascist sympathiser. Chris's doubts were based on physical appearance; he'd always understood a shared likeness between supposed father and daughter, but he began to recognise an alternative form of inheritance and an explanation for their difference in character. He also believed there was a genetic element to human sexuality and saw a source for his own orientation in the clumsy implications of the newspaper article describing Woodrow Jensen's death.

Before leaving Chris's flat, Jane asked that he let her know if any buried memories of his mother's past were to surface. In return, she said she would tell Herb Jensen she had found his lost great-nephew. She left it to Chris to establish contact between them. She felt obliged to warn that the old man might struggle with Chris's homosexuality, as he'd struggled with his brother Woody's for the last 70 years.

In her heart, Jane hoped Herb Jensen's Christian faith would guide him towards love and charity rather than preoccupying him with notions of sin or biblical prohibition. In her head, she wasn't convinced his deep-seated beliefs could be abandoned so easily.

Inspiration and adulation

Jane knew her meeting with Chris Aimson had provided little more than character sketches for some of the cast in the Dye family drama. He had confirmed there had been a falling-out, a fight of some description, and that it led to an irreconcilable separation. But that had already been clear. She was no nearer understanding the nature of the disagreement. What had been so unacceptably bad that Mary Dye's existence was forever denied by the rest of her family? There were clues in her husband's political leanings, but would that have been enough?

Jane studied the wedding photograph showing Mary, her husband and their two young children, hoping that it would somehow reveal one more secret. As Chris Aimson had suggested, James Smith and his adopted daughter were compellingly similar, but Jane began to think the likeness was based more on colouring than shared features. That jet-black hair could easily have come from elsewhere in the child's genetic make-up. The same explanation would also account for her strikingly blond brother, Ernald.

Staring hard into James Smith's face, Jane suddenly realised his appearance wasn't modelled on Clark Gable as she'd once assumed. She googled Oswald Mosley and his portrait confirmed the likely inspiration. James Smith had the same swept back hair and dapper moustache as the man whose middle name James had given to his son. In Britain, Oswald would have been as acceptable a name in early 1945 as Adolf would have been in Germany a few months later. James Smith presumably thought he would get away with Ernald, particularly when shortened to the more familiar and innocuous Ernie.

Ernald Smith was now dead. His son, Dean, now seemed Jane's only hope for making progress. Chris Aimson said that Ernald had taken after his father. Hopefully they shared the family secrets and these, in turn, had been passed down to Dean. She could put it off no longer: she needed to make another trip to Dowley.

Another encounter

Jane's Mazda was once again the only vehicle in the village car park. She made sure there were no valuables in sight and checked the doors were locked securely. Dean Smith was 'of no fixed abode', but had a conviction for drunk and disorderly so she assumed he was no stranger to his local bar. She therefore walked the short distance to the White Hart, where she'd taken refuge only a few days previously. Whilst it had unnerved her at the time, she'd now managed to stifle her memory of the large man with long black hair getting into the white van.

There was a similar vehicle parked untidily in front of the pub, partly blocking the road and with one wheel on the curb. It was like thousands of others and Jane hardly noticed it. She was mentally rehearsing how to ask about Dean without sounding like the policewoman she'd once been. Without the authority of a warrant card, people had no obligation to answer her questions and were more likely to clam up if they sensed her background.

The tall, bearded landlord greeted her with a smile. 'Hello again, duck. You're becoming a regular. It was white wine, if I recall correctly?'

Jane returned the smile. 'May I just have a soda and lime, please. I'm driving and I try to behave myself. I wasn't in the best of moods last time. I hope that didn't come across too much.'

'Not at all. You were charming.'

Halfway through the sentence, Jane thought she saw something change in the landlord's face. It was as if he had remembered something, something that worried him. His eyes flicked around the pub nervously and then he busied himself getting Jane's drink.

When he'd put it down on the counter, she tried to put him at ease. 'I don't think I explained what I was doing in Dowley last time. I'm a professional family historian, looking for ancestors and relatives, that kind of thing. In this case, I may even be looking for heirs, though it might be a bit early to say that.'

Jane had to raise her voice slightly over the sound of a rough diesel engine firing into life outside the pub door, but she could see that the landlord look relieved.

'Like that daytime TV show?' he said. 'They trace people due inheritances from family they never knew existed. Is it called Heir Hunters?'

'Yes. I've only seen it a couple of times, but yes. Maybe a cross between that and Who Do You Think You Are?'

The landlord had now relaxed totally. 'Wife loves them both. You must have a very interesting job.'

'Yes. I've only just started out, but it's certainly been interesting so far.' Jane hesitated briefly before proceeding. 'I'm currently trying to find someone who lives round here called Dean Smith, Dean Ernald James Smith to be exact. Ring any bells?'

The landlord's expression changed again. 'I know a Dean Smith. Couldn't tell you his middle names, but he puts a fair amount over this bar. He was here last time you came in. Haven't seen him today. He'll probably be in later, knowing our Dean.'

'You look concerned,' said Jane.

'He's a good customer, but not a particularly... pleasant man.' The landlord was now talking quietly and choosing his words carefully. 'Look, duck, it can be a bit rough round here from time to time. A girl, woman, about your age was found dead in what they call mysterious circumstances a while back. Face down in the river. She'd fallen on hard times, shall we say, and had been spending a bit of time with Dean. A lot of us thought her death was down to him.' The landlord's eyes scanned round the pub again. 'As it turned out, he had a foolproof alibi, but the fact we thought it tells you a lot about the bloke. A nice girl like you probably wants to make sure there are always other people around if you're in his company. In here would be a good place. I could keep a friendly eye out. He's not the sort of bloke to stand up to someone bigger than him.'

Jane nodded her understanding. 'Thank you for the information. And the offer. I'll take your advice. Any idea what time he'll be in?'

'All depends if he's bothered to get out of bed yet."

An hour later, Jane was still sitting in the White Hart, two empty glasses in front of her and feeling bored. In the police, she'd spent long hours on surveillance or simply waiting for something to happen, and patience had never come easily to her. Some people are happy alone their own thoughts; that was company she tried to avoid.

Her doldrums were broken when the two men walked in. She recognised them immediately from their slight build, thin pointed faces and closely cropped hair. It was the weasel brothers she'd encountered on her previous visit. She looked questioningly towards the landlord, and after a short delay, he reluctantly nodded and tilted his head to the left to confirm the identity of the man she sought.

The men bought their drinks and then moved over to their usual table. Jane went to the bar and returned her glasses.

The landlord looked stern. 'Be careful, duck. He can be a bit of a bugger if you wind him up. I can handle Dean, and his sidekick, but I'd rather have a quiet life, if at all possible.'

Jane smiled reassuringly. 'Don't worry. I'm just going to ask him some questions about his grandfather. It's all very tame and innocent.'

'Just be aware he's got strong views, even for round here. Try not to react, eh duck?'

Jane walked over to the corner where the two men were sitting and interrupted their conversation. 'Hi my name's Jane Madden. I understand you're Dean Smith? I'm a genealogist, and unless I'm wrong, your dad was called Ernald Smith? Do you mind if we have a chat?'

Dean looked up and a broad grin revealed uneven teeth. A blackened stump was just visible at one side of his mouth. 'Hello, pet. We've seen you in here before – couldn't forget that orange jacket you've got on, could we? Don't get me wrong, we like bright colours.' He winked surreptitiously to his friend before facing back towards Jane. 'Yeah, my dad was called Ernald. He was always known as Ernie, but Ernald was what they put on his death certificate.' He twisted his head again. 'Steve, mate, why don't you do one? The lady here would like to talk with me. She's a jeanie something. I've temporarily forgot what one of them is, but she's a very pretty lady and I'm always happy to oblige a lady. Go on, run along now like a good boy.'

After the briefest of complaints, Steve obediently stood up and sloped away. Jane took his place.

'You and Steve aren't related at all?' she asked. 'There's quite a similarity between the two of you.'

Dean looked offended at the suggestion and exaggeratedly shook his head.

'Sorry,' she said. 'Anyway, I'm a genealogist. I research people's family trees, you know, find their ancestors and long-lost relatives.'

'Like them heir hunters on telly?' Dean sounded interested.

'We use the same sort of sources and methods.'

'So, I could be in line for a windfall from some cousin I've never heard of?' Dean was now leaning forward expectantly.

'I'm really not sure about that. But I am working on behalf of someone I believe to be a cousin of yours, second cousin actually. He's a businessman based in the States and has asked to me to solve a family mystery.'

Dean's eyebrows rose at the mention of an American businessman. 'Anything I can do to help, Jane. Please, just ask. Ask away. I'm a helpful guy. Known for it.'

'That's really kind of you, thank you.' Jane studied his face and wondered where to start. 'What do you know about your grandfather, James Smith?'

Dean sat back in his chair smugly. He felt like a wise man in unique possession of knowledge. He liked to talk, to express opinions, to educate. And who knew how this attractive woman might show her appreciation?

He held up his hands like a priest beginning a sermon. 'I don't remember that well, personally. He died when I was a kid, but my dad was always talking about him. When my dad wasn't in the nick, of course. He absolutely hero-worshipped the bloke. Really handsome guy with charm to match. All the ladies loved him. Bit of a family trait, eh pet?'

Jane smiled in response, trying to keep her gaze from the crude and faded swastika tattoo that Dean had presumably inked on his own wrist at some stage in his youth.

Dean's eulogy abruptly shifted into diatribe. 'And he had the guts to speak his mind. Ahead of his time, he was. There's a right-wing uprising on the cards, mark my words. Lots of people, all around the world, have had enough of the liberal, leftie elite getting rich on immigrant labour, whilst we ordinary folk get kicked in the balls. He was warning about it years ago. Said we'd have been better off being mates with Hitler rather than bankrupting ourselves in that stupid war. We might still have an empire for a start. And he never believed all that bollocks about the holocaust. Go on the Internet today, ignore the official propaganda, and you'll find he was right all along.'

Jane could see that James Smith had never changed from the boy who marched in the streets of east London with Oswald Mosley. And the infected blood still ran through Dean's veins. She decided it was best just to listen, to see what else he would reveal.

Dean read her silence as agreement and the alcohol was fuelling his confidence. 'He used to get sick of people playing the old soldier. You know, "I was there at Dunkirk. It was a great victory. We didn't get our arse kicked by the Germans. Look at all me medals." That kind of thing. Well, my dad once told me that my grandad had a medal of his own. And not just one for turning up. Thing is, it was made of iron and shaped like a cross.'

Jane couldn't conceal her disbelief. 'An Iron Cross? A German medal?'

'That shocked you, didn't it? For services rendered, if you know what I mean. It wasn't something he flashed around, obviously, but my dad said he'd seen it. Mind you, he could be a lying bastard, my dad.' Dean smiled but there was a suggestion of bitterness in his eyes. 'I don't really know the full story, I guess. What I am sure of is that my grandad was a man of principle who had more balls than all them supposed heroes who marched around on Armistice Day.'

Dean seemed to be backtracking on the dubious medal story and Jane began to question how much he was extemporising on thin memories and his own prejudices. She thought it was time to steer him in a specific direction.

'James Smith's wife, your grandmother, was called Mary. Is that right?'

'She was always a bit on the wet side. I think her husband led her a bit of a dance, if you know what I mean. She did as she was told, but wasn't bright enough to understand his politics. God, I remember the times she used to drag me down to that old war memorial to show me her brother's name. Boo hoo.' Dean wiped fake tears from his eyes. 'My grandad used to laugh at her. Behind her back, like – he wasn't a cruel man.'

Jane tried to keep her face unreadable and her voice even. 'It's her family I'm working on behalf of. There was some row and they totally lost touch to the extent that the current generation didn't even know Mary existed. Can you tell me anything about that?'

'Not really. I guess the old dear would know.'

Jane moved forward in her seat. 'By "the old dear" do you mean your grandmother?'

'Yeah, my dear old gran. Silly cow.'

'And, sorry to question your grammar, but did you mean would know or would have known?'

Dean looked thoughtful. 'That's the million-dollar question. Sometimes her mind's as clear as a bell. Others she's totally gaga. But these days, I think it's gaga more often than not.'

'Your grandmother's still alive?'

'Well, unless she's popped her clogs in the few last weeks and the bastards haven't bothered telling me.'

Jane bought Dean another drink and let him talk. A story emerged of a squalid upbringing, with a shiftless father in and out of prison and a mother who ran off, leaving an insecure young boy in the care of his grandmother, a woman he grew to mock and belittle like his father and grandfather before him. The more Dean talked, the more he revealed his ugly bigotry and a bragging, bullying, morally vacant personality. The more Jane listened, the more he thought she was being won over by his compelling opinions and charisma. Explaining he was between flats at the moment, he eventually asked if she'd like to go back with him to Steve's place. He became loud and angry when she declined, so she stood up and walked back to the bar. The landlord gave Dean a hard stare, and he quietened and began silently mouthing obscenities at his pint glass. Steve returned to sit next to his friend and became the focus of his muttering resentment.

Jane hoped that would be her last encounter with Dean. He had served his purpose. She didn't trust his wilder claims, particularly the nonsense about an Iron Cross, but the picture was emerging from the jigsaw and he'd told her where she was likely to find the final pieces. He'd given her the name of his grandmother's nursing home.

Jane thanked the landlord and made her way towards the pub door. As she swung it open, she saw a white van parked outside. It was the one that had been there when she arrived, but it was now facing the other way and its hot engine was still ticking. The driver had just climbed out and had his back to her as he slammed the door with unnecessary force. He was a large, powerfully built man with long black hair, streaked with grey. Jane knew him immediately: it was the man she'd seen outside the churchyard, the man she'd felt had been watching her.

Jane froze briefly and then all reason, all control, abandoned her. She was consumed by one thought. A blind wildness entered her eyes.

She darted towards the man.

From behind the bar, the landlord saw what was happening and shouted after her. It was too late. She could hear nothing but a name, a childish term of endearment, screaming in her head.

Jane crossed the pub forecourt in under a second. She reached up and yanked sharply on the man's shoulder. He spun round instantly as if forever on his guard. His raised fists were clenched and his back was arched like a boxer poised to lash out.

Seeing Jane, he checked himself but didn't lower his hands. 'What the fuck do you think you're playing at?' he spat.

The madness on Jane's face receded almost immediately. 'I'm sorry, really sorry. I thought you... I thought you were someone else.'

'If you were a bloke you'd be on that floor with no fucking teeth by now. No-one lays their hands on me. No-one. And who? Who did you think I fucking was?'

'It doesn't matter,' mumbled Jane.

'I said, "Who did you think I fucking was?"'

'I thought… I thought you were my da… my father.' Jane struggled to hold back tears.

The man dropped his arms to his side and the aggression in his tone began to soften. 'I'm not your father,' he said.

Jane's own voice became lifeless and empty. 'I know. I haven't seen him since I was a really small girl, but I know you're not him. I just remember how big he was. His hair. Like yours. But, no, you can't be him. I'm sorry.'

What was left of the man's anger seemed to quell. 'You're the bird with the green sports car. I saw you in front of the church a few days back.'

'Yes, I remember.'

'As it happens, you reminded me of my own girl. She was tall like you, same colouring, same build. Until that slimeball drug dealer got his paws on her. She was like a fucking skeleton last time she came to visit me.' His expression became distant and regretful. 'And now she is a fucking skeleton, six feet under. I should have been around to look after her, but I wasn't. Shame on me. That drug dealer won't be poisoning anyone else's daughter, but it's too late. Too late for me, too late for her.'

'I'm sorry,' Jane repeated for the third or fourth time.

'Yeah, right. Leave me alone, eh love? Ask anyone round here. I'm a man you'd best leave alone. If you know what's good for you.'

He pushed past Jane and into the pub. She stood fixed to the spot, shaking like a lost and frightened child.

After a minute or so, the landlord came out and touched her arm. He spoke quietly, partly out of compassion but also so that his voice didn't carry inside. 'You okay, duck? I thought Michael had gone for the day. Christ, we had a lucky escape there. What was that about?'

'I thought I recognised him. I made a mistake.'

'Michael's not a guy you want to make mistakes with, duck, believe me. Sit down at one of the tables outside. I'll get you that white wine.'

'No. It's okay. I'm going home.'

Jane walked away without looking up. Her car was soon pulling out of the car park and onto the road. Only an insistent ringing from the dashboard reminded her to clip her seat belt into place. She drove like a automaton, unconsciously steering and changing gears as if programmed by clockwork discs and cams. Her mind was consumed by dark, repetitive thoughts that took hold and refused to let go. Once again, she reproached herself for her fixation with the father who had abandoned her so many years previously, sailing off on that huge ship to a far-flung land, never to return. Once again, she seethed with bitterness towards her mother, the woman who had driven him away. Once again, she questioned her own role in her father's desertion and sought the blame and guilt that must surely be hers. Once again, she hated herself for her own weakness and her inability to let childhood wounds heal.

When she reached her home in Nottingham she had no recollection of the journey. She blankly left her car unlocked, walked up the steps into her house, fumbled with her key and then shut the door behind her. She didn't open it again for three days.

Nottingham

Jane was lying on the sofa under a duvet. The TV was tuned to a bland daytime channel, but the volume was turned down. Her hair was unkempt and matted, and she was still wearing pyjamas despite it being mid afternoon. The curtains were slightly pulled back, but grey skies and a north-facing aspect meant the room was gloomy and dark.

The doorbell was ringing, but Jane seemed oblivious. Then she heard a familiar voice through the letterbox.

'Jane, it's me. Are you in there? Let me in, please.'

She pulled the duvet over her head for a moment but then relented. She lifted herself heavily onto her feet and trudged down the hall towards the front door.

She pulled it open a few inches and standing nervously on the doorstep was Tommy. When he saw her dishevelled appearance he knew his instincts had been right.

'Hi, Jane. Is it okay if I come in?' he asked gently.

Jane nodded and retraced her steps back to her living room. Tommy pushed the door open fully and followed.

As they passed the kitchen, Jane turned slightly. 'Do you want a coffee or something?' she said limply.

Tommy didn't, but said yes anyway. He felt any kind of activity, no matter how small, might help drag her from her stupor. She shuffled into the kitchen, lifted the kettle to check its weight and then turned it on.

A look of puzzlement crossed her face. 'I didn't know you knew my address, Tommy.'

He grinned apologetically. 'I hope you don't mind. It was something in your emails. I got worried when you didn't update me on the trip to Dowley and you just dropped off the net. Normally, you always reply to messages without fail. You could be laid low with flu, or the Black Death, and you'd have your phone or your laptop by your side. When you didn't respond, I feared the worst. That you'd slipped back again. Looks like I was right.'

Jane shrugged her shoulders and he continued his explanation. 'I knew you'd moved into your grandparents' old house in Nottingham. I do genealogy. It wasn't exactly hard getting your grandparents' names and then finding their address on the electoral register. So I got on a train and here I am.'

Jane felt a pang of guilt for what seemed like self-indulgent weakness. 'Oh, Tommy, that's ever so sweet of you. Thank you. I know it doesn't look it, but I was starting to get it back together again. I'd moved out of my bedroom into the living room. I was building myself up to have a shower.'

Tommy appeared encouraged. 'Why don't you have that shower now and I'll finish off making the coffee?'

Half an hour later they were sitting outside on the patio at the back of the house. Two half-empty cups were on the table in front of them. The sun had come out and its warmth was drying Jane's damp hair and raising her spirits. Talking Tommy through her encounter outside the pub helped her accept what she already knew. The man had borne a resemblance to a mental image that was probably distorted by decades of Chinese whispers in her mind. She didn't really know what her father might look like now, assuming he was even still alive. And why would he be stalking her? He had shown no inclination to seek her out in the past.

Tommy told her that the episode could be a blessing. Maybe its drama would lodge in her mind and prevent her succumbing to such irrationality in the future. It was a script she desperately wanted to believe. She made herself agree but knew her conviction was as fragile as sugar glass.

There was one positive she could not deny. Apart from grabbing a large, angry man by the shoulder, she hadn't done anything silly. No-one had got hurt.

When he sensed Jane had begun talking herself out of her darkness, Tommy tentatively steered her towards the case of the Dye family and their irrevocable split. He judged that an alternative focus might prevent her crawling back into the easy refuge of despair.

Jane led him through Dean Smith's revelation that his grandmother, the fourth sister at Margaret Stothard's mother's wedding, was still alive. Tommy shook his head out of disappointment at his own failure rather than disbelief. He'd played the odds and got it wrong. He knew that he'd never found a record of Mary Smith's death, but statistically a woman born in the early 1920s was likely to be deceased. The commonality of her name and the chance she might have remarried had seemed valid reasons for not trying harder to pin down the actual date and place. However, the fact that her two children had passed on might have clouded his judgement and made him assume their mother was dead too. He thought himself a slave to method and detail and didn't like it when he made lazy mistakes.

It was Jane's turn to be reassuring. 'I assumed she was dead too. She was called Mary Smith, for goodness sake. It must be the most common woman's name in the country. You wouldn't expect to find anything. I wouldn't have got anywhere on this thing without you. And we're almost there now. And Tommy…'

His eyes were in their habitual position, looking downwards at the table. She leaned across and gently lifted his chin to raise his gaze towards her face. 'Tommy, I know it's a struggle for you to leave your own flat sometimes. For you to get on a train and come all the way to Nottingham, to travel across a town you don't know and knock on a strange front door… Well I think that's the bravest thing anyone's ever done for me. I've told you before, you're a really good friend and I'm very lucky to have you. I don't deserve you.'

Tommy smiled but couldn't hold eye contact for long. He mumbled something about normal people thinking nothing of getting on a train. Jane didn't want to embarrass him further so reached for her phone to check the texts and emails she had been ignoring for three days.

In amongst several messages from Tommy, one email stood out. It was from Herb Jensen.

Dear Ms Madden,

Thank you again for tracking down Christopher Aimson. He has sent me a brief email introducing himself and to which I am yet to reply. Unfortunately, a good friend of mine is an attorney and he has advised me that, given the situation, I must take the precaution of getting a DNA sample before proceeding with any further communication. I am writing to ask if you would be prepared to act as my agent in this matter.

I look forward to your reply,

Herb Jensen

PS Please find attached a photograph of my brother. He's at the back, second from the left.

Jane read and reread the first paragraph trying to understand its motivation. Whilst his family had always harboured doubts about the parentage of Chris Aimson's mother, Herb Jensen had said he was prepared to respect his brother's acceptance of her. Now he seemed to be getting cold feet and introducing barriers. What had happened to change his mind? Had Chris revealed personal circumstances that had discomforted the old man such that he was looking for excuses to back out? Whatever the reason, Jane didn't yet feel strong enough to make anything resembling a decision. She typed a brief message saying she was away for a few days and would reply properly on her return. She then turned to Tommy.

'Thompson Ferdinand. I've just told someone I'm on holiday for day or two. I hate lying, so why don't you and I go somewhere? We might be justified claiming it on the project's expenses. If not, it's my treat. How about a nice country inn? Have you ever been to Norfolk?'

No longer East

Tommy made excuses about not having a change of clothes. Jane, fired by the irrepressible enthusiasm of a depressive whose mood has suddenly lifted, responded by taking him shopping to the nearest Primark. 90 minutes later, they were driving at speed down the A17 as it cut across the fenlands of South Holland, where Lincolnshire curved round the southern Wash.

The sun was losing its battle with the clouds, but Jane had the Mazda's top down and its heater up. Tommy sat huddled in the passenger seat, only the frame of the windscreen breaking his 360 degree view across endless acres of flat, fertile farmland, which had been stolen from the sea by generations of engineers and their ditches, dykes and pumps. Islands of high ground were as rare as in the open ocean, but the skyline was interrupted by walls of trees standing tall against the cutting wind. Also fighting the horizontal monotony were the irregular platoons of wind turbines, which seemed to be marching across the alien terrain like giant three-armed robots, scything their way through any and all resistance.

Tommy allowed himself an occasional look across at Jane. She was wearing superfluous sunglasses and her hair pulled back in a ponytail against the buffeting slipstream. She was enjoying the drive and looked strong and happy and beautiful.

They entered Norfolk and crossed the Great Ouse, as wide as the Danube at this point, but a waterway whose suspiciously straight banks betrayed man's dominance over its course and flow. Over the bridge, the A17 became the A47 and the scenery changed with it, gentle contours once more returning to the map and rendering a more familiar landscape.

It was early evening and cold by the time they arrived in the small market town of Dereham, and Tommy was grateful that Jane had relented and raised the Mazda's roof just outside King's Lynn. At such short notice, there'd been limited choice on the hotel websites, but she'd been excited to find availability in an 18th-century coaching inn just outside the town centre. The car park was in the old stabling area and was accessed through a narrow archway, whose brickwork was striped by the paint off numerous wing mirrors and bumpers. Fortunately, the little sports car slipped through easily. There was no reception, so Jane and Tommy checked in at the bar and were shown to rooms in a modern annexe. Whilst clean and functional, they lacked the beams and sloping floors of those in the original building, and which featured in the online photographs. Nonetheless, Jane was happy. The location seemed ideal.

Tommy would normally have liked to spend time carefully unpacking, but his luggage comprised a carrier bag with only the barest essentials, and Jane was keen to walk through the town before it got dark. The signs as you entered Dereham pronounced it the 'Heart of Norfolk', a claim that seemed to derive from its geographic location rather than any emotional bond. Its own heart was the keyhole-shaped market place, elongated but pinched inwards below the modern roundabout at its northern end, where previously cattle had been bought and sold for hundreds of years. Despite origins dating back to the Saxons and beyond, the central architecture was predominantly red-brick Georgian interspersed with more recent construction, most of it sympathetic, but some clashing with 1960s concrete arrogance. Throughout, modern shopfronts imposed conformity. The town had grown rapidly in recent years, promoting itself from East Dereham to Dereham, and had the standard complement of chain stores, supermarkets and pound shops, making its character blur with anywhere and everywhere else in the country.

And yet Jane was trying not to see 21st-century Dereham, but the East Dereham of 70 years before, a time of blackouts and rationing and individual little businesses, with hand-painted signs bearing local names of local shopkeepers: butchers, bakers, grocers, tobacconists, haberdashers and milliners, some struggling to fill their shelves in the face of wartime shortages, others benefiting from the proximity of nearby farms for their eggs, butter, meat and vegetables.

It was also a time of invasion, albeit friendly. Jane had read that there were tens of thousands of US airman stationed in Norfolk, its position on England's eastern bulge shortening the flight time to occupied Europe and Nazi Germany. Sergeant Woodrow Jensen was one of those men, based on an airfield only five miles north, putting East Dereham in easy reach by bicycle or jeep. It was in East Dereham that he died, shot in an unidentified cottage by his fellow countryman and assumed lover.

Jane had wanted a break, a night or two away, but Woody had determined where she'd put the pin in her map. Whilst she didn't yet know why Mary Dye had been ostracised by her family, the death of her first husband would have been a pivotal point in the young woman's life. As Jane walked Dereham's narrow mediaeval streets, she was looking for the ghosts of the past, visualising a Pathé-newsreel monochrome world of brave young men in American uniform, far from home and brashly living each day like it could be their last. Farm boys and city slickers, considered 'oversexed, overpaid and over here' by those they alienated, but charming the local girls with movie-star accents, nylons and chocolate. Jane pulled her phone from her bag and called up Herb Jensen's email. When she'd first opened it earlier that day, she'd concentrated on the words and his request for a DNA sample. This time she looked more closely at the file he'd attached, the photograph of his brother, Woody.

The crisp black-and-white image showed a group of ten men in front of large propeller driven aeroplane painted in a dull matt colour that could have been brown or green. They were in their smartest uniforms and smiling broadly. There was no obvious sign of the battle fatigue that led to Woody Jensen's 'weakness of character' suggested in the newspaper article reporting his death. The plane itself seemed surprisingly low to the ground, the cockpit section resting on a single small wheel. On the slab-sided nose, painted in a large cursive script, were the words: 'Mary Mine'. Precisely who Mary belonged to was unclear, but Jane allowed herself to imagine Woody's nine comrades naming the machine in honour of his new bride as a present for the couple's wartime wedding. The four men in the front row were kneeling and wearing peaked caps that Jane assumed marked them out as officers, though none of them looked older than 25. Standing behind them were the rest of the bomber's crew. Amongst them, second from the left, was Woody. Even if Herb Jensen's email hadn't identified him, Jane knew she would have singled him out from the line-up. She wasn't sure if it was his stature, he was a head shorter than the others and she remembered that his position in the cramped ball turret was the preserve of smaller men, or whether there was something about his face she recognised. His eyes in particular seemed familiar, but she couldn't place where she'd seen them before. One thing was certain: Chris Aimson's dark good looks were not inherited from the diminutive airman with awkward features and blond hair.

After their tour of the town, Jane and Tommy returned to their hotel. They ate well in its restaurant and then adjourned to the bar. Tommy reluctantly let Jane order him a pint of cider, and she continued with the Sauvignon Blanc that had accompanied her meal. They sat at a table with a hammered copper top and she looked around the room, trying to judge if the decor and fittings had genuine age or were more recent approximations of features that had been ripped out in times past for the sake of fashionable modernity.

'I think the bar itself, you know the bar counter and its wooden frame, are original. If not original, then pretty old,' she suggested.

Tommy nodded. 'It's got a few war wounds where it's been knocked about a bit. It's been there quite a while, I'd say.'

'I reckon he must have drunk in here. Propped up that bar with his crewmates between missions. Probably came in here with the guy who shot him. What was his name?'

Jane looked expectantly at Tommy, trusting the reliability of his memory. He didn't fail her.

'Corporal Henry Abrams. He was a clerk rather than airborne, if you remember. Presumably worked in the base HQ, sorting out logistics, parts, crew movements. That kind of thing.'

'That's it, and that newspaper article said he had a certain reputation amongst locals, or words to effect. I don't know if that means he was a bit camp or put himself around a lot. Either way, it must have been really tough being gay in those days.'

Jane looked at Tommy and tried to read his expression. Finding it inconclusive, she hesitantly asked a direct question.

'Tommy, I'm sure you're not, but someone asked me a few days ago and... I guess I realised I'm not 100% sure. It's not as if it matters these days, but you're not gay are you?'

'Who asked you?'

'My old friend Sarah. We were at the tennis club, and I was talking about what I was doing now and mentioned you. And she asked if you were gay. I said no, but then…'

Tommy shook his head. 'No, I'm not gay, Jane.'

Jane was beginning to redden. 'I don't know why I asked. It doesn't matter, does it? I'm sorry. And I'd forgotten about your online friend in South America. What's she called again? Gabby something.'

'Gabi1701.'

'That's it. So describe her to me again. What does Gabi1701 look like?'

'She's a really nice girl. Kind. And she likes the stuff I do. A bit of programming, computer games.'

Jane could tell she was pushing Tommy in a direction he didn't want to go and relented. 'Okay, I'll shut up and get us another drink.'

As she stood waiting to be served, Tommy stared at her in profile, hoping her peripheral vision didn't detect his gaze.

When she returned to the table, they chatted about the case they were researching and their plans for the following day. As always when they got together, Jane did most of the talking but Tommy contributed factually and by checking things on the Internet using his phone. Gradually, as the large wines began to have their inevitable impact, Jane began to discuss the person she hoped was sponsoring their trip, Julian Stothard.

'Between you and me, he's rather good looking. And rich and successful. Oh, and separated from his wife. Who, his mother intimated, is a total bitch. So, what do you reckon, Tommy? Do you think I stand a chance? Independence is good, but a girl doesn't want to be single forever. I think I could cope with a move over to the States.'

She twinkled and Tommy wasn't sure how much she was teasing him. He stared into her eyes very briefly and then shrugged his shoulders.

Jane looked guilty. 'I'm sorry, Tommy. You don't want to hear all this girl talk. I thought I was with Sarah for a minute. I guess I ought to shut up again and definitely make this my last drink. Or I'm going to be anybody's.'

Not long after, they said goodnight and retired, relatively early, to their respective rooms. Tommy lay on his bed staring into the darkness and saw who he always saw in the sleepless nights that plagued him. It wasn't Gabi1701. It was someone he'd fallen for the day he met her. It had been at a group therapy session, but even then, at her lowest ebb, the vibrant, happy Jane was only partially obscured, just below the surface, waiting to bubble back into the daylight. Her husband, Dave, had collected her that day. He was a big man, with the powerful and confident air of a military officer or a rugby player. He chatted easily with the therapists and staff. He charmed the other patients. He was everything Tommy knew he wasn't. Dave knew it too. When he came over and introduced himself, Tommy recognised the condescension in his smile. Both men had instinctively sized each other up. Each had pigeonholed the other. Both were largely right.

And yet it didn't matter. It didn't matter to Dave because Tommy could never be any kind of threat. It didn't matter to Tommy because he knew the Daves of this world left you alone if you stayed out of their way. It didn't matter that Tommy was in love with Dave's wife because Tommy accepted she was forever out of his league, with or without Dave.

Dave and Jane were now divorced. Tommy was well aware of the maxim about faint hearts and fair ladies, but that was guidance for men like Dave. Tommy had Jane's friendship and it was a relationship he dare not risk by speaking out, voicing something that could never be reciprocated. He wasn't proud of it, but he knew he needed his unrequited feelings as a distraction from his anxieties, to sustain him through his dark nights and as a block to the obsessive negativity that might otherwise consume him. But he also knew he'd set a time bomb whose fuse was ticking. He'd let himself get in too deep. Somehow, it had been easy to accept the status quo of Jane and Dave being together. Though Tommy had ruled himself out of the competition, he foresaw heartbreak when she found someone new. When she'd moved away to Nottingham, he thought that distance might enable him to rein in on his emotions, but she'd pulled him into her world again. Being with her now made him as happy as he had ever been. He accepted that he would soon be sad. Life would go on. He would get over it.

Jane would normally pass on a full English breakfast, but her hangover demanded something more substantial than muesli and yoghurt. By contrast, the two pints of cider had eventually helped Tommy sleep and he was feeling fresher than usual. They were both in good spirits by the time Jane steered her car back out through the archway and onto the main road. Their journey was a short one. Tommy had been researching Woody Jensen's World War II airbase on the Internet and Jane wanted to see what remained, 70 years after the last American bomber had lifted off into the sky.

Google's satellite image showed three overlapping lines of concrete forming the elongated bars of what looked like a huge letter A stamped on the countryside. Two of the runways appeared well preserved, but the third and longest became little more than a suggestion as it continued off under ploughed fields. Some sections of the perimeter road were intact, including a few of the frying-pan shaped dispersal areas where individual planes would be parked, their separation minimising the impact of a bomb or strafing attack. An industrial estate to the immediate north contained several structures that could have dated back to the war. On a website of old Ordnance Survey maps, a sheet from the late 1940s had a disappointing white space where the airfield should be, but by a decade later, its disused status had rendered censorship unnecessary and the details were clearly drawn. Three of the largest buildings on the industrial estate had indeed been hangars and the control tower stood close by.

There was a security gate at the entrance to the estate, but Jane sweet talked the guard and he let them through. From ground level, the hangars were unmistakable, and despite having been reroofed, the peeling paint and rust on their walls and huge doors confirmed their age. The control tower was reduced to a sad windowless shell, though it looked like some work had been done to prevent it collapsing entirely to rubble. Tommy protested but Jane insisted they climb its open-sided concrete staircase to stare across the airfield from its upper levels. Once more she conjured up images of the past and imaged Mary Mine and her drab sisters lumbering into the air, lifting their cargoes of death and young men out towards the east with no guarantee of return. Mary Mine had always brought Woody Jensen home, but after his murder she would have flown on without him. Jane wondered whether the plane's luck had eventually run out and what became of the crewmates whose faces smiled eternally in the picture on her phone.

From their high vantage point, Jane and Tommy could see a cluster of light aircraft and gliders around a small building on the far side of the airfield. Tommy found it marked as a museum on the present-day map and was relieved when Jane agreed they should descend and make their way across to it. Other than walking straight down a runway, the only route now available involved leaving the site. They got back into the Mazda and drove out onto the meandering country lanes until they found signs pointing to a flying club.

There was a single vehicle parked in front of the clubhouse, which lay on part of the original perimeter road. Jane could tell the car was old and well loved, but Tommy explained it was a Bristol and very exclusive and expensive in its day. He suggested it probably still was.

They were looking around for signs of life when a red-faced man in his sixties appeared at the door of the building.

'Can I help you?' he said. It was more accusation than offer of aid.

Jane smiled. 'Good morning. We understand there's a museum. We were very much hoping to look round.'

The reply was terse. 'By appointment only, I'm afraid. You need to email the club secretary. It's all on the website.'

Jane was about to try the charm that had won over the security guard at the industrial estate when she noticed a small wooden cutout of an aeroplane, fixed above the door. It was painted in a faded olive green with US markings. She recognised the shape of the cockpit and the nosewheel below it. 'That looks like Mary Mine,' she said almost involuntarily.

The red-faced man looked impressed. 'She's just a generic Liberator, but we've got some pictures of Mary Mine inside. May I ask what your interest is?'

'We're doing some research on behalf of, well, the grandson and the brother of one of the men who flew in her. Forgive me, what's a 'liberator' in this context?'

Tommy chipped in. 'It's a type of American heavy bomber. Four engined, long range, lots of machine guns. Most people have heard of Flying Fortresses. You know, the plane in that film, the Memphis Belle? The Liberator was designed to do a similar job.'

'Not as popular with its crews as the Fortress. Sometimes called the "Flying Coffin" because she was an absolute bastard to get out of in a hurry. Forgive my French.' The red-faced man had become avuncular and animated. 'I'm Roger by the way. Club secretary. I can let you in the museum as you're here. I'm not the most knowledgeable on what's in there, but I can point you at the stuff we've got on Mary Mine. I warn you, it's a sad story. But you probably know that already.'

The museum was housed in one main room, with framed pictures and artefacts round the walls. One prominent set of charts showed the layout of the runways and buildings as it had been at the height of operations in 1944. In the centre of the room were freestanding green-baize display boards onto which a large number of smaller photographs had been mounted. These were all annotated and included several views of the base during the war, including the hangars, huts of various sizes and the control tower when it still had windows, railings and a greenhouse-like structure on its roof. There were a few aerial shots taken during air raids, but the bulk of the display was devoted to images of the men and machines of the bombardment group which had been based at the airfield.

There were ground crew maintaining engines, loading bombs and bullets, and inspecting damaged planes. There were men marching in smart uniforms and smaller groups looking anxious or tired in thick, fur-lined flying jackets, helmets and goggles. Most of all, there were pictures of big Liberator bombers, predominantly in drab camouflage but some in naked shiny aluminium, all with their names proudly painted beneath their cockpit windows, many with lewd cartoon artwork in accompaniment.

Roger led them to one particular panel and introduced it gravely. 'There she is, Mary Mine. Before and after.'

The before picture was familiar: it was on Jane's phone. There was Woody Jensen and his smiling comrades lined up in front of their plane. Their names and ranks were listed below and Woody's position, second from left on the back row, was confirmed. Mary Mine's squat, dark bulk in the background made her look solid and impregnable. But the adjacent photograph, Mary Mine's last, showed the truth. She was nothing but a fragile, flammable shell.

As Jane and Tommy silently digested the brief text below the image of the burnt-out wreck, Roger decided to elaborate. 'She was on her way back from a daylight raid over Germany and got caught by fighters. She was badly shot up. Several of her crew were wounded. The pilot somehow managed to get her home. They should have bailed out rather than trying to land her in the state she was, but they decided to bring her down. Undercarriage gave way and she burst into flames. No survivors. Plus, one the firefighters on the ground was killed trying to pull the burning men out of the wreckage. All pretty hideous really.'

Jane turned to Tommy. 'Have you seen the date? It was only a month after Woody died.'

Tommy just nodded, but Roger looked confused. 'So, the person you're interested wasn't part of Mary Mine's crew?'

Jane's answer was half question. 'He was the ball turret gunner. It was underneath somewhere?'

Roger pointed at the later picture. 'Yes. Tiny Plexiglas sphere in which they squeezed a man and two big machine guns. Wouldn't get me in one. They were supposed to winch it up and down on the Liberator, but it looks like it wasn't fully retracted when Mary Mine came down. I hope to God they'd got the poor chap out. Not that it made any difference in the end. Still, doesn't bear thinking about.'

'His name was Woody Jensen.' said Jane. 'There he is, in the first photograph. He should have been on the plane when it crashed, but he'd just been killed in Dereham by another American airman.'

Roger clicked his fingers to indicate recognition. 'We've got something on that. We don't have it on display for obvious reasons, but it's in one of the cabinets in the office.'

He left them for several minutes and then returned with a cardboard folder. In it was a newspaper cutting and two photographs. The cutting was the article Tommy had found online, and which reported the story of Woody Jensen's death at the hands of Corporal Henry Abrams. The first picture was just a duplicate of the one on display showing Mary Mine's crew including Woody. The other was one that Jane and Tommy had not seen before. It was taken in a bar, a bar that they knew, the bar in their hotel. Standing there were several men clustered around a central figure who was holding aloft a pint glass and grinning broadly. On the back was a handwritten explanation: 'This round's on me! Corporal Henry Abrams Jr, son of oilman Henry Abrams Sr, stands everyone a drink on the occasion of his 21st birthday.'

Jane and Tommy looked at each other. It wasn't just the setting they recognised. Immediately to Henry Abrams' left was a strikingly handsome man with jet-black Brylcreemed hair and a dapper moustache, a look that most would assume was modelled on Clark Gable. But Jane and Tommy knew the inspiration lay elsewhere. They also knew the man's name. It was the ardent supporter of disgraced British fascist Oswald Mosley, and the man who would marry Woody Jensen's widow, Mary. It was Dean Smith's grandfather. It was James Smith.

The twisted spire

Jane had put Tommy on a train back to London and then phoned Mary Smith's nursing home. She was told that the old lady had gone to hospital for 'tests', but was not being kept in and would be available the following day. Jane explained that Mary's grandson had suggested she visit and the youthful voice on the other end of the line seemed happy.

'Mary doesn't get many visitors, but she loves to talk. It might cheer her up.'

It was a large Victorian villa with a modern flat-roofed extension pinned to its side and back. Over a tall fence, a cul-de-sac of box-like townhouses occupied what had once been extensive grounds. Only a small plot remained at the front of the original house, but the garden was immaculately kept with beautiful flowers and pretty shrubs around a paved patio area. From there you could just make out the feature which dominated Chesterfield's skyline and reputation. Above the rooftops, the tall mediaeval spire of St Mary and All Saints appeared to be toppling sideways, its twisted frame and herringbone of lead tiles being only anecdotal at this distance.

Jane rang the bell and was greeted by a lady wearing a lilac polyester smock who tersely quizzed her in a South African accent on the purpose of her visit. Jane was immediately struck by the smell of boiled vegetables, which took her back to her own grandmother's last few weeks in a similar home in Nottingham. Having signed the visitor's book, Jane was shown down a corridor whose elegant mouldings and cornices abruptly gave way to the plainness of the modern annex.

As they approached the door to room number 12, the care assistant in the lilac smock became more loquacious.

'Mary's a lovely old dear, though her health's not... Let's just say it's not good. And you must remember her age. She's sharper than many of our ladies, some of whom are much, much younger, but she inevitably gets confused from time to time.'

'That's what her grandson said,' replied Jane.

'Are you a friend of his?'

'Not as such,' said Jane, noncommittally.

'Well, let's just say I don't how that one would know what Mary's like these days. He only comes to visit her when he's after money, and that must have run out because I can't remember when we last saw him. Not that we miss having him around. Trouble is, she's got no-one else.'

Jane saw her opportunity to be reassuring. 'I'm working on behalf of a lady who I believe to be Mary's long-lost niece. She only lives in Matlock Bath. She's got a son and daughter. I'm sure they'd want to meet Mary, assuming Mary wants to see them. Something happened years ago that caused a split in the family.'

'Family arguments, eh? Mary's not the sort to hold a grudge. I can't believe she started it.'

With that, the assistant turned away from Jane and opened the door after a token knock. The room was small, but freshly decorated in a bright floral wallpaper and light was flooding in from a large picture window. A thin and frail looking woman with wispy white hair was sat in a winged armchair, seemingly staring into space.

The assistant's voice became gentler. 'Mary, my love, here's that visitor we told you about. A nice young lady called Jane. She knows your family. Shall I bring you both a nice cup of tea, so you can have a nice little chat together?'

The old lady smiled and nodded.

The assistant turned to Jane and affected a conspiratorial stage whisper. 'I warn you dear, you won't get a word in edgeways when our Mary gets going. Now, plonk yourself down next to her.' She winked and left the room.

There was an old wooden dining chair close to Mary's and Jane sat whilst simultaneously introducing herself. 'Mrs Smith, my name's Jane Madden. I met your grandson and he suggested I talk to you. About your family. Is that alright?'

'I haven't seen Ernie for a long time.' Mary's voice was surprisingly strong.

'Your grandson is called Dean, Mrs Smith. I think Ernie was your son. I'm afraid he passed away some time ago.'

'Sorry dear, you're right. It's always the names I have trouble with. What's was yours again, my dear?'

'Jane, Mrs Smith.'

'It very sweet of you calling me Mrs Smith, dear. No-one in here ever does. I find it a bit, what's the word? Patronising, I think that's it. I'm not a little girl. And those doctors at the hospital. They're young enough to be my grandchildren and they immediately assume we're on first name terms. The world's so informal these days, isn't it? When I was a girl, only a husband and wife used each other's Christian name. Between adults, I mean. Oh, and brothers and sisters. For everyone else, it was Mr So-and-so and Mrs So-and-so. You'd go into the grocer's and it would be, "Good morning, Mrs Smith. How are you today? And how's Mr Smith? Is he keeping well?" These days, it would be "Hello, darling" or something like that. I miss the old courtesy sometimes. Everyone's got so much these days. We had nothing during the war, but I can't help but feel we treated each other better.'

Mary's eyes seemed to drift away and a questioning frown crossed her brow.

'Mrs Smith, it's those days I wanted to talk to you about. About your family and your sisters. Is that okay?' said Jane.

'My sisters? I haven't told anyone about them for a long time. I was the pretty one, you know. And maybe the silly one. The oldest is supposed to be most sensible, to set a good example. But I had my head in the clouds. He was a film star, you see, Britain's answer to Clark Gable and Errol Flynn. I used to watch him up on the silver screen.'

'A film star?' Jane looked puzzled.

'Yes. You wouldn't think it to look at me now, but I married a film star. No-one here believes me when I tell them.'

'Are you sure, Mrs Smith? It's just that I've been researching your family, looking at births, marriages and deaths, and I don't remember finding anything about a film star.'

'Perhaps I am getting confused. Everyone said he looked like film star, that was it. I was a goner from the first time I saw him. My sisters never liked him. I thought they were just jealous, but they were right. Maybe they were jealous, too. They're all dead now. I feel it in these old bones of mine. Still, I'll be joining them very soon. Those doctors said as much. Well they didn't say it, but I'm not stupid. I know what "let nature take its toll" means. About time, too. Do you believe in life after death, dear?'

'I don't know. Probably not,' replied Jane.

'When you get to my age you think about it a lot. I think about little else, if I'm honest. I've convinced myself there's nothing awaiting us. I say convinced, but it's more wishful thinking than certainty. I really hope there's nothing. It would be... easier. I can't face them. Maybe my brother, Kenny. He died at sea before I messed everything up. He still loves me. He'll forgive me.'

Mary Smith suddenly clapped her hands together and sat up in her chair. 'My dear, I'm so sorry! I'm getting really maudlin in my old age. A pretty young girl like you doesn't want to hear me wittering on about death and the afterlife. It's not something you'll have to think about for a long, long time. What did you come here to talk about?'

'Your family, Mrs Smith, and your relationship with them. I'm here on behalf your sister Anne's daughter. She's called Margaret.'

'Little Annie. She was the clever one. Got into grammar school. My mum and dad were so proud of her. She got her brains from my dad, but he had to go down the pit as soon as he was old enough. Always struggled with that rotten leg of his. A very timid man, my dad. My mum reckoned it was because he was bullied as a boy. He had these three cousins... No, they were actually his nephews, but the same age as him. Nasty piece of work they were. Died in the war, all three of them. I don't think my dad was sorry, though he'd never say so.'

Jane found herself distracted onto a storyline she no longer thought significant. 'Was that the First World War?'

'Yes, dear. Kenny, my brother, died in the second one.'

'Was their surname Oakley?'

Mary paused whilst she searched back through nine decades of memories. Experience told her to give up after a few seconds. 'Names, dear. I told you I'm not good at names. And we didn't have anything to do with that side of the family when I was growing up.'

Jane persisted. 'Did anyone ever blame your dad for not fighting in the war, the First World War?'

'How could they? Anyone could see he wasn't fit. My poor dad!"

Mary seemed on the verge of getting upset and Jane steered the conversation back to the relationship she'd actually come to discuss. 'I'm sorry. It doesn't matter. Please tell me some more about your sister Annie.'

Jane saw Mary's expression calm, but somehow it was a look of resignation rather than fond reminiscence.

'Ah,' sighed Mary, 'our little Annie. Wore glasses, of course. Clever people do, don't they? She married a sergeant-major. Well, he had been a sergeant-major. Much older than her, bald and barrel-chested. One of those men with ramrod up his... Well, that's what he used to say. They didn't get on. He absolutely hated him. Him and his Military Medal. That silly lump of metal caused it all in the end. Him bragging about it. Well, he always thought he was bragging about it, even when he never mentioned it. Something about the look on his face, the way he carried himself. It made him so jealous.' Mary Smith shook her head slowly as she remembered ancient conflicts.

Jane probed as softly as she could. 'Why did you fall out? You and Annie and your other sisters, what went wrong?'

'He had a wicked temper when he was drunk. It wasn't so much the rage; it was that he lost control. He'd always shout the odds, say anything, upset anyone, to come out on top. I came to realise, eventually, that he was a very insecure man. He looked like a film star, but it wasn't enough. They say film stars can be very insecure, don't they? He had to show off. On the rare occasions we had any money, he'd buy something flashy to say, "Look at me, I'm special." Silly things, from a little biro pen, when they were a novelty and no-one else had one, to big cars we couldn't afford to run. When he lost them, his looks I mean, it broke him. And it broke his spell over me, but by then it was too late.'

'What exactly did he do, when he was drunk?' pressed Jane.

'He did terrible things. I didn't know the full of it until much, much later. If the sergeant-major had've known what he'd really done, he wouldn't have kept quiet. It was only Annie begging him that stopped him going straight to the authorities. "It's my wedding day," she said. "The war's over," she said. "He's all talk, he's making it up," she said. "She's my sister," she said. By the time I found out, what he'd really done, he told me I was in too deep, that I was an accomplice. He said he'd make sure that I'd hang along with him. We'd dangle and kick side by side, if I ever told a soul.'

Mary paused only briefly before continuing. 'And here I am, telling you. Perhaps it is time for my final confession. But you can't absolve me of my sins, can you, my dear? Still, I guess they're not going to hang me now, are they?' She chuckled mirthlessly and answered her own question. 'Don't worry. I know they haven't hung anyone since before you were born. And I guess I'm already in a prison of sorts, a prison called decrepit old age, and on death row, at that. There's nothing they can do to me now. And there's certainly nothing he can do to me anymore. Not unless he's waiting for me. On the other side, I mean. You don't believe in life after death, do you dear?'

Jane shook her head. 'The man we're talking about, it's your second husband, James Smith, isn't it?'

'He was such a good-looking man. You'd have fallen for him too, and I'm sure you're not a silly girl like I was. I sometimes think Annie was in love with him. That's why she stood up for him. But maybe that's me being silly again. Maybe it was simply that she loved me, her big, silly sister. She thought she was protecting me, when all along she was condemning me. Call me Mary, dear. Why not? We're friends now aren't we?'

'Alright, thank you, Mary. So what did James do that was so terrible?'

'He liked boys as well as girls, of course. Lots of film stars do, don't they?'

'Is that what caused the rift in your family?'

'No, they never knew about that. I didn't find out for years – he was very good at covering his tracks – and I wasn't about to broadcast it to the world.'

'But you thought it was terrible?' persisted Jane.

Mary Smith shook her head, her eyes staring at a blank wall as if it were a window on the past. 'He ruined those children. Well, he ruined one of them and drove the other away. Maybe that's my biggest regret. He treated little Ernie so badly, beating him, calling him "ugly, pasty bastard" all the time. "Ugly, pasty, little bastard".' Tears formed in her eyes as she repeated the phrase. 'Yet Ernie hero-worshipped him. He became the same sort of man, but without the looks. Without the luck, too. Ended up in prison, of course. And then, he did the same to my grandson, Dean. Dean's mother ran off when he was only young. I tried my best with him, but the influence was too strong. And I was too weak. Nature or nurture, that's what they say, isn't it?'

'Mary, what about your daughter, Lois? The little girl you had with your first husband, the American airman, Woody?'

'Nature or nurture,' reiterated Mary thoughtfully. 'I never actually loved Woody. He wasn't good looking at all. Pale, very small, quite effeminate really. But he was twice the man James was, I can see that now. I only married him because I was pregnant. Woody adored her when she was born. She was such a beautiful girl. And then, that terrible thing happened. I became a widow with a small child. James said he loved me, but he only married me so he could run away and hide. He treated Lois so much better than Ernie. He was always buying her presents and pretty dresses, but she eventually saw him for what he was and she ran away from him. I tried to keep in touch, but he found out. He frightened me when he was angry, so I chose the easy way out. And I chose the film star. Again. Silly, silly girl. She's dead too, isn't she, my little Lois?'

'I'm sorry, yes.' said Jane quietly. 'But I think you know she had a son, Christopher. He's a very handsome man, too. His health isn't great, but—'

'You won't tell them, dear?' Mary suddenly sounded frightened. 'Where I am, I mean. I can't face them, you know. I can talk to you, you're... Forgive me, you're no-one. But I can't face my family. Not after all this time. They'll see what a shameful, weak, silly woman I was and they'll be right. I just want to die peacefully and hope the lights just go out and stay out. I can't do anything for them, not now. I've got nothing and it's too late. Please don't tell them.'

'If you don't want me to say where you are, I won't,' promised Jane. 'But one thing you can do for them is to tell me your story, answer their questions. You didn't fall out with your family because of the way James treated your children. I know he had strong political views. Was that what caused the trouble?'

Mary's mind was still focussed elsewhere. 'I don't want them coming to my funeral, either. I don't want everyone milling around talking about me, saying nice, respectful things and thinking something completely different. No more lies. I'd like you to come, dear, but not my family, not the ones I've wronged. I just want to be burnt and my ashes scattered and forgotten. I burnt him, you know. He always wanted to be buried with a fancy gravestone in black marble, but I burnt him...'

Mary went quiet. Jane spent a few seconds gathering her thoughts and then gently resumed her questioning.

'Mary, you said something earlier about hanging. Was that just an expression, or did you really mean it? What did James do that could possibly merit hanging?'

'They hanged Lord Haw-Haw, didn't they?'

'Lord Haw-Haw?' Jane's brow furrowed as she struggled to place the aristocrat with the familiar but strangely comical name.

'Yes. You remember, dear. He was on the wireless during the war. "Germany calling, Germany calling." Despite the plummy accent, he wasn't even British. He was Irish or American, or something, but we still hanged him for treason. James was so upset. They'd been friends, you see, before the war.'

'Yes, of course, I remember now.' Jane's eyes opened with illumination. 'William Joyce, nicknamed Lord Haw-Haw when he broadcast Nazi propaganda from Berlin. And James was a friend of his?'

'Well, he said they were friends. I think they met once. Lord Haw-Haw was a lot older than he was. He visited him in hospital after he'd been beaten up by those filthy Bolshies.'

'Bolshies? You mean Bolsheviks, as in communists? James was beaten up by communists?' Jane remembered Chris Aimson saying his grandfather had lost the sight in one eye after a fight with anti-fascists, but hadn't appreciated the revolutionary polarisation of the time.

'Beaten very, very badly. It changed him, I think. Lord Haw-Haw was one of the top British fascists before the war and had a terrible scar on his face where he'd been slashed with a razor by a communist gang. James felt it was bond between them. They both hated, hated Bolshies. And Jews, of course.'

'Why was James beaten up by these Bolshies?'

'He was only a teenager. It was 1935 or maybe 1936. He wasn't old enough to be a Blackshirt. He was a cadet. They wore grey shirts – he told me how his ended up blood red. He was selling party newspapers on a street corner in the East End. That's where he came from. His father had been gassed in the First World War. They were promised a home fit for heroes and what they got was poverty and the Depression. I know fascism seems wicked now, but the government, democracy itself, didn't seem able to cope and Mosley promised change, a new order. Anyway, there he was, my James, on that street corner. I think he had one Blackshirt steward with him. They were jumped by four or five of them and beaten so, so badly. He was only a boy but they hit him on the head with an iron bar.'

'That was when he lost the sight in his right eye?'

Mary nodded. 'And he was forever plagued by terrible headaches and dizzy spells. He hated them for the rest of his life, Bolshies. I think Haw-Haw hated Jews the most and went straight over to the Nazis. Mosley just wanted to avoid war and preached that we strike a peace deal with Hitler. They interned him and most of the British fascists, but James was too young, too unimportant to be of interest.'

Mary paused and seemed lost in her thoughts. There was a look of concern on her face as if she was questioning her memories, or perhaps it was her judgement in revealing them that she doubted. Jane was about to speak when the older woman resumed her story unprompted.

'He kept his head down until Hitler declared war on Russia and then he felt he had to do something, something to help in the fight against communism. It got worse when America joined in and loaded the odds. I didn't know what he was up to at the time, dear, honestly I didn't. I didn't know he was a fifth columnist until much, much later.'

Solution

Jane tried to get Mary to focus on James Smith's wartime activities, but the old lady increasingly jumped around the decades as individual thoughts came to her. Jane was forced to take scribbled notes in an effort to keep track. The story seemed to be that one of his pre-war acquaintances had put him in touch with a Nazi spy who'd been parachuted into England and was building up a network of fascist sympathisers to gather information on allied invasion plans. At that time James was already hanging around American air bases, buying and selling black-market goods. Unfortunately, some of what Mary said was contradictory and she seemed more interested in talking about his later life, their troubled marriage and the impact it had on their children. Mary described how they'd been forced to move away from Dowley and James had dragged his family from place to place, as he strove to avoid the consequences of various dodgy money-making schemes catching up with him. Eventually they'd returned to Dowley, but only when Mary's family had dispersed to more prosperous parts of the country.

Gradually it became clear Mary had exhausted herself and her confusion was returning. Clouds drifted over the seemingly clear blue sky of her deep-seated memories, and she once again became insistent that her husband had been a film star and that she'd seen one of his black-and-white films on television only days previously. The South African care assistant came in to say that Mary's lunch was ready, and Jane thought it best to leave.

Now back home in Nottingham, Jane tried to process Mary's account of family estrangement and weigh it in the balance of likelihood and doubt.

It did seem very probable there had been a fight at Mary's sister's wedding. For Mary and her husband to be effectively purged from the family, the cause had to be extreme. But James simply expressing pro-Nazi views to a decorated war hero could easily have been sufficient, given that it was so soon after a terrible conflict in which so many people lost so much.

Jane had enough to go back to the Stothards and claim she'd solved the family mystery and completed her work on the case. It would beg the question, however, of whether Mary's wilder claims were true. Could James Smith really have been a fifth columnist, a spy feeding information on US air force movements back to the Germans? Margaret and Julian Stothard would surely want to know. Jane needed to know too.

Dismissal

Hi Jane

Thanks for the update. I appreciate you've only given me the abridged version, but it's quite a story. I particularly liked the bit about meeting Lord Haw-Haw. If I were a sceptic, I'd say someone was just pulling famous names from a hat. Or had watched too many spy films. Sorry if I sound a little grumpy, I've been awake for 48 hours (bastard insomnia – moan, moan, moan). Anyway, the rational answer to your question is a simple no. James Smith was not spying for the Germans. He couldn't have been because <u>no-one</u> was.

Check out 'Double Cross' using the URLs below and you'll see what I mean.

Glad to hear you're feeling well,

Tommy x

Double Cross

Jane followed Tommy's links to various web pages which described the Double Cross system run by British intelligence in World War II. She realised it was history she'd heard of before and felt stupid that she'd fired off an email without doing some simple research herself. But whilst the basic premise of Double Cross was coming back to her, she'd never fully appreciated the totality of its reach.

Just south of Nottingham was a heritage railway where volunteers ran steam locomotives on tracks abandoned by British Rail long before it, too, was lost to denationalisation. Jane and Dave had visited the line to attend a beer festival, which was spread across the various stations such that different selections of ales could be reached by climbing onto a passing train. At least one of those stations was forever stuck in 1940 with displays of wartime paraphernalia, including, most memorably, a baby doll in a pram gas mask. Thinking back now, Jane could also visualise the backdrop of a weathered propaganda poster proclaiming that 'Careless talk costs lives'. People were warned that Britain was awash with cunning and virtually undetectable spies funnelling secrets to their German masters. Newspapers and novels fed the paranoia. Watch what you said in front of the man who looked like an incorruptible bank manager with his pinstripe suit and impeccable accent. He could have polished his vowels in Munich and learnt his politics at Nuremberg. The myth had persisted in many people's minds, despite contradictory wartime files gradually being declassified over the years.

The reality had been one of incompetence, exposure and betrayal. Nazi agents had often been ill prepared with a poor command of English. When they arrived in Britain by parachute or submarine, or posing as refugees, they did not blend into the landscape. They stood out: they looked and acted like spies. They became even easier to spot when Bletchley Park cracked the Enigma code. MI5 monitored radio traffic from German military intelligence, the Abwehr, which gave them prior notice of incursions. Some of the would-be moles surrendered themselves on arrival; the rest were simply rounded up. They were all interrogated and then either imprisoned, executed or turned.

The ones who turned, that is, agreed to act as double agents, fed back misleading information to their controllers in Germany. This was the Double Cross system.

At the Tehran Conference in 1943, the leaders of America, Britain and Russia met to discuss the strategy of the war, including the opening of a second front. Winston Churchill famously remarked to Josef Stalin that, 'In wartime, truth is so precious that she should always be attended by a bodyguard of lies.' Operation Bodyguard was adopted as the name of the deception plan to disguise the date and location of the D-Day landings. As part of Bodyguard, one of the main achievements of the Double Cross system was to help confuse the Nazis into thinking that the Allied assault was likely to be focussed in Calais rather than Normandy. Even after the invasion, the Abwehr still trusted one of the double agents and his fictitious network of subagents to the extent that he was radioed congratulations for a job well done.

This much was vaguely familiar to Jane. What she had never realised was the completeness of Double Cross. From their deciphering of Abwehr transmissions, British intelligence believed they effectively controlled the entire German espionage system in this country. They were right: analysis of post-war records confirmed that only one agent had escaped MI5's attention and he was a failure, committing suicide in 1941 when he ran out of supplies and money.

Jane closed the lid on her laptop and leant back in her chair. Tommy had been correct. To all intents and purposes, there were no Nazi spies operating in Britain, certainly not by the stage of the war when James Smith was supposedly gathering information on US air force movements. It had been a tall story all along. Assuming it wasn't habituated to lying, Mary Smith's aged mind was muddling memory with mirage. Her husband hadn't been a spy, just as he'd never appeared on the silver screen. But what had planted the idea? There was something about the way the narrative held together, the logical sequence of events, the names, dates and places, that made Jane think there was some kernel of truth at its heart. She was still intrigued. She felt compelled to visit Mary again.

The shoe box

Once again, Jane phoned ahead. She was met by some initial hesitation, but the call was transferred to the nursing home manager, who was cautiously positive.

'She's been asking when you were coming back, Ms Madden. She said she hadn't finished her story. It seems very important to her. I said she could tell me, but I won't do, apparently. She's...' There was a heavy pause on the line as the manager considered her words. 'Let's just say she's not feeling her best. But, at this stage, if it's going to make her happy then who am I to stand in the way.'

Before she left her house, Jane checked her emails. Nothing new of interest had arrived, but there was one existing item in her inbox that made Jane's heart sink. It was the message from Herb Jensen asking for a DNA sample from Chris Aimson to prove the blood link between them.

Jane had heard once of a swimmer denied an Olympic gold medal by the precision of modern clocks and the fact he'd cut his fingernails. Technology might lead to increased accuracy, truth even, but it didn't always result in justice.

Jane felt a wave of doubt that broke into resentment. She knew she couldn't ignore Herb Jensen's request for much longer.

As on her previous visit, Jane was shown into the room by the South African care assistant. This time, Mary Smith was still in bed, propped up by pillows. She was wearing a thick, knitted cardigan in a bright shade of pink that seemed to emphasise the cold ashen-grey of her face. She looked deathly tired.

Life flickered in her eyes when she saw Jane and her thin lips smiled.

'My dear, thank you for coming back. Forgive me, I can't remember your name.'

'It's Jane. And you said I could call you Mary. Because we were friends, which was kind of you.'

'Yes, Jane. I remember that much. I also remember not finishing my story. I got sidetracked into that silliness about my husband being a film star. When you're old and you've wanted to believe something for so long, you can talk yourself into it. I am a silly old woman aren't I?'

'Not at all. It must be difficult when things happened so long ago.'

'Yet some things come back to you so clearly, as if they were yesterday.'

'Mary, I wanted to ask you about one of the things you told me. About your husband, your second husband, and what he did in the war.'

'Yes... sorry, I've forgotten your name again, dear.'

'It's Jane, but don't worry. It's just that you told me he'd been giving information to a German spy and I just wondered if that was, well, similar to you getting confused about him being a film star. You see, what we know now, what people weren't told at the time, was that they were all captured. All the German spies who came to Britain. Before they could do any harm.'

'But what about his medal, Jane? That Iron Cross he was so proud of?'

'You never actually saw that, did you, Mary?'

'He kept it hidden under the floorboards. His dying wish was to be buried with it, under that black marble headstone he wanted so much. But I think I told you, I had him burnt. And I kept it as a reminder that I'd got my revenge, petty as it was.'

Jane's eyes narrowed in confusion. 'You've actually got the medal?'

'Under the bed. In my little box of mementoes.'

Jane bent down and surveyed the carpeted shadows beneath the pine bed frame. At the head end, against the wall, was a cardboard shoe box. She got down on her knees, stretched her arm past the bedside cabinet and pulled the box out. It had a layer of dust and she could feel her eyes begin to itch. She was about to open it when she abruptly stopped herself.

'I'm sorry, Mary. I should have asked. Do you mind if I look inside?'

'It's too late for secrets, dear.'

Jane removed the lid and placed it on the floor beside her. Inside the box were postcards, letters and photographs, two of which immediately caught Jane's eye. One was very familiar: it was the black-and-white image she'd come across two or three times before. It showed Woody Jensen, Mary's first husband, and his crew of in front of Mary Mine, the US air force bomber. The other was a snap in the grainy colour of a cheap Instamatic camera from the 1970s. The angelic though plain-looking toddler with straight blond hair was instantly recognisable. It was Mary's grandson, the now far from innocent Dean Smith.

'Look for a manila envelope, dear,' instructed Mary. 'You can keep it if you like. It's no use to me anymore.'

Jane found it doubled over at the bottom of the box. It was starting to become fragile with age and she opened it out carefully. Somehow it was an odd size, like A4 but slightly longer and narrower. Something heavy lay at the bottom and she slipped it out onto her lap. On a ribbon of red, white and black, hung a metal cross of unmistakable shape. Within an outline of silver, it was painted black and embossed at its centre was a Nazi swastika. The medal and ribbon were pristine as if never worn.

Jane stared at it for a few seconds before she realised there was something else in the envelope. She gently slid her hand in and retrieved a folded piece of yellowing paper.

She had started to dismiss the medal as a trophy purchased by James Smith sometime after the war, perhaps from a returning soldier who had stolen it from a corpse or bought it for a few cigarettes from a disillusioned captive. This second item was harder to explain. It was a note, handwritten in neat copperplate using fountain pen. The letterhead featured an imperial eagle holding a garland in its talons. Within the garland, the swastika once again announced its sinister presence.

Incongruously, the writing was in English. Jane read it twice.

To my old comrade,

I wanted personally to write to you in gratitude for your heroic efforts in the war against International Jewry and the contagious putridity of the Bolsheviks with their subhuman Slavic hordes. When we met those few short years ago, I saw in you a mirror of myself, a patriot prepared to stand for the greater good and not fall in behind a myopic, spineless British Government owned and manipulated by the Jewish financiers who caused the wholly unnecessary conflict between Germany and her natural friend, England.

It gives me great pride to see that my faith in you was well founded. I salute you and congratulate you on your award of the Iron Cross, an honour you share with the Führer himself!

Do not believe the propaganda peddled by Churchill and his lickspittles in the BBC. German strength grows daily and her forces remain unvanquished. I look forward to meeting you again when the Reich triumphs and we can stand side by side as victors.

Your friend,

William Joyce

Jane looked up from the note and towards the old lady lying in the bed beside her. 'When did you first see this, Mary?'

'It was after my sister's wedding. When he'd been beaten up by the sergeant-major. James was angry and hurt, emotionally as well as physically. He showed it to me as evidence of his... courage, I suppose. He wanted to prove what a big man he was.'

'So that was just after the war?'

Mary said something affirmative, but Jane wasn't listening. Her attention was focussed on how James could have forged such a document back in the 1940s. Nowadays, with modern computer technology and rudimentary IT skills, anyone could download symbols representing the Third Reich and generate convincing-looking headed paper. But this note had age. Could it be genuine? Could James and the Nazi agent he worked for possibly have slipped through the net of accepted history?

Mary interrupted Jane's ruminations. 'That wasn't the worst thing he did. Well maybe it was – I guess I don't know how many American airmen died because of his spying. But it wasn't the worst thing he did to me. It wasn't the worst thing he did to my children. They could have grown up, happy and decent, in America. Their lives would have been so different. That's why I wanted to talk to you again. There's more I have to tell you, while I still can.'

Adders' nest

Despite her frailty, Mary Smith had talked for over an hour, though she once again went round in circles of repetition and occasionally contradicted herself. Unlike Jane's first visit, Mary hadn't drifted into obvious fantasy, yet some of what she said was still very difficult to believe. When Jane left and climbed into her car, she found herself fixated on one revelation. It, at least, was more than plausible: it was convincing. And it threatened to affect the future, not just the past.

Jane knew she should drive home. She should calmly digest everything she had been told and think carefully how to proceed. There was one thing she should not do.

She pulled her phone out of her bag, scrolled through the list of contacts and dialled. The call was answered after three rings.

'Yeah?'

'Is that Dean Smith?'

'Who wants to know?'

'It's Jane Madden, Dean. We met in the pub in Dowley, if you remember. You gave me your number.'

'And then you told me to fuck off, pet.'

'You were coming on a bit strong, Dean. That's all. I didn't mean to cause offense. I am a married woman, you know.'

'I didn't see no ring.'

'Look, let's have another go at getting on. There's something I need to ask you. I'm pretty close by in Chesterfield and I wondered if I could buy you another pint. Hopefully we'll separate on better terms this time.'

'That landlord and me aren't on the best of terms at the moment. I'm doing my drinking at home. But you're welcome to bring a few tins of Stella round. Then you can ask me whatever you want. Pet.'

Jane hesitated. A bad idea was in danger of becoming an act of irresponsible stupidity, like walking up to an adders' nest then taking off your boots.

'Okay, give me the address,' she said.

It was an estate of 1960s social housing, whose narrow roads were bordered by wide grass verges planted with stubby cherry trees. The architecture was uniformly functional and plain, with only a few properties embellished by extensions and non-standard decoration that advertised their transfer to private ownership. Jane pulled up in front of a two-storey block that could have been taken for a row of terraced houses were it not for the single entrance centrally positioned and surrounded by six brown wheelie bins. The UPVC window frames looked relatively new, but the wood cladding around the first floor appeared to be stained with damp and starting to decay.

Jane pulled a transparent polythene envelope from the glove box and put it and its contents into her handbag. The tins of lager were still cold from the corner-shop fridge, and she lifted them off the passenger seat and climbed out of the car.

There was evidence of hinges in the door frame, but there was nothing barring access to the communal hallway. Hanging heavily in the air was the unmistakable sweet-herb, burning-rope aroma of marijuana that Jane felt she'd been catching everywhere since the police softened their attitude to possession. She took the bare concrete stairs to the first floor and found the entrance to Dean's flat immediately on the left. She remembered it was actually his friend Steve's apartment and wasn't sure if it was better that the two of them were home or just Dean. Either way, she did know the sensible thing was to go back to her car and drive away.

There was the sound of loud, angry voices coming from inside, but then applause broke out, indicating a

TV programme rather than a live argument. Jane pressed the bell; nothing seemed to happen, so she knocked sharply three times. There was abrupt silence and the door opened almost immediately.

'Jane, thanks for popping round. Please come in. Sorry we're in a bit of mess. Steve's an untidy bugger. I keep telling him to sort it out, but you can't get the staff these days, can you?' Dean smirked with appreciation at his own joke.

'Is Steve in?' asked Jane.

'Nah. Told him to fuck off. You didn't want to talk to him, now did you?'

Dean stood back and Jane walked into a small sitting room with a window overlooking a graffitied yard at the back of the block. Immediately facing her was a battered sofa with what appeared to be a duvet roughly crammed into the gap between it and the wall behind. As well as a matching armchair, there was one side table and a huge flat-screen TV that would have dominated a much larger space. It was still on, showing a channel Jane didn't recognise, but the sound was muted. Dean's assessment of untidiness was accurate and there was a pile of clothes dumped in one corner, partially hidden by the chair. The room smelt of body odour and cigarettes, half-heartedly disguised by a recent blast of air freshener. There was also an undertone of pot, but Jane felt that had probably drifted in from outside.

Jane sat in the armchair and handed the tins of lager to Dean. He cracked one open and offered it back. Jane declined and he shrugged, then slumped down on the sofa and took a swig.

'So?' he asked.

'I've just been to see your grandmother,' replied Jane.

'How is the silly old cow? Still in the land of the fairies?'

'She's had some tests at the hospital. I don't think they went terribly well. I guess there's not a lot they can do for a woman her age, and she seems to be going downhill rapidly. If you want to see her again, let's just say I'd go sooner rather than later.'

'Is that what you wanted to see for me for? To tell me to visit my barmy old gran? Fuck off!' Dean's tone was one of amusement rather than aggression.

Jane shook her head. 'No. I just thought you should know. The reason I wanted to see you was to do with some of the things she told me. About your family.'

Dean became defensive. 'You don't want to believe everything that silly old woman says. She lives in a dreamworld most of the time. Did she give you the one about my grandad being a film star? Was he on tele last week? How about him winning the Iron Cross?'

'You told me that one, Dean.'

'Maybe I was just winding you up, pet.'

Jane leant forward. 'Look, she said a lot of things and I don't know what to believe. Some of it seemed very far-fetched, but there was one thing that rang true. When you look at old photographs it's very obvious. I'd been explaining it away, but when she told me how it happened, the pieces slotted into place.'

'What do you mean, "old photographs"?' Dean was beginning to sound irritated.

'Your father looked very different from your grandfather,' said Jane, cautiously.

'What are you inferring?'

'Your grandmother was married twice. Her first husband, an American, was killed in the war. She had a young baby and so she married James Smith. Only she was pregnant again—'

'Big deal! Woman being knocked up on her wedding day. Never heard of that before.'

Jane ignored Dean's sneer and continued. 'She was pregnant with her first husband's baby. James Smith either pretended or wanted to believe it was his, but when it was born he couldn't pretend the child, your father, looked anything like him. The way your grandmother explained it, James Smith became very resentful of your dad and treated him badly. Your dad's reaction was to try ever harder to be like him, to please him. Maybe your dad would have had a different life, not gone to prison for example, if things had been otherwise.'

Dean said nothing and his face had become impassive and unreadable. Only a faint twitch in his right eye betrayed the surge of anger and resentment swelling within him. He'd been brought up to idolise his grandfather. Dean knew the same blood flowed in his veins; he would not have that taken from him. Some days it felt like all he had.

Jane reached into her bag and brought out the transparent polythene envelope. 'I hope this hasn't come as too much of a shock and I suspect it's difficult for you. There's one way to prove it. This is a DNA test kit. I'd bought it for someone else, but if you could give me a saliva sample—'

'I'll give you a fucking sample, you bitch!' Dean leapt across the room and grabbed Jane by the shoulders, yanking her upright out of her chair. He pulled her into him and pressed his face hard against hers. She was an inch or two taller so he had to use his weight to forcibly bend her at the knees. He began to lick her cheek and she could taste fried food and stale cigarettes on his breath.

'Dean! No. Get off me, please.' Jane tried to wriggle out of his grasp.

'You think you're so fucking clever, don't you, pet? Well, now I'm going to teach you a little lesson you won't forget.'

'Dean. No! Stop this! You'll be sorry, Dean. Don't do this.'

Dean grabbed Jane's face with his right hand, squeezing her cheeks together painfully and distorting her mouth into a vertical line.

'Shut up!' he hissed. 'You're the one who'll be sorry if you don't do exactly what I say. The last woman who messed me about ended up face down in the river with her head smashed in. And smart old Dean here got away with it, so you be a good girl and behave. Maybe you'll enjoy yourself. Eh? It's why you came here, after all.'

Dean's senses were focussed on one thing as he ripped open her blouse with his free hand and began fumbling at the belt of her jeans. He didn't notice her right leg slip round the back of his calves. If he felt her hands slip onto his chest, he might have convinced himself it was the beginning of an embrace.

The next thing he knew, he was tumbling backwards. He hit the floor awkwardly and the words, 'You bitch!', were half out of his mouth when he sucked them back in again. Jane had followed him down and landed heavily with both knees slamming hard into his stomach. He twisted his head to the side and retched but Jane's weight prevented the contents of his gut spewing out.

Prostrate, sweating and between rapid, heavy breaths, he resumed his threats. 'I'll make you pay for this, you bitch. You'll wish—'

He stopped abruptly. Something sharp was pressing into the socket just beneath his right eye. It felt as if the skin was being pierced and the eyeball was being pushed up and out. He lay motionless as Jane shifted her position so that she was astride him with her knees pinning down his shoulders. He was seeing double and the image was partially blurred, but he could just make out her face. He saw flared nostrils, wide eyes, bared teeth. It was a look verging on madness. He forced his breathing under control in fear of any violent movement jarring whatever weapon was cutting into him and threatening his sight.

His voice was weak and shaking. 'Calm down. Let's not get silly. I was only playing.'

By contrast, Jane's tone was steady and cruelly measured. 'I'm not playing, you filthy little scumbag. You make me sick.'

Dean tried to sound soothing but he croaked and swallowed with anxiety. 'Look, just think for a minute. You'll have my eye out and that's a prison sentence for sure. You wouldn't like prison. Trust me, I've been there. You wouldn't like it. Not a nice girl like you. So let's just calmly talk about this.'

'You're not the only one who gets away with things, Dean. I pretty much blinded a suspect in a police cell once. Did I tell you I used to be a policewoman, Dean?' She paused more for effect that in expectation of a reply. 'I guess not. Anyway, he pissed me off, too, Dean. And I got away with it. And he hadn't just tried to rape me. Had he, Dean?' Another pause. 'Here I am, a poor, defenceless woman, fighting off a known lowlife scumbag. I think I'd get the benefit of the doubt in court, don't you, Dean? If my old chums in the force let it get anywhere near court, of course, Dean.'

He was begging now. 'Please just stop this. Please. You're scaring me.'

The red mist in Jane's mind was lifting and she began to see an alternative path to retribution. 'So, tell me about the woman who ended up in face down in the river.' Jane gently increased the pressure against Dean's eyeball causing him to whinny like a frightened horse.

'Okay, okay. She was a junkie. Do anything for the price of a fix. This one time she was playing all hard to get and I gave her a bit of a slap. Then she started threatening me...'

'Keep talking.'

'Her dad, he was due out of prison. The bloke you had the run in with outside the pub. Michael's a total animal. A big, angry, vicious animal. Been inside for

169

manslaughter. She said she'd tell him it was me that got her on the heroin…'

'Keep talking.'

'I was scared, so I think I just pushed her. Just to make her shut up. We were by the river. She hit her head on the rocks. She didn't move. She was in the water. I was scared. I heard someone coming. I ran away. I was scared.'

Dean felt the pressure on his eye socket recede and Jane's weight shift off his body. He began to breathe deeply again and touched his face. His vision slowly cleared and he managed to focus on a small drop of blood on his fingertips. Looking over, he saw Jane kneeling alongside him and putting a jagged Yale key back in her bag.

He lifted himself onto his elbows, all fight seemingly knocked out of him. 'Good luck proving that to anyone, by the way. I've got a watertight alibi. I was probably lying to you anyway. Just to get you off me, you mad fucking bitch.'

In one final act of defiance he spat angrily into Jane's face.

She felt the saliva dripping down her cheek. 'Thanks for that,' she said and stood up.

Another phone call

She left it until the following morning before making the call. A bottle of wine had stopped her shaking and got her off to sleep. She awoke with a rough head and a feeling of anxiety. It was a conversation she could do without, but she knew it couldn't be avoided. She sat staring at a half-drunk cup of coffee and then reached for her phone.

'Dave speak...' There was a slight pause as he registered the name that came up on his mobile's screen. '...oh hi, Janey. Look, I'm at work. Is this urgent or could we talk later?'

'Hi, Dave. It's a work-related matter. You remember you said you were friends with that DI in Chesterfield? The one who gave you the lowdown on Dean Smith, the guy I was trying to trace?'

'Please don't ask me for any more favours, Janey.'

'I've got something for you this time. A lead for your friend, something on Dean Smith.'

'Go on.' Dave had begun to sound interested.

'A girl was found dead in a river in Dowley a while back. Dean admitted to me that he did it. Said he just pushed her and got scared, but he is a total scumbag so maybe he did do it on purpose. He said he had an alibi but there must be a hole in it.'

'Dean just admitted this to you in passing, did he?'

Jane hesitated before replying. 'It's a long story. My testimony wouldn't be accepted in court, but—'

'But what, Janey? That suggests you forced it out of him somehow? What was going on?'

Jane sighed. 'I guess there was an element of duress. Look, he attacked me and I fought back.'

Dave replied angrily. 'I warned you about him! What was your supposed partner, Tommy, doing while all this was going on?'

'I was on my own. It was a spur of the moment decision. I can handle the likes of Dean Smith. He'll think twice before attacking another woman.'

'Oh, my God! What does that mean? What did you do to him, Jane?' Dave lowered his voice. 'Please tell me you left his fucking eyes alone. No, it's not eyes, is it Jane? It's just eye. Always the right eye. Please tell me he's not in a hospital ward somewhere with half his face covered in bandages.'

Jane felt her own voice beginning to crack. 'It's fine, Dave. Don't worry. I stopped myself this time. That's good, isn't it? I just nicked his skin a bit. He might have a slight bruise. He tried to rape me – he won't be making any complaints. I didn't want to make this call, but I couldn't ignore what he told me. And it was the truth. I know it. He killed that girl.'

The line went silent for a full ten seconds before Dave replied. He sounded calmer now but was still whispering to avoid being overheard. 'What am I going to do with you, Jane? When you attacked that guy in the cells… You know you were lucky to get away with just losing your job. If he hadn't been doped out of his head, if the desk sergeant hadn't pulled you off him, if the hospital hadn't been able to save the guy's sight, if I hadn't stuck my neck out… All these ifs… It could have been very different. We both know that.'

'I know, Dave. But Dean attacked me. And I stopped myself, don't you see? That's good, isn't it?'

'If you say so,' said Dave without conviction. 'Okay, I'll call my mate in Chesterfield and say I've got an anonymous but reliable tip-off. But maybe you need to do something for me. Maybe you need to go back and see that psychiatrist again. What do you say, Janey?'

'He'll just get me talking the same old crap about my father and my mother. And he'll put me back on those horrible pills. I'll be a zombie again. With a memory full of holes. I'm not going back there. Please don't ask me to do that, Dave. I can't go back there.'

'Okay, okay, I get it,' said Dave, defeatedly. 'But promise me one thing. Stay away from Dean Smith.'

'I will.'

The line went dead. Jane's grip relaxed and her phone slipped out of her hand and dropped onto the carpeted floor. She left it where it lay and walked over to her laptop. She'd made the call, now she had an email to type.

She'd thought of ringing Tommy too, but given his nocturnal habits there was a chance she'd disturb him whilst he was catching some much needed sleep. An email also allowed her to organise her thoughts, pushing Dean Smith to the back of her mind so she could try to make sense of the scribbled notes she'd made in Mary's company. In amongst the rambling recollections, tangential asides and dubious claims, there had to be a core of accuracy and truth. Tommy had previously dismissed the suggestion that James Smith had been a spy. But that had been before Jane had seen the Iron Cross and William Joyce note. Could they possibly be taken at face value?

Three threads

Hi Jane

Wow! Your email made quite some reading. No need to apologise for it being a bit complicated. It sounds like Mary was talking to you for hours, and you know I like complicated.

I agree that Mary isn't what a judge would call a 'reliable witness'. She had to have been mistaken in at least some of what she told you. Your question, of course, is: how much? There's a lot to comment on, but I think there are three main threads to address:

Thread #1. Was James Smith a German spy?

I can't help but feel things hinge around this. If you believe it, even partially, the rest of it makes much more sense.

Which takes us to the medal and the letter you scanned purporting to be from William Joyce. The Germans didn't engrave a recipient's name on Iron Crosses, and I agree one would be relatively easy to get hold of. The letter is more puzzling. I was able compare the writing with a genuine document written by Joyce. Unfortunately, it's on the Web as a poor quality image and I'm no graphologist, but they certainly look similar. Would James have had the skills to forge the letterhead and make a good fist of the handwriting? And why would he bother? One interpretation is that he was a complete and dedicated fantasist. Perhaps Mary was taken in by – or shared – those fantasies.

I need to dig into this some more. I'm still convinced the Double Cross system means he can't have been (working for) a German agent, but maybe I'm missing something. Leave it with me.

Thread #2. The parenthood of Mary's children.

You seem quite unhappy about what Mary told you. She jumped around a bit, so let me see if I can summarise the story.

Mary moves to Norfolk to work as a Land Girl. There she meets James Smith. He's originally from London but earning a dodgy living as what they used to term a 'spiv'. He buys otherwise unobtainable goods from GIs on US air bases and then sells them on the black market. He's not been called up himself because he's lost the sight in one eye. He's charismatic and looks like a film star. Mary is besotted and has an on/off relationship with him. She gets pregnant, but then he wants nothing more to do with her.

Mary has also slept with American airman, Woody Jensen. He marries her and is registered as the father of the child, Lois, when she's born. Despite her obvious resemblance to James, Woody accepts the baby as his and absolutely adores her.

Mary gets pregnant again, this time she says the father is Woody, but he's killed almost immediately afterwards. James Smith steps in this time, marries her and they go back to her home village, Dowley in Derbyshire. She says he's trying to hide under the anonymity of his surname, off the beaten track in a remote mining community. When the child's born it's a boy, whom he can't resist naming Ernald after Oswald Mosley's middle name. James has himself registered as the father, but treats him badly because he's not his real son. Ernald doesn't exactly grow up a pillar of the community, a trait he passes on to his own son, your friend Dean Smith.

I think that sums up what Mary told you. If true, we'll have to amend the family tree, but I sense you're reluctant to do so. Unfortunately, this sort of thing happens, Jane. If it helps, I'll try to lay out the evidence for and against:

Evidence for, photographic. Lois looks like James Smith; Ernald looks like Woody, compellingly so when you've heard the explanation. That said, children don't necessarily take after their parents, genetics is a complicated business.

Evidence against, birth certificates. Official documents aren't always right, but Mary's saying the paternity of both her children is incorrectly recorded, i.e. the wrong way round. One big problem is that Ernald's date of birth is a full ten months after his supposed father, Woody, died. You pointed this out, and her answer – eventually – was that James simply delayed the registration, perhaps because he was trying to distance himself from the name Woodrow Jensen. I guess it's possible; he sounds dodgy enough, spy or not.

On balance, I think we should probably accept Mary's account, but DNA testing is the only way of achieving any certainty. I'm assuming that's why you wanted the sample off Dean Smith. You'll still need to get one off Lois's child, Chris Aimson, of course.

Thread #3. Woody Jensen's death.

I definitely need to think about this some more. As I suggested, if we don't think James Smith was working for the Germans, then this part of Mary's story seems like another fantasy and even harder to accept. You mentioned that photograph we saw in the Norfolk air museum, but that's circumstantial evidence at best.

Give me a day or so and I'll get back to you.

All the best,

Tommy x

PS and more importantly, are you OK? I get the impression it didn't go too well when you went round to Dean Smith's flat. He doesn't sound a very nice man. I hope he didn't upset you.

Case closed

Jane was sitting on the patio at the back of her house. It was within range of the wifi signal and the laptop was open on the wooden slatted table, shaded from the sun by the large umbrella that had once been a vivid orange but had long since faded to khaki. Her grandfather and latterly her grandmother had lavished much love and attention on the small walled garden. Jane struggled to do little more than keep it under control and its once bright summer colours were gradually being reduced to a monochrome palette limited to various shades of green. Nonetheless, it was her oasis and she sat out there whenever the weather allowed.

She'd read Tommy's email twice and was composing a reply in her head when her phone rang. Dave's picture appeared on the screen and she reminded herself that she'd meant to delete it.

'Hi Dave.'

'Jane. It's just a quick call. I'm outside the station having a quick fag.'

'What are you doing back on the cancer sticks?' Jane heard herself nagging and backed away. 'Not that it's any of my business anymore.'

'Correct. Look, I spoke to my mate, the DI in Chesterfield, about Dean Smith killing that girl.'

'Is he going to pull him in?'

'Jane, now don't get wound up about this, but he's not interested.'

'He's not even going to pull him in and talk to him?' Jane made no attempt to disguise her anger.

'It's like this. Dean was a known associate, that is customer, of the girl. She was on the game to fund her habit. But he does have a solid-gold alibi. He was caught on CCTV on the other side of the county at the time she died—'

'We both know time of death can be way out,' interrupted Jane.

'Not in this case. She was found quite quickly. There was only a small window when it could have happened. And at that time Dean was doing over a car accessory shop. I told you about it before. Someone grassed on him and the stolen goods were found in his flat along with the hoodie he was wearing on camera.'

'He told me he did it, Dave.'

'Under duress, i.e. you were scaring the shit out of him at the time. He'd probably have said he was the Yorkshire Ripper if you'd told him to. Look, Janey, the coroner recorded an open verdict. It was suspicious but maybe she just fell. And there's something else.'

'What else?'

'The girl's father is a local gangster type. You know, he supposedly runs a building company, but he's also a bare-knuckle fighter who sorts out disputes and collects debts through threats and violence. There were stories of him getting out of prison and butchering the pusher who got his daughter hooked. They didn't find a body and no-one would talk, but he's not a man you want to wind up without cause. If, just for example, he heard that someone had been reinterviewed about the death of his daughter, then who knows what he'd do if he got his hands on them. His line of questioning might be a little more robust, shall we say.'

'You're telling me the local plod are scared of this guy?' Jane sounded exasperated.

'They just think Dean Smith's got an alibi and they need more than a dodgy confession before prodding this particular wasps' nest.'

'And the girl was just a junkie prostitute from a criminal family, so let's not try too hard.'

'That's not fair, Jane.'

The line went quiet for several seconds. It was Dave who broke the silence. 'There was something else I wanted to talk to you about. Your mother wrote to me a while back.'

'She wrote to me too. I threw the letter straight in the bin,' snapped Jane.

'I knew that would be your reaction which is why I didn't mention it at the time. Look, she's back in the UK, living in Dorset. Nice place on the coast by the sound of it. She wants to build bridges and I just thought—'

'Thought what?'

'I just thought it might help you get your head together if you went to talk to her. Maybe you could sort out this thing you've got about your father. Maybe you could stop… Well, stop doing what you almost did to Dean Smith.'

'I stopped myself, I told you,' replied Jane, plaintively.

'But what about next time, Jane? What about the next Dean Smith?'

'He was an extreme case. He attacked me. It was self-defence.'

'Please just think about it. I'll email you her address and phone number. Yeah? Just think about it. It's starting to rain – I'd better go back inside. I'll email. Bye now.'

Jane sat and stared at the ivy which had begun to dominate the far wall of the garden. But the colours she saw were not green and brick-brown; they were the silver-grey of a huge ship and the yellow-white-blue of a glaring, sunlit sky haloing the black silhouette of a huge man towering over a little girl.

Tears welled and began to overflow her reddened eyelids.

'Please don't go, Daddy,' she said.

Heroes and myths

Dear Ms Madden,

I have been waiting patiently, but it is has been some time since I requested that you collect a DNA sample from Christopher Aimson. Please can you give me an update with some urgency or I will be obliged to enlist the help of an alternative agent to progress this matter.

Regards

Herb Jensen

Sarah was a lady who lunched. Fortunately, a cancellation had left a slot in her busy social calendar. It was Jane who suggested the castle. It was somewhere they'd frequented as teenagers and she had a sudden urge to retrace old steps.

The sun was still shining, and Jane found Sarah sitting at a cafe table on the wide stone terrace at the back of the building. To Jane's slight surprise, her friend was not alone. Under a rather grand Panama hat was an imposing grey-haired man of ample frame, whose intransigently black moustache was thick with cappuccino froth from the large cup he had just returned to its saucer.

On seeing Jane, Duff wiped his face with a napkin, stood, doffed his hat and beamed warmly. The sequence of motions appeared seamlessly fluid and graceful as if choreographed and endlessly rehearsed.

'Jane, my darling,' he said, 'you look gorgeous. Now, don't worry. I'm not stopping.'

'No, please stay, Duff. It's good to see you,' replied Jane.

'No, no. I know you wanted to have a woman-to-woman chat with old Ginge here. It was just that she told me you were meeting at the castle and I said, "It's on our doorstep, yet I haven't been up there in donkey's yonks, my little ginger currant bun. Why don't I take the morning off work and we'll have a wander round. See if the old place has changed."' Sarah rolled her eyes, but Duff ignored her. 'Ginge doesn't often agree with me, as you know, but on this occasion she thought I'd hit the old nail on the head and here we are.'

'I know who I'd like to hit on the head, you rambling old fool,' interjected Sarah.

Duff ignored his wife's comment and started gathering his things. 'But commerce calls. I'm needed back at the coal face, so I'll leave you chaps to matters feminine.'

'Please don't rush off on my behalf,' persisted Jane.

'Please do, Duff. I'm starting to find your conversation somewhat tiring,' counteracted Sarah.

'You're a very tiring woman, my love,' returned Duff, grinning broadly.

'Yes, yes, Duff. So just buy Jane a nice Americano and then toddle off to that dull little business of yours so we girls can be rude about you behind your back.'

'At once, my cuddly ginger porcupine.' Duff pulled back his chair for Jane and then strolled away towards the cafe door.

Jane sat down and took in the magnificent view. It was one she'd not seen for years, yet it was as familiar as the face of a long-lost school friend encountered at a class reunion, briefly unrecognisable then unmistakably the same. It caused Jane's mind to drift into its dustier archives.

The castle sat on a bare sandstone cliff that gave it a commanding position overlooking the old town of Nottingham. But the mediaeval fortress occupied by the sheriff and besieged by Richard the Lionheart was long gone. Parliament ordered its slighting after the civil war and it was replaced by a grand ducal palace. Today, Jane knew many visitors were disappointed when seeing it for the first time. Apart from the outer gatehouse, there was nothing that could be used in any Hollywood depiction of Plantagenet conflict. The backdrop was more Downton Abbey than The Adventures of Robin Hood.

Whilst the sheriff and King Richard I had documented, historical involvement with the site, it was the mythical outlaw who had earned a statue in the castle grounds. Aiming his bow for over 60 years, the squat bronze archer had been deprived of his arrow several times, until a replacement of stronger alloy was securely welded into place to deter the souvenir hunters. Nearby, and treated with considerably more respect until his memory faded, was the metal likeness of another local hero. Albert Ball, VC, was a World War I flying ace who crashed to his death over the Western Front in 1917, aged just 20. Jane's Nottingham-born great-grandmother had also been a Ball, and the fighter pilot had always been talked of as a cousin. One of Jane's earliest forays into family history had been to establish the exact genealogical link, but she had been dismayed to find the ancestral lines drifting apart to villages on opposite sides of the county. Ball was a common surname and any shared genes appeared to predate the available parish registers, if they existed at all.

All those thoughts, of history personal and civic, flashed through Jane's head in a fraction of the time it would have taken her to voice them out loud. To Sarah, it was as if her friend had merely paused to scan the horizon.

Duff reappeared with a coffee cup in one hand and a plate in the other.

Sarah looked concerned. 'What on earth have you bought, Duff?'

'I thought Jane might like a little slice of chocolate cake.'

For once, Sarah seemed genuinely cross. 'It's like a doorstop! And we're going to have lunch soon.'

'Ah, it's just it was the last piece. It looked particularly appetising and they couldn't really cut it into two. Well maybe they could. I wouldn't have bought it for you, my love. I just thought Jane might enjoy it. She's such a skinny waif of a thing.'

'Unlike me, of course?'

'That's not what I meant, my little ginger sausage...' Duff was beginning to look uncomfortable. '...no, not sausage. Something thin. My little ginger cheese straw?'

Sarah looked at him coldly and Duff continued to dig. 'Look, you know I think you've got the perfect figure. It's just that you worry about it so much. That's all I meant. Honestly, Sarah. My love.'

Jane thought it best to cut in. 'The cake looks wonderful, Duff. It's ever so sweet of you, but it is a little on the large side. It might well spoil my meal.'

'I'm an old fool – I simply didn't think. It is a slab, you're right. But there's an easy solution. Ladies, I bid you goodbye and trust you'll enjoy your luncheon.'

Duff grabbed the cake off the plate and took a large bite. He nodded appreciatively and with his free hand lifted his hat as a gesture of farewell. He then strolled off, munching chunks of cake as he went.

Jane smiled as she watched him go. Sarah shook her head to suggest disbelief but she, too, couldn't help grinning. 'Silly old duffer,' she said.

They chatted about old times for a while and then bought lunch. Sarah picked at a salad with the enthusiasm of someone in mortal fear of calories, whilst Jane ate with the hearty appetite of one whose metabolism and nervous energy had, so far in her life, helped her maintain the same dress size she'd been at 16.

Sarah pushed her plate away after a couple of mouthfuls and steered the conversation onto more serious topics. 'You said you had a dilemma you wanted to discuss with me.'

Jane swallowed carefully before replying. 'Two dilemmas in fact. Should that be dilemmas or dilemmae? You had the expensive education.'

'Which, as you well know, was wasted. Apart from the lessons in deportment and how to get out of a sports car without flashing your underwear. Latin, in particular, was frightfully, frightfully dull and totally impenetrable. And the word might actually be Greek. Anyway, tell me about dilemma number one and dilemma number two.'

Jane took a sip of mineral water and her expression became more serious. 'Dilemma number one – Dave says I should go and see my mother. He thinks it would help clear up some of the nonsense in my head. Maybe I'd come to terms with my hang-ups about my father.'

'I think you told me your mother had come back from Australia and was living somewhere near Bournemouth?'

'That's right. She buried her fourth husband – he was the richest of the lot, if you remember – sold the place in Sydney and came home. She wrote to me, but I didn't bother replying.'

'I know you were upset she didn't come to your grandmother's funeral, but she had a reason,' ventured Sarah.

'Yes, her husband was very ill and she was on the other side of the world. But to not attend your own mother's funeral is unforgivable. It's not as if she couldn't afford the flights. She always put her love life first – her relationships with men were always more important than anything, certainly more important than me.' Jane took another sip to slow her emotions. 'Until she got bored and moved onto the next one. Three divorces is quite good going.'

Sarah shrugged. 'I only met her a few times when we were young, but she was certainly glamorous. It's no surprise men were attracted to her. Like mother, like daughter, in that respect at least.'

'I know you mean that as a compliment, but I have no desire to be like my mother. She certainly didn't think I was attractive. "Poor, plain little Jane" she used to call me. "Shoulders like a boy" was the other one.' Jane let out a brief groan. 'Oh sorry, Sarah. It was all a long time ago. I shouldn't moan – I was very lucky to have my grandparents to raise me. The only time I really spent alone with my mother was when she took me on one of those shopping trips to London or Paris. When she was between men and needed a companion.'

'Well you're not plain Jane anymore. Duff was telling me he's never seen you looking more attractive. So tell me about your love life. You had a choice of two men, as I recall. What were their names? Tommy and Justin?'

Jane shook her head. 'I told you, Tommy and I are just friends. We're chalk and cheese romantically. I'm really not his type. Though he was ever so sweet a few days ago. I was feeling a bit, well, under the weather and he came all the way from London on the train to check I was alright. He used to suffer from really bad agoraphobia, so it was a big thing for him.'

Sarah raised her perfectly drawn eyebrows. 'I told you he was in love with you.'

'No, he isn't. He's just a nice guy. Oh, but he's not gay like you suggested last time. I asked him.'

'You're very naive sometimes. If he's not gay, then he's in love with you. So, tell me about the other one. Justin?'

Jane shook her head again, but somewhat less convincingly. 'I think you mean Julian. He's the client for the project I'm working on. I'm sure I only mentioned him in passing.'

'It was the way your eyes went all distant that gave it away, darling.'

'Well, he is gorgeous. And more my type. Oh, and loaded.' Jane paused while she digested what she'd just said. 'Oh, Sarah! I'm sounding just like my mother after all. Looking for rich men to marry. You bring out the worst in me! Let's get back to my dilemma. Should I visit my mother or not?'

'Obviously you should visit your mother. It's not healthy to run away from your past. It's not healthy to bear grudges. If you talk things through with her, it might help you come to terms with your upbringing. You might even forgive her and forgiveness can be quite cathartic, to both give and to receive. And it's not as if Bournemouth is on another continent.'

'It's just outside Bournemouth. A place call Sand... Sand Dunes or something?'

'Sandbanks!' Sarah suddenly sounded excited. 'Sandbanks is one of the most expensive places to live in the country, in the world, in fact. That football manager, you know, the one with the gorgeous son who got divorced, he lives there. John Lennon bought his Aunt Mimi a house in Sandbanks in the sixties. It's millionaire central. I know you said your mother married money, but I didn't realise how much. Jane, darling, you're an only child. You won't need to worry about finding a wealthy husband.'

'I don't want my mother's money.'

'No, of course not,' said Sarah dismissively. 'But that's one dilemma sorted. You're going to visit your mother. What's the other one?'

Jane took a deep breath and her expression became solemn again. 'It's a question of honesty, from a professional and a moral standpoint. I can't ask Tommy. He's far too straight, and nervous. He'll want me to tell the truth. It's just that, in this case, it's simply not right.'

Sarah tilted her head thoughtfully before replying. 'White lies make the world go round. Where would we be if we told the truth all the time? "Do I look fat in this, dear? Well, yes actually, but it's not the dress – you look fat in everything. Dear."'

'But what about dirty-grey lies?' The question was rhetorical and Jane continued after the briefest of hesitations. 'It's complicated. There's this old man in Minnesota trying to track down the English descendent of his brother, who was a US airman killed in World War II. The man who appears – on paper – to be the airman's grandson is gay and the old man has a big hang-up about homosexuals.'

Sarah looked perplexed. 'It's the 21st century, for God's sake. Can't he get over it?"

'It's just that his brother was murdered. By a gay man, his lover. At least that's what they thought at the time. Now, I don't know what to believe. But the old man is harbouring 70 years of pain, resentment and prejudice. He's looking for obstacles and has asked me to get a DNA sample from the grandson.'

Sarah's face now suggested slightly bemused concentration. 'You mentioned something about the grandson being related "on paper"?'

'The airman's English wife had a relationship with another man. She had two children.

The first was, according to her birth certificate, fathered by the airman, though she probably wasn't. The second was – in all likelihood – but the other man's name is on that certificate.'

'In all likelihood?'

Jane nodded slowly, as if questioning her own assertion. 'I'm pretty convinced it's true.'

'Then surely this second child, or its descendents, are to whom the elderly American would want to make contact?' The intonation on 'surely' conveyed Sarah's doubt not her certainty.

'There's one descendent. Trouble is, he's a total lowlife shit. I knew that already, but then he tried to rape me—'

Sarah looked shocked. 'Rape? Are you okay, darling? Have you been to the police?'

'Yeah, I'm fine. I won. He lost. The point is, he's almost certainly done worse. Whereas the gay guy seems a decent, deserving person. His partner was killed in a road accident and now he's struggling with serious illness and raising a young child on his own with very little money. He needs all the help he can get.'

'So what are you suggesting, Jane? Notice how I'm not asking what "He lost" means. I suspect I don't want to know.'

'Don't worry. I didn't do him any permanent damage. But I did get a DNA sample off him. It's not ideal, the bastard spat on my face, but I'm pretty confident it'll be okay.'

'And you're thinking of sending it to the elderly American, so he hasn't got an excuse to disown the man you judge to be, quotes, deserving?'

Jane shuffled uncomfortably in her seat. 'I had a rush of blood to my head, a sense of injustice. I thought it was a good idea. Or maybe I just wanted to have the option. And now...'

Jane went quiet so Sarah prompted, 'And now?'

'And now I'm having second thoughts. But here's the thing – mister lowlife shit ended up confessing to me that he'd killed a girl, albeit accidentally. Maybe. I can't get the police to accept that confession – there's some crap about an alibi – but I can do him out of any chance of inheritance and help someone who is much, much more deserving and, as far as the official documents are concerned, is the legal heir.' Jane slapped the table in exasperation. 'For God's sake! It must happen all the time – fathers leaving everything to kids who, if you DNA tested them, wouldn't actually be theirs.'

Sarah began twisting one of her dark-auburn locks between the fingers of a perfectly manicured hand. 'I remember when we used to play in the tennis leagues. You'd get quite cross if I made a dubious line call.' A naughty smile flashed over her face. 'Or tried to put the opposition off by commenting on their frizzy hair or buck teeth.' Sarah savoured the memory and then her expression became earnest once more. 'What I'm saying is, you had integrity. You wanted to win fairly or not at all. I seem to recall you joined the police because you wanted to do something worthwhile.'

Jane sighed. 'Yes, but I was young and stupid. You discover life isn't a game of tennis. There are rules, but the people making the dodgy line calls seem to get away with it. They're the ones who prosper. They're the winners.' Jane briefly cradled her forehead in her left hand. 'Or maybe I'm just being cynical. We don't all have a trustworthy, reliable, lovable Duff to prop us up when we feel the world's against us.'

Sarah feigned a look of horror. 'Don't ever let him hear you call him lovable! He's conceited enough as it is. Loathsome is much closer to the mark. Laughable, perhaps.'

Jane's face broke into a reluctant grin. 'Alright, the word will never pass my lips.'

'So, what are you going to do, Jane?' said Sarah, her seriousness returning. 'I've always been prepared to sacrifice honesty for expediency, but let's look at it from a practical viewpoint. What if the American asks for another sample further down the line when you're not involved? What if, despite the apparent evidence, the birth certificates are right and the guy you're promoting really is a blood relation and you send DNA from someone who isn't?'

Jane didn't reply. She turned her head away from her friend and looked again at the view across the rooftops of Nottingham. The white Portland stone of the town hall dome gleamed in sharp contrast to the dark frame of sky behind it. The sun still shone brightly over the city, but heavy, threatening clouds were beginning to assemble on the northern horizon.

Jean Paul

The MX-5's fabric roof was doing its job. There were no leaks, though it thrummed with a sound like muffled applause. The air conditioning had been winning over the condensation, but with the engine off, the windows were rapidly surrendering their transparency to what Jane's grandfather had always called wet steam, to distinguish it from the hot, transparent gas. The mist of water droplets was emanating from Jane's laboured breaths, as she struggled to get into her raincoat within the tight confines of the cramped front seat. Her bag was made of green canvas, and fearing its permeability, she stuffed it beneath her coat before pulling the hood over head and opening the door. Almost instantaneously, the torrential rain angled into the car and soaked everything it could reach. Jane clambered out, slammed the door with her hip and began running for the shelter of the apartment block's doorway. She'd been able to park in a prime position and it was little more than a few paces, but the path was submerged beneath a small lake and her shoes were drenched by the time she reached cover. They squelched unpleasantly as she dripped her way up the half-exposed staircase and across the landing to flat number six.

When Chris Aimson opened the door he was wrapped in a thick winter cardigan and noticeably shivering despite its unseasonal protection.

'Oh God, Jane. It's disgusting out. Come in quick. I'll make you something warm. Tea or coffee?'

'Coffee please.'

Chris set off down the hall, his stick tapping a pulse on the laminate floor. Jane shut the door behind her, removed her coat and slipped off her ruined shoes. She left them in a soggy heap and was aware of leaving wet footprints as she followed into the kitchen.

Jane wiped her hand over her face. 'The heavens opened just past Watford. There was so much spray on the motorway, and it got so dark, I had to slow right down.'

'Yeah, I used to hate driving in weather like this,' said Chris over his shoulder as he filled the kettle.

'Used to?'

'They took my licence away because of the illness. I can't afford to run a car anyway, so what the hell. Being in London we do alright for buses and tubes – it could be worse.' He looked down and noticed Jane's sodden stockinged feet. 'Do you need a towel?'

She shook her head. 'A couple of sheets of kitchen roll would be fine.'

'We're out, I'm afraid. Here, this tea towel's clean.'

Jane dabbed her feet as dry as she could, and Chris threw the damp cloth into the empty washing machine. He led her into the sitting room and she cradled her coffee as she walked slowly behind. The television was on at low volume, and brightly animated cartoons were dancing across the screen. In the middle of the room, sitting on a cushion with his back to the door, was a spellbound toddler with bushy black hair.

'Jean Paul, come and say hello to Jane.'

The little boy turned, then scuttled over to his father and shyly clung to his leg.

Jane crouched down, smiled broadly and held out her hand. 'Hello, Jean Paul. You're a gorgeous boy. You look just like my friend Tommy. Well, he's all grown up now, but I bet he looked just like you when he was your age.' She ruffled Jean Paul's hair. 'And he's got a cool Afro, too.'

'It does need a cut, I'm afraid,' said Chris apologetically. 'It suits him, but he'd probably be more comfortable if it were short. Come on, Jean Paul. Say hello to Jane. She's a very nice lady.'

The little boy mumbled something resembling hello and then buried his face in Chris's trousers.

Chris bent down and gently lifted the boy's head. 'Now Jean Paul, turn off the TV and do some drawing. Jane and I need to talk.'

Jean Paul obediently walked over to where he had been sitting, lifted a small silver remote control and the TV went blank. In corner of the room were some loose sheets of paper and a square plastic box that had once contained biscuits but now held an assortment of wax crayons of varied colour and length. He flopped onto the carpet beside them, pulled out a piece of paper and the brightest orange crayon and began scribbling enthusiastically. His tongue protruded between his teeth as he focussed intently on the image he was trying to create.

Jane felt herself melting. 'I think I'm in love. I don't often get maternal, but he's adorable. Can I take him home?'

She turned towards Chris, expecting to see a look of proud appreciation. In its place was a mask of contemplative sadness.

'Sorry, Chris. Did I say something wrong?'

'No, no. I'm being silly. It's just that someone is going to take him home some day. When I can no longer look after him because of this bloody illness.'

'Oh, I'm sorry. That was tactless of me.'

'No, of course it wasn't. It's not your fault.' His tone became matter-of-fact as the melancholy ebbed away. 'You said you needed to get a DNA sample for Herb Jensen. I wrote to him as you know, but only got a very cursory reply.'

'Let's sit down, Chris.'

Jane felt like she was back in uniform, breaking news of a fatal accident to a relative who already fears the worst. She sank onto the settee and Chris sat alongside her, lowering himself with a sigh like a man 20 years his senior.

'Chris, since I last saw you I found out your grandmother was still alive. She's in her nineties and very frail, but living in a nursing home in the... In the Midlands.'

'In the Midlands?'

'Yes, I know that's vague. I promised I wouldn't tell her family where she was. She's ashamed of her past. She's tired and I think she just wants to die quietly.'

Chris looked nonplussed. 'But I could take Jean Paul to see her. Surely she'd want to meet her great-grandson? He's good at cheering people up.'

Chris looked towards the little boy drawing happily in the corner, and Jane followed his gaze before replying.

'I'll contact her again. Maybe she'll have a change of heart.' Jane paused. She resumed slowly but gradually the tempo picked up. 'But... she is a little confused now. She's quite a talker, and some of what she said I believe, some I don't. You remember I told you last time that your mother's father wasn't James Smith, the man who raised her – I use the phrase loosely – but your grandmother's first husband, Woody Jensen?'

'Of course. Herb Jensen's brother, the American airman killed in the war.'

Jane smiled apologetically. 'It's certainly Woody's name on her birth certificate. Unfortunately, your grandmother cast doubt on that. She suggested that James was probably the father after all. She was pregnant when she got married, though she might not have been totally sure who the father was at the time.'

'Oh,' said Chris.

'Yes, oh,' said Jane. 'We've always known your mother looked very like James. It seems like the obvious explanation could have been right all along.'

Chris's face remained impassive. 'So that's why Herb Jensen wants you to get a DNA sample. You've told him that, in all likelihood, we're not related.'

'I haven't told him anything yet. But you see, there's always been doubt in Herb's mind because of the lack of family resemblance and the apparent implications of Woody's death. He said he was prepared to ignore it, for the sake of his brother's love for your mother. Brief as it was.'

Jane waited for Chris to nod his understanding before resuming. 'And now he seems to have changed his mind. When you wrote to him, I assume you told him you were gay?'

'Obviously. That's who I am.'

Jane picked her words carefully. 'He's always struggled with his brother's supposed homosexuality. I've got no evidence he's holding that against you, but who knows? He's an old man. He's from a different world. It's not right, but ultimately, it's his money. He can give it to whomever he wants. And he doesn't have to explain.'

There was still no anger on Chris's face. 'Ah, well. I guess we just have to send him a DNA sample and hope for the best. It was a silly fantasy anyway. A hitherto unknown benefactor coming to the rescue. And the fact is, no amount of money is going to cure me of this miserable disease. It's just that, being ill with a bit of money seems a damn sight better than being ill without. And I worry so much about what the future holds for Jean Paul.'

Chris stopped talking, his attention drawn to the window as an increase in noise indicated the rain had intensified once again. A smile of acceptance crossed his face. 'So how does this test work then?'

Jane waited for a partial lull in the weather and dashed back to her car, running over muddy grass to skirt the swelling puddle that had lain in ambush on her arrival. Her shoes were now filthy as well as wet and cold, but she hardly noticed. She was remembering the sense of injustice that had caused her to call on Dean Smith, on her own in that sordid flat. It had been a reckless decision that she'd barely gotten away with. She'd taken a big chance for the gobbet of spit that ran down her face. Dean's saliva was still sitting in a sample bottle back in Nottingham.

Two cousins, two samples of DNA, Jane was trying to calculate odds and risks. She felt an almost irresistible temptation to tilt the scales in favour of Chris Aimson. She knew it was dishonest; it just felt right.

Answers

After a temporary intermission, the rain had returned and now battered the flat roof over the extension Jane's grandfather had built at the rear of the house. The deadened thudding rolled in waves across the covering of rubberised felt that had withstood the elements for more than double its predicted lifespan. She was scanning the ceiling nervously for damp signs of its capitulation, when her mobile phone began to ring.

'Hi, Tommy. Give me a sec.' I'll move somewhere quieter.'

After some muffled noises, Jane's voice reappeared. 'Sorry about that, it's raining tigers and Great Danes up here.

'Sorry?'

'Cats and dogs, big ones. How are you anyway? You don't normally phone. Everything okay?'

'Yeah, it's brilliant. Sun's shining here. I'm outside the National Archives in Kew, looking at the swans and ducks on the pond.'

'Hope you've brought a raincoat. I think this weather's coming your way again.'

'Jane, I've found it! The explanation for the Iron Cross and that letter from William Joyce. Everything, really.'

'Tommy! That does sound brilliant.'

His enthusiasm bubbled down the line. 'So, we were worried about the conflict with operation Double Cross and the fact that it mopped up all the German spies in Britain. There was something nagging at me in the back of my mind, something I'd read somewhere. I had a dig around on the Internet and that led me to come over to Kew.'

'Go on,' said Jane.

'So, during the war, there was an MI5 agent, known by the alias Jack King, who infiltrated a network of British fascists. Most of Mosley's chums were interned but some escaped the net, including a few hardliners who never thought Mosley was pro-Nazi enough. It was these men, and women, that King made contact with. He posed as a Gestapo agent and convinced them to feed information to him rather than doing anything more damaging.'

'What sort of information?'

'Well, he received some leads that would have been of genuine value to the enemy, including observations of jet aircraft research and amphibious tanks being tested in Welsh swimming pools. Significantly, after the war the authorities decided not to prosecute the 100 or so people he'd smoked out, because it wouldn't end fascism in this country but would make it harder to investigate in future.'

Jane tried to process ramifications of Tommy's words and he took her lack of response as a cue to carry on. 'That much was on the Web, but I've just been reading specific files associated with King's work. One has recently been declassified and refers to a contact codenamed Hollywood. King describes him as "vain and arrogant" and says, and I quote, "the fake Iron Cross and the forged letter from Joyce made his one good eye gleam with childish delight". King also says that Hollywood was supplying him with "worthless tittle-tattle" about US airbases in Norfolk gained through "an unnatural relationship with a feckless American sodomite". Hollywood disappeared late in the war. King puts this down to a realisation that Germany was doomed after D-Day and recommends that "no great effort is wasted in tracking down such a minor pawn".'

'Wow!' said Jane.

'Yes, wow.' agreed Tommy. 'Interestingly, the date of Hollywood's disappearance is soon after Woody Jensen is killed.'

'Is James Smith mentioned anywhere by name?'

'No, I think part of the file might be missing, but all the facts fit with our man, especially the bit about him having lost the sight in one eye. And if Mary Smith was telling the truth about him working as a German spy – well, he believed he was – then I think we now have to give credibility to her story about how Woody died, particularly as King's account appears to substantiate it, circumstantially at least.'

'Tommy, you are brilliant! Not only are the nicest person I know, but the cleverest. I owe you a huge kiss next time I see you.'

There was a tangible delay before Tommy replied. 'I'll email you some stuff. Look, my battery's getting low, so I'll ring off. I just wanted to tell you what I'd found. See ya!'

He hung up.

A few minutes later, an email arrived in Jane's inbox. It was from Tommy and attached to it were digital photographs of the documents he'd been reading in Kew. Two minutes after that, a second email arrived. The subject line read 'PS'.

Hi Jane

Almost forgot. I found the attached picture online. It's from one of Oswald Mosley's rallies in the mid 1930s. You'll recognise Mosley as the one marching past in the peaked cap, black tunic and jackboots. Good-looking devil, wasn't he? In amongst the line of Blackshirts there are a few youngsters wearing grey. Look at the lad on the left, giving a fascist salute with almost unbearable enthusiasm. Now, draw a moustache on him and add a few years. Look familiar?

Tommy

Jane maximised the image on her screen and zoomed in on the figure Tommy had highlighted. The handsome, dark-haired boy looked like he would break many hearts when he grew up. He looked like he could become a Hollywood film star. He also looked compellingly like a young James Smith.

The pieces interlocked. The puzzle appeared to have been solved and she could wrap up the case with Julian Stothard and his mother. Before she did so, there was another call Jane wanted to make.

Jane had told Chris Aimson she would contact Mary Smith to see if she might have second thoughts about meeting him. Little Jean Paul was a lever that might break anyone's resolve. Jane also felt that Mary deserved to know the truth about her second husband's wartime activities. He had been an ineffectual dupe played by British intelligence. Whatever else his crimes, he had not caused American bombers to be shot down nor allied soldiers to be killed on the beaches of Normandy. Jane hoped the knowledge might in some way assuage the old woman's shame before she died. It might also make her more amenable to reconciliation with her family.

The phone rang four times and was answered by a woman with a South African accent. 'Kirkspire Lodge nursing home.'

'Hello, it's Jane Madden here. I was wondering if it was convenient to come in to see Mary Smith again?'

'Sorry, who did you say you were?'

'Jane Madden. I visited Mrs Smith recently. We had a couple of very long chats about her family history, and there are some things I've subsequently found out that I think she'd like to know.'

'Yes, of course. You made quite an impression on her. Your visits seemed to take a weight off her shoulders somehow. For a short while, at least.' The line went briefly silent. 'I'm afraid I have some bad news. Mary passed away the day after you came in. We knew she was ill, of course, but didn't expect things to move quite so quickly. We're all very sad. We miss her very much.'

'I'm sorry to hear that. That Mary's dead, I mean. Obviously.' Jane's awkward response stemmed from surprise and genuine sorrow.

'Will you be able to come to her funeral? There won't be many there. I'm sure she would have really appreciated it.' The South African accent had lifted in expectation.

'Of course,' said Jane, without thinking.

Contractor/client relationship

Jane had been trying to get in touch with Margaret Stothard for two days. There had been no response to Jane's answer phone messages, and then she remembered a holiday being mentioned. Jane hoped the older woman had gone somewhere far; the weather in England had become what the TV forecasters liked to call 'changeable': frequent downpours interspersed with fleeting sunny spells just long enough to tease you out of doors prior to being caught in the next deluge.

Not knowing how long Margaret might be away, Jane emailed her son, Julian. She'd had no direct contact with him since they'd had lunch by the river in the beautiful tree-lined gorge at Matlock Bath. Whilst she welcomed the excuse, she found herself struggling with words like a 12-year-old schoolgirl trying to impress the best-looking boy in class. She wanted to appear friendly, available even, but without seeming desperate. After three or four rewrites, she told herself to grow up and settled for simple and businesslike. That was the truth of their relationship after all: she was a contractor reporting back to her client.

Julian

I trust you are well and hope Pittsburgh's avoiding the rain we're having over here.

I'm confident we've now got to the bottom of why your mother's aunt was totally disowned by her family. I've interviewed the surviving members of that branch of the tree and we've also found supporting documentary evidence.

It's quite an incredible story and I think it's best relayed in person. I was hoping to arrange a meeting with your mother. Unfortunately, she's not returning my calls and I think she's away? If so, please could you tell me when she'll be back.

If you prefer, I can obviously email you a report of what I've found and you can pass that on.

Please let me know how you would like to progress.

Jane

Hi Jane

Great to hear from you. Sorry I've taken a while to respond. I wanted to confirm some arrangements before coming back to you, and they took a little longer than I'd hoped.

You were right; my mother has been away. We've got a little place in Cape Cod and I flew Mum and her carer over for a break. I was intending to spend more time with mum myself, but something big happened to divert me and I only managed a few days. Still, she got to see the boys and the weather has been kind, so I'm sure she enjoyed herself. There's an old world feel to that part of the Cape and the pace of life suits her.

My mother's really excited that you've solved the family mystery and is happy to wait until you can talk us through it. She doesn't want to get it second-hand from me. Thinks I'd get all the details wrong. She's no doubt right.

I'd like to hear the story myself and I've sorted it so we can all catch the same flight back to the UK. We land at Heathrow in the morning of Thursday next week. Would you be able to get to my mother's on Friday around lunchtime? That would give my mother a day to get over the jetlag. Perhaps we could go out for a meal afterwards?

I'm really impressed that you tracked everyone down and managed to speak to them. I knew I'd found the right woman as soon as we started chatting on that first video call. It's always nice to have your instincts confirmed about these things.

I'm looking forward to seeing you again.

Julian

Artificial light

Jane found herself with time to kill. Inactivity made her restless, so she decided to decorate her bathroom. The tiles were white and innocuous, but her grandmother had decided to brighten the room by having the one exposed wall painted a strident shade of pink that somehow glowed orange under artificial light. Jane felt it had faded with time; nonetheless, it still made her wince every time she saw it. She knew taste was individual, and also generational, but she often thought age must have adjusted the colour setting on her grandmother's eyesight when she scanned through the paint charts and stopped there.

The weather was still flipping between wet and dry, but the rain dancers seemed to be praying harder than the sun worshippers, and Jane was happy to stay indoors for what she convinced herself was an afternoon's job. It wasn't. Two days, three coats and pink still ghosted through the layers of brilliant-white emulsion, particularly round the edges where the roller wouldn't reach.

Feeling dejected, Jane sank down on the toilet seat. Her hands and arms had a misty rash of tiny paint spots, and some strands of her hair had stuck together after she'd accidentally leant her head against the wall. She'd forgotten how much she hated decorating. She hated the monotony, and she hated the fact that things always took much longer than you ever thought they could or should. She'd hated it when she and Dave had shared the load. It was worse now she was on her own. She also suspected she'd bought the wrong sort of paint. Why, she asked herself, did there have to be so much choice? Dave was always talking about not using matt on silk, or perhaps it was silk on matt, but she'd dismissed it as irrelevant boys' talk like the number of cylinders in an engine or absolutely anything to do with cricket.

Jane looked at her watch and calculated there was time for one more quick coat after this one had dried. With any luck, the pink would finally surrender and she would be left with an inoffensive bathroom and a fading memory of temporary hardship. She wondered if she could be bothered getting clean enough to make herself something to eat and decided she wasn't that hungry. Instead she listened to her grandmother's old transistor radio, now flecked with white, and scanned the newspapers she'd scattered over the surfaces she wanted to protect.

On one page, pulled from inside a local weekly that had become 90% adverts, was a news story asking for help identifying the perpetrator of a supermarket break-in. A grainy black-and-white CCTV image showed a slightly blurry young man in a hoodie staring upwards into a camera. His pupils glowed like cats eyes in the road, as the retinas behind bounced back the infrared that shone unseen in the darkness. In her time as a policewoman, Jane had studied many such images. Sometimes a positive identification was possible. More often, it gave you only a rough idea of who you were looking for: their colouring, size, a suggestion of facial features. Someone might recognise this thief from the photograph, but more evidence would be required to avoid an innocent lookalike suffering wrongful conviction.

As Jane looked at the image and gently rubbed at the paint on the back of her hands trying to peel it away, she felt a sudden spark of illumination.

An end and a new beginning

Jane was standing in front of the full length mirror mounted inside the door of her bedroom wardrobe. Black blouse, black skirt, black scarf, black shoes, it was too much she realised. She wasn't family. She wasn't even a friend, just an acquaintance, and a very brief one at that. She wasn't sure who, if anyone would care but thought she should tone down the outfit all the same. Looking through her hangers, she was struggling between tops in dark green and muted burgundy, when she heard her phone ring downstairs. Grateful for an excuse to delay the decision, she raced down the staircase and managed to catch the call just before it switched to voicemail.

'Hello?' she said, slightly short of breath.

'Is that Miss Madden speaking?' The voice was raised in the unwarranted assumption of a poor long-distance line and had an American accent. Jane knew it immediately.

'Yes, this is Jane Madden.'

'Miss Madden, this is Herb Jensen. I'm phoning you from the USA. I hope this isn't an inconvenient time. If you'd rather I rang back, please say.'

'No, now's good. I'm going out in a while, but I can talk.' Jane was aware of a slight anxiety creeping into her speech and hoped it didn't transmit across the Atlantic. 'What can I do for you Mr Jensen? I assume the DNA sample has reached you by now. Have you been able to get it looked at already?'

'That's what I wanted to talk to you about.'

'I see,' said Jane, cautiously.

'It's not right.'

'Not right, Mr Jensen?' Jane's throat was becoming dry and she put her hand over the phone's microphone so she could swallow quietly.

'No, dear. It's just not right.'

'Mr Jensen, as I tried to explain in my letter—'

'I spoke to our local pastor. He's an old friend, a good friend, and he got me to see the truth of it.'

'A pastor?' Jane was struggling to see why a clergyman would advise on the scientific testing of DNA.

'Yes. Reverend John Foster. I felt I had to tell him what you said, that my brother probably wasn't a homosexual after all. Obviously, I'd never mentioned anything about it before. I told him I felt a great shame had been lifted from my family.'

'I see,' said Jane.

'So I showed the pastor your letter, including the photograph you sent of Christopher and Jean Paul, and when he'd read it he looked at me like I was the personification of sin.'

'Er... okay.'

Herb Jensen nodded unseen at the far end of the line. '"That's what you've come to tell me?" the pastor said. "All you care about is a label that was put on your poor brother 70 years ago? What about the reaffirmation of his courage? What about the son of the daughter he loved so much, albeit for such a short time? What about this dear, innocent child?"'

Jane kept her silence. The old man clearly wanted to answer the questions he'd just revoiced.

'The pastor's wife was a free spirit when she was younger. It was the 1960s – you know how things were back then. She fell in with an irresponsible man, gave birth to his twin girls and he promptly left her to pursue his idea of love and peace with someone else. The pastor took her and the girls in, and he's always loved those children like his own. They are his own. Because that's what's in his heart and that's more important to him than cells and chemicals and genetic codes. My brother loved his baby daughter. He always knew, we always suspected, there was a question over her biological father. And yet I started demanding a DNA sample. I think we both realise why. Because I forgot about love, and charity, the cornerstones of my Christian faith.'

Herb Jensen stopped talking, allowing Jane to respond. 'As I said in my letter, Mary Smith couldn't be 100% sure who the biological father was, but there did seem a strong probability it wasn't your brother. It's your decision what to do with the sample. As I told you, there is another potential branch of the tree, through Mary's second child, but if you're looking for someone to carry forward your brother's memory, I wouldn't look there. I think you'd only find pain and irredeemable corruption.'

'It's in the trash,' said Herb Jensen.

'Sorry?'

'I've thrown the DNA sample in the trash. Woody put his name on his daughter's birth certificate. Who am I to start questioning that?'

'So you're going to get in touch with Chris Aimson?' Jane's optimism had been building and she felt a sudden rush of relief.

'I've just had a long chat with him. Before I called you. You were right, he seems like a fine young man, with a good heart. I've never been to Europe. I thought my long-haul flying days were behind me, but I'm going to get on a plane and come over, while I can still get around on my own two feet. We're going to visit Woody's grave together. You know, Jane, when you reach my age you tend to get sentimental, but I'm very, very…'

The words had become faltering and then they stopped altogether. Jane could hear a faint sobbing down the line before Herb Jensen managed to gather himself.

'…I'm very happy, Jane, and I wanted to thank so much for your help. I feel a purpose to however many days or years the good Lord chooses to allow me. And when the time comes and I see Woody again, me an old man and him a fresh-faced youngster in his prime, I'll finally be able to look him in the eye.'

Laid to rest

In keeping with her wishes, Mary Smith's mortal remains were to be cremated. Herb Jensen's call having delayed her, Jane pushed her car over the motorway speed limit, exploiting the 10% + 2 mph margin she hoped the traffic cops still observed. She liked to know where she was going and usually found time to check a route in advance. Today she was blindly relying on the robotic voice of her mobile's satnav. She'd never felt comfortable taking map reading directions from her ex-husband; somehow she begrudged the disembodied but all-knowing woman in her phone even more.

The crematorium was on the town's northerly outskirts. With minutes to spare, Jane pulled into a wide gateway that finally broke a mile-long stretch of dry-stone perimeter wall. She found herself on a drive that curved though gently undulating folds of extensive wooded gardens and lawns, a backdrop of arable farmland creating an impression of rural isolation. Jane had once seen a film where the botanic gardens at Kew had convincingly stood in for heaven, and immediately felt a similar sense of serenity and peace, as her tension from being late ebbed away. Like at Kew, there seemed to be tree species of infinite variety. Hazel stood alongside Scots pine, sycamore and rhododendron. Several specimens of weeping birch and willow added their sorrow to the purple-red warmth of Japanese maple.

Across the lawns, concentric circles of rose bushes carried plaques of dedication to loved lives lost. The ashes of Mary's husband James had found their way onto the rose gardens when, like the then-young trees, their rings were fewer, but no memorial bore his name; no-one had ever stood over his last resting place to pay their respects or confide their thoughts.

When Jane climbed the flight of stone steps from the main car park she found a crematorium building that could have been taken for a 1950s primary school, complete with a newly acquired roof of solar panels, were it not for the central chimney, a tall and angular bulk of bricks architecturally suggesting a church tower, albeit one devoid of ornament or aperture.

Jane entered the chapel quietly and slipped into one of the open wooden pews at the back. There were no more than ten mourners in front of her, all facing towards the altar with its simple brass cross flanked by two lit candles. The wall behind was pierced by a triptych of narrow rectangular windows coloured by the green of a tall oak, set back to fill the view without blocking the light. It had taken decades to fulfil its purpose but now spoke of the wonder of creation more eloquently than the finest stained glass.

Jane scanned the heads in the front pews and, on the left, recognised the hair colour and style of the South African care assistant who had shown her into Mary Smith's room and later told her of Mary's death. Only two people were sat on the right of the central aisle. They were both men, with similar close-cropped hair and narrow shoulders. They were hunched together and furtively giggling like naughty schoolboys sharing a dirty joke in assembly, their barely suppressed laughter frustrating the mood of the lilting organ music being softly piped through loudspeakers high on the walls either side of the altar.

Jane hadn't been sure Dean would come to his grandmother's funeral. In fact, she'd thought his indifference more likely. For herself, she considered that she'd made a commitment to attend. She was not minded to be intimidated, not by the presence or otherwise of Dean Smith. She'd forgotten another promise. She'd told Dave she would keep away from the man who had tried to assault her and nearly caused her to lapse into vengeful violence.

The coffin was plain and simple and was brought in on the shoulders of the undertaker and his assistants, looking suitably mournful in expression and attire. They laid the wooden box on a catafalque set in a bay to the left of the altar, then bowed and walked respectfully away. An elderly man who had been sitting unnoticed behind a lectern stood, placed his palms together as if in prayer and looked around the room. The arrival of the coffin had not silenced Dean and Steve; the headmasterly glare of the retired cleric caused them to look sheepishly at their feet and their joking stopped.

The service was brief and only Reverend Carter spoke. Jane had identified no religious belief in her long conversations with Mary Smith. Indeed, the elderly woman had expressed her hope that death was final and the afterlife a myth. Nonetheless, she had no doubt prayed obediently as a child and her first marriage had been under the auspices of the Church of England. An Anglican funeral was an easy default, inoffensively meeting social expectations without the D-I-Y involvement of a humanist ceremony.

The first hymn on the order of service was All Things Bright and Beautiful. Jane judged this an appropriate choice as there had still been something childlike about Mary, despite her reaching her tenth decade of life. It was also something that everyone would know. The last wedding Jane attended had featured modern words and tunes. Whilst fitting in their themes of love and togetherness, their unfamiliarity had resulted in the non-churchgoing congregation whispering and mumbling in musicless embarrassment.

Any fears Jane might have had about awkwardness during the singing were quickly allayed. The South African care assistant proved to have a fine voice and her confidence and volume encouraged those around her.

Surprisingly, Dean joined in with a gentle and pleasing baritone. Jane doubted he'd ever been a choirboy but briefly wondered what sort of man he might have grown into had his background allowed it.

Reverend Carter read the eulogy with sincerity though Jane suspected he'd never met its subject. Mary was a loving wife to a man who reputedly had the looks of a Hollywood star. She was a caring and devoted mother and grandmother. Dean was singled out for mention as her only surviving descendant and our thoughts were with him in his time of loss. The Reverend focussed on Mary's last years in the nursing home, her cheerfulness and popularity with the staff and other residents, because Jane realised, his words had been suggested by someone who had only known that final stage in Mary's life. It was almost certainly for the best. Mary wanted to forget her earlier years and dreaded being reunited, in life or in death, with the family she'd felt she'd wronged. Lacking Herb Jensen's faith, Jane sensed the lights had gone out as Mary had wished. The darkness inside the coffin was absolute and unending.

The second and final hymn was Amazing Grace. This time the South African care assistant sang with such power and passion that everyone else soon quietened and simply listened. A cynic might call it a party piece, but it was genuinely moving and Jane found tears welling in her eyes. She reached into her pocket for the boiled sweets she'd purchased as insurance the day before. From a time of stiff upper lips and backbones, it had been her grandmother's tip to avoid losing one's composure and crying at funerals. They'd shared a similar bag when her grandfather was laid to rest. Jane had not really expected to need it today but was caught off-guard. She was still sucking as Reverend Carter read the committal and curtains drew themselves around the coffin and it slipped from view.

The service ended with a few final words of prayer, and Dean immediately nudged his friend to stand up and leave. As Dean turned he saw Jane for the first time. His expression was of surprise more than anger. He walked down the aisle with his eyes fixed on her face, and she did her best to look calm and unflustered. The boiled sweet, now flat and sharp-edged against her tongue, was a fortuitous accomplice in the deception. Dean paused when he reached her and seemed about to speak, but something changed his mind and he continued on and out of the door. Jane watched him leave, and when she turned back, the South African care assistant was standing in front of her, smiling warmly.

'I'm so glad you could come!' she said, shaking Jane's hand vigorously.

'I was happy to. I liked Mary and was very sad when you told me of her… passing.' Jane normally preferred the directness of the word death, but the euphemism seemed more appropriate in the company and surroundings. 'And you have a most wonderful voice. Amazing Grace was heart-stopping. Can I book you in advance for my funeral?'

They exchanged a few more pleasantries, during which Jane declined the invitation to attend the buffet that was being laid on in the nursing home. She had done her duty by Mary Smith and wanted to get home. Jane thought about lingering so she would have an escort back to the car park, but people seemed to be dawdling and impatience took hold.

She wondered if Dean might be waiting outside the door, but there was no sign of him. She crossed a wide patio area and turned to descend the stone steps she had climbed on her arrival. Halfway down, out sight of the chapel and leaning against the wall smoking, were Dean and Steve. Like the first time she saw them, she was struck by their similarity and remembered how she thought they might be brothers. She considered turning back, but it would have been an obvious retreat so she kept going.

Dean threw his cigarette on the floor as she reached him. He wasn't sure who might be in earshot above, so he kept his voice low. 'You've got a fucking nerve coming here.'

'I came for your grandmother. I really wasn't sure you'd bother,' replied Jane, evenly.

'I ought to give you a fucking slap. Right now.'

'Last time you laid a hand on me it was you that got the kicking.' Jane turned her face towards Steve. 'Did he tell you that? Your mate here, rolling on the floor, gasping for breath, begging me not to hurt him.'

'Fuck off!' spat Dean, his involuntary increase in volume causing him to look nervously up the staircase to see if anyone else appeared.

Jane was still talking to Steve. 'He got so scared he started telling me about a girl ending up face down in a river. It was like being in a confessional.'

'I was spinning you a line just to get you to…' Dean hesitated, not wishing to confirm Jane's accusation of physical submission. 'What matters is that I told you that I had a cast iron, solid gold alibi.'

Jane shrugged. 'It took me a while, but I worked that out. You were caught on CCTV doing a bit of thievery at the time that girl was killed. Only it wasn't you, was it Dean? It was someone who looked very like you, certainly when wearing a hoodie and under infrared light. You were panicking, and that someone gave you the stolen goods and called the police to say where to find them. It turned out to be very convenient.' Jane turned back to Steve. 'Don't you think?'

Steve looked nervously at Dean who quickly replied on his behalf. 'He doesn't think nothing. 'You're fishing. You can't prove anything.'

'As it happens, you're right. And the police don't seem interested without something more concrete. But maybe they'll come knocking on your door – I wouldn't sleep too easily. In the meantime, what do you suggest I do?'

Jane waited but neither Dean nor Steve answered

'Well, one thing I could do is tell the girl's father. What was his name again? Oh yes, Michael. I could tell him my suspicions and he could, shall we say, ask you about it. I imagine he can be quite persuasive.'

'Deano?' Steve voice had become high-pitched and tremulous.

'He's an animal.' Dean's response was minimal and seemingly emotionless but its implication was clear.

Jane's eyes flicked from one man to the other. 'Fortunately for you, I can't be 100% sure what really happened, and assuming you don't push me, I don't believe in vigilante justice. Also, I don't think you killed that girl deliberately. You're scum but you haven't the balls for murder. I've heard this Michael's reputation. I've met the man. I know what he'd do to you.' She paused while she considered her words. 'So I've had to find some other way of getting back at you. It's not enough, but it's all I've got.'

Jane turned away and continued down the steps.

Dean called after her. 'Maybe you need to watch your back, you smug bitch!'

Jane kept her eyes straight ahead, her reply drifting over her shoulder. 'Don't think so, Dean.'

The two men watched her walk off towards her car and kept their silence until they saw it start and drive away.

'What do you think she meant about getting back at you?' asked Steve.

'I don't know. It was probably a load of bollocks. One of them empty threats.'

'Who the fuck is she anyway, Deano?'

Dean thought for a moment. 'Ex-copper turned jeanie… I don't know, jeanie something. Oh, I remember. She said she was one of them heir hunters, like on the telly. She was working for an American businessman. It sounded like he was minted.'

Film star looks

As on Jane's last visit, there was another vehicle in front of Margaret Stothard's bungalow. Once more it was a smart Mercedes, this time in metallic grey. It wasn't as considerately parked as before, and Jane had to squeeze the little Mazda perilously close to fit into the remaining space.

She twisted her rear-view mirror and checked her appearance. She'd spent ages on her hair and changed outfits at least three times. 'This is as good as it gets,' she said out loud before climbing out of the car and walking up the steps. As she'd hoped, the door was answered by Julian. He was looking tanned and even more blond, and she hoped for a moment he might kiss her on one or both cheeks like an old or, perhaps, intimate friend. Instead, he just smiled and shook her hand.

'Jane, lovely to see you again. You're looking well. We can't wait to hear what you have to say. My mother's very excited, and I confess, so am I. Please come through.'

Jane followed into the sitting room and was surprised to find another woman sitting alongside Margaret Stothard. It wasn't Caroline, the live-in helper, but someone much younger and considerably more glamorous. Jane thought for a moment it might be Julian's sister, up from nearby Derby, but there was something about the sheen of her immaculate hair, the perfect makeup, the personally trained figure, the clothes that screamed expensive through cut and quality rather than designer labels. She was breathtaking and Jane flashed a look at Julian that he would have read as 'How could you do this to me?' had she not caught herself in time.

The introduction, when it came, was superfluous. 'Jane, I'd like you to meet my wife, Shelley.'

Jane waited, albeit momentarily, for a few words of explanation. They were not forthcoming. Julian was reconciled with his wife and it was a story he was not going to relate. Jane felt foolish for thinking it was owed to her and then ridiculous for thinking she could ever be in the running in a competition where the standard was so high.

Jane forced a smile. 'Nice to meet you,' she said.

Shelley seemed to look through Jane and see everything. She was pigeonholed like Tommy had once been by Dave.

'So you're the lady my husband's paying to dig through the Stothard family tree. I do hope you've got some good answers for us. I was expecting to be in Paris by now, wasn't I Julian?' Shelley looked at her husband proprietarily. Her accent was part southern drawl, part Katharine Hepburn at her most condescending.

Sensing an air of friction to which her son was oblivious, Margaret Stothard interceded. 'Jane's very clever, Shelley dear. Don't you worry about that. Make yourself comfortable, Jane, then spill the beans. What juicy dirt did you manage to unearth?'

Jane proffered a file of documents but said she would summarise the tale as concisely as she could. She started with a brief recap, mainly for Shelley's benefit.

Jane reminded them of the main players in the family mystery: Margaret's previously unknown aunt, Mary; Mary's two husbands, Woody Jensen and James Smith; her two children, Lois and Ernald; and her grandchildren, Chris Aimson and Dean Smith. Mary's existence had been hidden by Margaret's family, but what had she done to merit such exclusion? That was the question that Jane had been trying to answer since last she met the Stothards.

'I have a confession to make,' she said, cautiously. 'We hadn't been able to find any actual record of Mary's death. We thought it was because Mary Smith is such a common name—'

Margaret interrupted with near-accurate intuition. 'She'd be well into her nineties. Are you saying she's still alive?'

'No, but she was until very recently. I attended her funeral a few days ago,' said Jane, feeling a guilty glow on her face.

'But why didn't you tell us, dear? Julian, we could have flown back from America earlier – couldn't we?' Margaret turned her unseeing eyes to where she knew her son was sitting.

Jane responded first. 'I'm sorry. I didn't tell you because it was her express wish that no-one from her estranged family attend. She felt a great deal of shame and didn't want to be judged. She also made me promise not to tell you where she was living and then... She died soon after. It was sudden but she knew she was very ill.'

'So you actually met her?' It was Julian's turn to sound shocked.

Jane nodded in confirmation before remembering Margaret's disability. 'Yes. Yes, I did. I tracked down her grandsons and Dean Smith told me where to find her. She was in a nursing home. She was somewhat confused and I couldn't believe half of what she told me at first. It made me doubt the other half. But we've been able to substantiate a lot of what she said. It's a sad story, certainly sad for Mary.'

Julian was about to speak again when Shelley put a discouraging hand on his knee. 'Can I make a suggestion?' she said. 'Why don't we just let Jane tell us what she's found out and we can express our approval or otherwise at the end.'

Shelley's authority established, Julian kept his peace and Jane continued her revelations. She told of Chris Aimson, his situation and his potential salvation in the form of Herb Jensen. Margaret said she was also keen to get in touch with her cousin's son and Jane was suitably encouraging. When they discussed Dean Smith, however, she guardedly painted a darker picture and countenanced against any form of contact.

Dean had at least fulfilled his purpose in leading Jane to his grandmother, in her Chesterfield nursing home. Jane tried to compress her long interviews into a few minutes.

'Despite her frailty, she talked and talked. It was difficult to know what was fantasy and what was fact. At first, she told me her second husband, James Smith, had been a film star. I knew that wasn't true, and it turned out people just used to say he looked a film star. Mary certainly idolised him like one. But he was poisonous, with poisonous ideas. We're pretty certain this is him at a fascist rally in the East End of London before the war.'

Jane opened her laptop and showed them the image of a handsome boy, arm thrusting in a fascist salute, whilst a man in a black uniform marched by.

'It's a photograph of Oswald Mosley and a bunch of Blackshirts, Mum,' said Julian. Then, remembering their conversation by the river, he turned his focus back towards Jane. 'Didn't Smith call his son Ernald after Mosley's middle name?'

'Yes,' she confirmed. 'He never lost his ultra right-wing sympathies. Passed them onto poor Ernald and then the inheritance continued down another generation to Dean. Dean still thinks of his grandfather as a role model of political far-sightedness. Which leads us to Margaret's parent's wedding in 1948...'

Jane reminded them that Churchill had made his Iron Curtain speech as early as 1946, signalling the start of the Cold War. Russia was the new enemy, and James must have felt vindicated in what he saw as his anti-communist activities during World War II. In a fit of drunken envy and insecurity, he blurted out his pro-Nazi allegiance and bragged of an Iron Cross. No-one believed the full story, but the sentiments were damning enough. He was given a beating by Margaret's father, and Mary was told to choose between her husband and her family. She chose the film star and banishment.

Jane explained that, contrary to all her expectations, James did have an Iron Cross, but it was a fake made by British intelligence. James had died always believing it was genuine. When he'd shown it to Mary she'd not gone straight to the authorities, and he'd convinced her that made her an accomplice who would hang alongside him if it ever came out.

Jane laid out the evidence, including the medal itself and the forged note from William Joyce, otherwise known as Lord Haw-Haw.

It had taken 30 minutes for Jane to recount all the details and she paused to let them sink in.

Eventually, Julian spoke. 'You sound convinced, Jane.'

'When you look through the documents, the dates and the places, everything seems to fit. It corroborates what Mary told me, though she and her husband never found out he was working for MI5, not the Germans. In her defence, she didn't actually know he was a spy, or thought he was a spy, until after the war had ended.

So that's the family scandal. I'm glad it was all 70 years ago – it's shocking even now.' Julian looked at his wife, Shelley. He was hoping to see a look of empathy and understanding. It wasn't there.

'I'm afraid it gets worse.' Jane felt like she was twisting a knife in the Stothards' emotions. 'Mary told me something else. It was about the death of her first husband, Woody Jensen.'

'He was the American airman. Didn't he die in the war, dear?' Margaret's facial expression was less pained than Julian's had become.

'Yes and no. He wasn't killed on a bombing mission. He was killed in Norfolk, in a town now called Dereham.

The conclusion at the time was that he was shot by another US serviceman who then turned the gun on himself. The evidence suggested it was an argument between lovers.'

'Mary wasn't exactly good at choosing men,' chipped in Shelley, who'd been avoiding comment up to this point.

'Maybe she wasn't that bad,' countered Jane. 'She married Woody and he seems to have been fine and decent. He didn't have James Smith's looks, but he was the better man in every other way. If Woody hadn't been killed, her life would have been totally different.'

'Forgive me, dear.' Margaret's eyes were pointing towards Jane. 'When you can't see you have to listen intently. You said "the conclusion at the time"?'

'Mary told me a different story. She said it was something James revealed much later. He was drunk, but also confident of his hold on her. Like everything else, we didn't know whether to believe it at first, but having substantiated the other things she said, we've now no reason to doubt it.'

'Go on, dear,' prompted Margaret.

'James Smith was bisexual. He seduced an American air force clerk, Henry Abrams. We've seen a photograph of them in a bar together. Abrams worked in the office dealing with the deployments of US bomber squadrons. He was the source of the information Smith thought he was feeding back to his spymaster. Somehow Woody Jensen found out. Mary had already had a relationship with Smith, so Woody was probably wary of him. Woody goes round to Abrams' flat and finds him in bed with Smith—'

'And like James Bond, Smith pulls a semi-automatic and blasts away,' said Shelley, with a certain relish.

'He was a little cleverer than that,' said Jane. 'He grabbed Abrams' service pistol and forced Woody to get undressed. Smith then shot Woody followed by Abrams.

The gun is found in Abrams' hand. He has a reputation as a homosexual and when the US Military Police see the bodies they jump to the conclusion they're supposed to. It's 1944 and their prejudices probably tell them that's the sort of thing homosexuals do.'

Jane had reached the end of her story and felt an emotional ambivalence. She was confident in her conclusions and the thoroughness of her methodology, but worried she'd lost the sense of humanity in the story she was telling. These had been real people and their lives reached through into the present day. Mary Smith had, of course, died only recently. Dean Smith was still arguably the victim of his antecedent's crimes. Margaret and Julian Stothard were having to confront uncomfortable truths from a past perhaps too close to be dismissed as colourful rather than shameful.

After a thoughtful silence, Margaret and Julian asked a series of questions and Jane did her best to answer. Gradually the mood became lighter. Margaret expressed her delight that the family mystery had been solved more thoroughly than they could realistically have hoped. Julian agreed that Jane had earned her money and also her stripes as a professional genealogist.

Shelley, however, thought it necessary to add balance to the praise. 'It is what you were paying her to do, Julian darling. If you hire someone, you expect them to do the job.'

Julian's response was to suggest they all adjourn to a nearby restaurant for a celebratory meal. Shelley looked uncertain and Jane declined the invitation. She explained she needed to get home in preparation for a long journey to the south coast the following day. Julian showed her to the door and walked down the steps with her to her car.

As she climbed into the driving seat, he said his farewells. 'Jane, you've been remarkable. I knew I'd found the right woman. You were a bit circumspect about what happened between you and Dean Smith, perhaps for my mother's benefit, but I suspect you went above and beyond what might be expected of your average family historian. I think I've definitely got my money's worth.'

'Thank you. I'm glad you're pleased. And I'm glad you're back with your wife. She's stunning. Looks like a movie star. Bye Julian.'

The car rolled down the short hill and turned out onto the main road, and Jane found herself suddenly wincing at her reference to Shelley and her film star looks. She hoped Julian didn't think she was bitchily hinting at an unwarranted comparison with James Smith. It had not been intentional, though she thought, maybe at some subliminal level it had.

The ferry

After a protracted period of disappointing weather, the forecast was for a fine weekend. Jane was en route for the south coast. Unfortunately, so was half the population. The motorway traffic was heavy but it moved more or less steadily. Even London's M25 failed to live up to its reputation as an elongated car park, fulfilling instead the orbital intent of its designers. Jane was obliged to slow at times and feared an accident or roadworks ahead, but the delays had no apparent cause other than weight of vehicles, and she was soon on her way again. It was a phenomenon that Tommy had once explained as compression waves flowing through cars and lorries like sound through air molecules, but she'd never really understood.

Any hopes Jane had of arriving at her destination in reasonable time began to fade when she reached a place called Rufus Stone, where William II supposedly met his suspicious end hunting in his Conqueror father's then New Forest. The blue signs of the motorway network had just given way to the green of an A-road, and the traffic ground to a turgid crawl as car after car of eager sunseekers, beachcombers, surfers and boaters were funnelled and trapped on the main route across the national park and down to the seasides beyond.

After one mile and nearly fifteen minutes, Jane pulled into a lay-by. The Mazda's hood had been up for travelling at speed; she decided it might as well come down for a slow but scenic crossing of an area of quasi-natural beauty that was new to her. She also took the opportunity to silence satnav woman. It was a long trip and Jane had decided to put up with her, but now the traffic jam was trying enough on its own.

From the A31, the New Forest appeared more open scrub and heath than ancient woodland. Jane vaguely remembered reading somewhere that forest meant a royal hunting ground rather than an expanse of trees, but the landscape stretched to the skyline and was a calming distraction as she and her fellow drivers nose-to-tailed their way forward.

Eventually the jam thinned, and the traffic began to move freely. Jane resisted the temptation to speed. If she was late, she was late.

She reluctantly had to re-enlist satnav woman for the final, fiddly part of the journey. She was directed onto a narrow peninsula of land, covered with expensive-looking houses and semi-tropical gardens. Beneath the bricks and soil lay a sandspit stretching across the mouth of a vast natural harbour, leaving only a narrow channel for the passage of boats and ships. Jane had almost reached the chain ferry that bridged the final gap, when she was told to turn right and, after a few yards, stop.

Jane scanned the house names and saw the entrance she was looking for, flanked by high stone walls. She was able to pull off the road onto the start of the driveway, but her access was blocked by formidable iron gates. About four feet off the ground was an intercom, and she had to climb out of the car to reach the button.

An electronic beep prompted through the speaker.

'Hi, it's Jane. Sorry I'm late.'

After a short delay a familiar voice replied. 'I can see you, darling. Come on in.'

Jane looked up to see a CCTV camera pointing down from a short mast. Her attention then switched to the gates as they rolled back, only the faintest whirr betraying their mechanical impetus. Jane climbed back into the Mazda and continued down to the end of the drive.

All down the street, the houses occupied long, narrow plots and their architects had typically pushed close to the boundaries to make maximum use of the space available. As a result, Jane was very aware of the imposing mansion-like properties that sat to each side of the relatively modest bungalow in front of her. Strategically planted firs and palms provided little more than a token screen.

Jane parked on a gravel area big enough for three or four vehicles. She climbed out, locked the car and then questioned the necessity when she saw the iron gates were once again barring intrusion.

'Darling, it's wonderful to see you again!'

Jane turned back towards the front door. A glamorous woman, immaculately dressed and coiffured, looking older but not old, stood with her arms open in greeting.

Jane smiled as warmly as her confused emotions would let her. 'Mother, you're looking wonderful. But then you always do.'

'Thank you, darling. And you're looking as nice as I've ever seen you. Our ugly duckling seems to have matured into something much closer to a swan. And your outfit… It's certainly bright and colourful.'

Jane felt her smile cracking. She didn't care if her clothes were too gaudy for her mother's taste. She should have taken the suggested improvement in her appearance as the compliment intended. Instead, all that echoed was the reminder of a plain child, with 'shoulders like a boy', forever in the disappointed shadow of a woman for whom looks were all-important.

Jane blinked something approximating warmth back onto her face but didn't reply. She stepped forward and gave her mother a perfunctory kiss on the cheek and let herself be shown through the door and into the main room beyond.

'Wow!'

Jane's mood had instantly shifted from resentful melancholy to open-mouthed awe. The bungalow had been extended rearwards and the whole of the far wall was open. Bi-fold glass doors had been slid back such that the internal space merged with an external patio and then down into a beautifully manicured garden. A sprinkler rainbowed back and forth over a shining lawn that seemed to flow almost seamlessly into the glistening waters of the wide harbour beyond. Yachts bobbed at anchor on the opposite shoreline, and one skipper was raising his mainsail as he motored into the main channel towards the sea. Jane could see him frantically cranking his windlass as he passed less than 50 yards from where she stood.

Jane was still spellbound. 'Oh, Mother! The view's stunning!'

'It's not quite Sydney Harbour, but it's the next best thing. The neighbours have all built up and out, but I just wanted somewhere cosy. When you're on your own, you don't want too much space – it's just more rooms to clean. But the view is wonderful here.'

Jane doubted her mother did much cleaning herself and was almost surprised when she was led into a vast kitchen and her mother turned on a kettle.

'You prefer coffee, don't you, darling? Tiny bit of milk, but no sugar.'

Her mother's memory was accurate because it matched her own preference. Her supposedly big-boned daughter had also been obliged to eschew the fattening tyranny of sugar and too much milk.

They chatted politely like vague acquaintances and moved outside to a pair of wicker sofas, the older woman having carefully donned a large sun hat to protect her complexion from the ageing rays. It was she who made the first move. She knew the responsibility lay with her, and it was a conversation she'd rehearsed many times. She'd no idea how it might conclude.

'Have you forgiven me, darling? For not coming to your grandmother's funeral?'

Jane's eyes didn't meet her mother's, focussing instead on the coffee in her hand. The elephant in the room had been unchained. 'I still find it hard to believe you didn't come. She was your own mother.'

'Keith was so ill at the time. I know I could have just jumped on a plane, but Australia's so far away. I didn't feel I could leave him.'

The elephant began to stampede through the dark jungle of Jane's mind. 'It's just that your men always came first. When I was growing up… You dumped me on Granny and Grandad. You always seemed to be away on holiday with some bloke. In Paris, Rome…' Jane stopped abruptly, struggling to regain control.

'We never really bonded, you and I.' Jane's mother was gazing distantly across the harbour. 'I was very ill after you were born. They kept me in hospital for weeks. My mother looked after you. You and she were always much closer. And then there was your father, of course. You always loved your Daddy. You were his little princess.'

'Pirate princess,' corrected Jane emphatically, before regretting the seemingly childish distinction.

'Gosh, I'd forgotten that. Yes, you were his little pirate princess and he was your pirate king. It seems so long ago and, in the scheme of things, was such a short period of time. But, I do understand, darling. When you're a child years seem like a decades. And those years, they make us who we are.'

Jane dabbed at her face with the back of her hand, trying to disguise the tears welling in her eyes. 'Why did you have to drive him away, Mummy?'

Jane's mother hesitated before answering. 'He was a brute of a man. A businessman he reckoned, but always doing dodgy deals, sailing close to the wind. He used to hit me, of course. I'm not the first woman to be attracted to a villain. It's the gangster's moll syndrome, I guess.'

'I didn't know he hit you. He never laid a finger on me.' There was a clear incredulity in Jane's voice. 'Is that why you made him leave?'

'I didn't make him leave. He left of his own accord.'

A white wall of steel suddenly began to enter Jane's field of vision. Taken aback, she twisted her head to take in its full vastness.

'It's the Cherbourg ferry, darling. They come very close to the shore at this point. Everyday people gawping down on you. It's still a breathtaking sight, though.'

'I remember saying goodbye to him at the dockside,' said Jane, as she was drawn into the image that haunted her. 'Looking up at that huge grey ship, not understanding that I'd never see him again.'

'Don't be silly, darling.'

'No seriously. I know I was young but it's one of my earliest memories.'

'He didn't sail anywhere.'

'But I remember the ship. Standing under the curve of the bows. Being scared it would topple over on top of me.'

'No, darling, no. You're getting confused. Grandad had been in the navy in the war. He took you to an open day at Portsmouth when you were about four. He told me how scared you'd been standing next to an aircraft carrier. The deck arched over you and there was an optical illusion that it was tilting. I remember your upset little face when you were talking about it.'

'But I remember Daddy standing there with me.'

'He wasn't there, darling. You're conflating two different memories. Your father never sailed anywhere.'

But you and Granny always told me he emigrated to South Africa on a boat.'

'It seemed kinder. You were always such a sensitive child. But did my mother never tell you the truth? After all these years?'

'She always refused to talk about my father. She said it was better to let things lie. That I'd only upset myself.'

The stern of the ferry shifted into view as she turned hard to port to follow the deep water channel. Jane's mother's eyes followed it for several seconds before she replied.

'She always mollycoddled you. I'm afraid I'm not really the mollycoddling type.' She hesitated again. 'The bastard never went anywhere, or not far anyway. He found another woman and decided he wanted to make a clean break. He used to make a big fuss of you when it suited him, but having a child cramped his style. He never married me as you know, so he just upped sticks and took his fancy woman to London. That's why I married Uncle Trevor so soon after. I needed the money.'

'But London was only a couple of hours away, he would have come to see me,' pleaded Jane.

Jane's mother paused between each word of her reply. 'He, simply, couldn't, be, bothered.'

Jane no longer tried to hide her tears. 'So he's been in London all this time. I used to live in bloody London!'

'I heard he moved to Spain, probably when you were in your teens. God knows where he is now. Hopefully he's smoked or drunk himself to death. Or perhaps one of his dodgy friends has done for him. I don't know and I don't care.'

'All this can't be true. Granny would have told me.'

'She used to write telling me that the sensitive little girl had been become a sensitive woman. You've been ill, darling, I know you have. Perhaps she didn't want to make things worse. Maybe I should have been more careful just now. But—'

'I don't even have a picture of him,' interrupted Jane. 'I know he was big, with lots of black curly hair. Whenever I smell cigarettes on someone's clothing it takes me to that dockside and him towering over me. Only now you tell me that never happened. But I don't really know what his face looked like. I don't know what my own father looked like!'

Jane's mother stood and walked slowly back into the house. Five minutes later she returned holding a single photograph. She laid it on the table in front of her daughter.

'There he is. Stephen Jones, your father.'

Jane picked it up and studied it through her still moist eyes. There were two figures: her mother looking young and beautiful in an elegant evening dress; next to her a huge man, with thick, black hair pulled back into a tight ponytail, his heavy-set body squeezed into a smart dinner suit with a bow tie round his bull-like neck.

The face wasn't handsome, nor was it ugly. Jane recognised it immediately. It was her own. Bigger, stronger, harder, but the family resemblance was incontestable. And there, in the photograph, was the one thing she remembered about her father above all else: the black triangle acid-etched onto her consciousness. Like the pirate he seemed to have been, he wore a patch strapped in place over his brutally scarred and ruined right eye.

The lychgate

Dean Smith was sitting watching the lunchtime news on TV. He prided himself on keeping abreast of current events, and he liked to swear at the liberal, left-wing bias he saw in most of the reports. As always, Steve's living room smelt of sweaty men and cigarettes. Obliviously, Dean drank cheap lager from a can while Steve played a game on his mobile phone.

'Oi, Steve. Listen to this.'

The programme had switched to a local newsreader, a face once familiar to national breakfast-time audiences, but now reduced to stories about traffic congestion and human interest on a regional scale. He was talking about a father and his young son being reunited with an elderly American relative. They were filmed visiting an American war cemetery. Buried there was the American's brother, who was grandfather to the British man. It was made clear that the Briton had a serious long-term illness, and a lot of focus was on his delightful child, though the boy's charm was lost on Dean.

The local connection was through a Derbyshire woman, born in the village of Dowley, who had married an American airman during the war. It was his grave that was depicted in the short clip. The woman was named as Mary Dye.

'I'm pretty certain that was my grandmother's name, you know, before she was married,' claimed an excited Dean. 'This is it! This is what that heir-hunting bitch meant when she said she'd found a way of getting back at me. They're making it clear the old Yank's got pots of money and he's going to leave it to that poof so he can look after his brat.'

'Fucking hell,' said Steve.

'Fucking karma, mate. Justice. I'm due a cut and I'm going to get it.'

Steve looked unconvinced. 'What if she's done something, you know with records and stuff, to do you out of it?'

'I wouldn't put it past the slag, but I'm not going to be cheated. I've been shat on all my life – my mum pissed off and left me, and my dad was fucking loser. Useless bastard!'

Dean suddenly threw the TV remote and it smashed violently against the wall. One final, perceived injustice had cracked the dam holding back a lifetime of grievance and rage.

'And he made me a fucking loser too,' he snarled. 'Well, this is my chance to have something for once. I will not be fucking cheated this time! Do you hear me?'

Steve had never seen his friend so out of control. It frightened him.

'What can you do, Deano?' he said, nervously.

'The Yank'll be back in America, out of reach. But I'm going to track down that sick waste of space. What was his name? Chris Aimson. And I'm going to lean on him so fucking hard, him and his precious kid, that he's going to be begging me to take what's mine.'

'But how will you find him?'

'I don't know. Facebook, everyone's on fucking Facebook. I'll pay someone to ferret him out if necessary. But I'm telling you, mate. Not this time. I will not be cheated this time. I'll kill that bastard before I let him steal my fucking birthright! They can lock me up forever – I've got nothing to lose. Literally, nothing.'

'Maybe you should calm down, Deano. Look, are you sure your Gran's name was Dye?'

The question made Dean falter. 'Yeah, well, almost. Shame the selfish bitch has pegged it or we could just go and ask her. Hang about…'

'What?'

Dean's eyes glinted with enlightenment and relief. 'That old war memorial in front of the church.'

'The bronze thing we ripped out and had melted down.'

Dean's head bobbed manically. 'But, don't forget, some do-gooder made a fuss and they put another one up. In stone or something. Something not worth nicking.'

'So what good is that to us?'

'What good it is to me, Steve, is that the old dear used to haul me down there as a boy to look at her brother's name. And her brother's name will be the same as her maiden name. Shit, but I'm a smart fucker! Talk about written on tablets of stone...'

In a matter of minutes they were in the lychgate of the church, just across the road from Dowley's village green and its reminder of its mining heritage. They'd half-run, half-walked and the exertion had made them breathless. Steve lit a remedial cigarette and Dean snatched it to take an anxious drag before switching his attention to the replacement plaque.

A few weeks earlier Jane had stood in the same spot, tearfully recognising names from the First World War to whom Dean did not know nor care he was related. Her eyes had drifted lower, and she'd noticed something odd before being abruptly distracted by her first sighting of Michael, the local builder turned gangster, whose back and bulk had disturbingly evoked images of her father.

Had Jane's emotions not been racing, she would have placed her fingers into the carved granite letters to make sure they were not distorted by shadows. She would have contacted the parish council to report the stonemason's error. It was not to be. The discrepancy was forgotten. This version of history remained unchallenged.

Trusting the hardness of the evidence, Dean rapidly scanned the four columns of names, digging back into his memory of childhood visits with his grandmother.

'I remember it was at the bottom left, under World War II. Here we go, Stevie boy – Atkins, Baker, Brown, Brown, Pye, Self, Skelton, Spencer.'

Dean's shoulders dropped and he sank dejectedly to his knees. 'Her name was Pye, not Dye…'

Made in the USA
Coppell, TX
16 June 2020

28034386R00142